The Old Royal

by

J.R. McLemore

Copyright © 2012 J.R. McLemore

All rights reserved.

No part of this document or the related files may be reproduced or transmitted in any form, by any means (electronic, photocopying, recording, or otherwise) without the prior written permission of the author.

This story is a work of fiction. Any resemblance to real persons, living or dead, is purely coincidental. All characters, names, places, and incidents are products of the author's imagination and are used fictitiously.

ISBN: 1467957135
ISBN-13: 978-1467957137

DEDICATION

This one's for Lara.
For believing in the idea and helping to
rescue it from a life spent in the desk drawer.

ACKNOWLEDGMENTS

This book would not be possible if it weren't for the help of several people who not only aided in validating the facts from my research, but also took the time to proofread the early manuscripts and provide their opinions, which helped shape the story. I thank my wife for her first-rate editorial skills, and for her overall support and enthusiasm. A huge thanks to Geb and Mark for being such invaluable beta readers. And I want to thank my brother Charlie for not only proofing the final draft, but for lending me his support in this endeavor.

OTHER BOOKS BY J.R. MCLEMORE

 Hush, Hush, My Love

 *An Adverse Anthology: Strange & Disturbing Short Stories*

 *Majoring in Murder*

Available at **Amazon**, **B&N**, **Smashwords** and wherever books and eBooks are sold!

CHAPTER 1

All of the items for sale in the store had two things in common: they were dusty and they were old. Anthony Jessup moved slowly through the aisles, looking at the broken down relics taking up space on the shelves. The floorboards creaked beneath his feet as he moved between the fragile items. There was no particular order to the way things were arranged for display. They were simply placed wherever there had been an available space. Among the motley collection of knick-knacks were Depression era bowls, glasses, pitchers, and plates; porcelain dolls; rusty woodworking tools; chests; lamps; and some items that Anthony had never seen before but guessed were some sort of farming implements. He found the dolls to be especially creepy. Most of them were missing patches of hair or an eye, or in a few cases, both. A majority of the porcelain dolls had flaky faces and looked ominous staring back from that chipped and peeling finish. Most were missing limbs and dressed in dingy, frilly dresses. A cold chill crept up Anthony's back when he saw the head of a bodiless doll nailed to one of the support posts. One of its winking eyelids didn't open completely and seemed to say "Come here often?"

Objects hung suspended from the ceiling with chains or rope. The biggest was an aged-looking wooden canoe suspended over two or three aisles by chains. Anthony wondered if it would stay afloat, but doubted it, given its appearance. Metallic signs that advertised long-gone brands, from cigarettes to soap and half a hundred other things, were nailed to other support beams. Animal traps hung on the walls, everything from small leg traps to large bear traps, complete with ragged teeth designed to bite into flesh. These were rusty with age, and threatened tetanus. Among the traps and doodads on the walls were stuffed animal heads surrounded by more antique signs. It seemed this place had cornered the market on them. Altogether, the collection of junk reminded him of a couple of horror movies he'd seen, mainly *The Texas Chainsaw Massacre* and *Wrong Turn*. Places where piles of junk lay abandoned because their owners had been murdered in some gruesome and disturbing fashion.

Anthony thought the building was probably an antique in itself, only rented out as a last-ditch attempt to make a little money instead of bulldozing it. When he made his way closer to the front of the store, Anthony noticed that the man behind the counter was occasionally peeking over his newspaper to stare as Anthony wound through the aisles—as if he'd make off with any of the crap from the shelves.

He'd have to pay me to take it.

Anthony couldn't shake the creepy vibe he'd detected while walking around inside.

Damn, all it needs is Leatherface to run out of the back with a growling chainsaw.

Anthony couldn't help himself; he was a horror fan.

He wasn't just a scary movie aficionado. He also had a bookcase filled with horror novels which he enjoyed reading again and again. As Anthony ran his finger through the layer of dust on one of the shelves, the floorboards creaked behind him. His heart skipped a beat. As he turned, he caught a peripheral glimpse of someone standing behind him. His heart kick-started with a rush of fear-induced adrenaline.

"Come here." It was his girlfriend, Susan. "I found something I think you'll like."

"Damn, you scared me!" he said, keeping his voice low so as not to let the man behind the counter hear him.

Susan grabbed Anthony by the hand and led him to the back corner of the store where old books and records littered the shelves, all of which had definitely seen better days. Anthony thought it looked more like garbage that should have been thrown out years ago. The few books that caught his eye were trashy romance novels. Those that still had covers showed some variation of a muscle-bound man with long flowing hair cradling some big-breasted damsel, probably in distress. Water-stained and tattered thesauruses and dictionaries lay among the romance novels, as well as a few classics, the kind Anthony was made to read in high school. It was like someone had collected all of the books that really bored him.

The record albums were no different. At first glance, Anthony identified several worn, but legible artists' names: Conway Twitty, Loretta Lynn, Dolly Parton, Jerry Reed, and Ernest Tubb.

Oh God, I've died and gone to trailer park heaven.

In addition to the country albums were Strawberry Alarm Clock, Perry Como, Judy Collins, Neil Sedaka, Marty Robbins, and Sonny & Cher. When Anthony sifted through a few covers, he wasn't surprised to find a record from Zamfir, master of the pan-flute. He couldn't help but think of these albums as cast-offs in the twenty-first century where people like Britney Spears, Kanye West, and Pink ruled the top 40 list. Today, hip-hop seemed as popular as Starbucks coffee. Even country music had revamped its image since these records were produced. Anthony observed Dolly Parton's rhinestones and beehive hair on the album cover. Today's singers wouldn't be caught dead looking like that. He tossed the record down with the rest of the junk.

Still holding his hand, Susan bent and picked up a paperback from the many scattered books on the bottom shelf. The novel Susan had singled out was one by Roger Kurrey. She knew he was Anthony's favorite author. She also knew Anthony had nearly every book Roger Kurrey had ever written. Because Anthony was an aspiring writer himself, he held Kurrey in high regard and looked to Kurrey's first published book as inspiration. Anthony had often told Susan that if he could just get his first book published, his writing career would be on its way, just like Roger so many decades ago. Currently, Roger Kurrey had more than twenty-five books in print, many of which had been optioned into movies and television miniseries. This was Anthony's dream, to follow Roger Kurrey's footsteps and become a famous full-time author, a household name.

The book Susan pulled from the pile was called *When the Clock Strikes Three*. It was Roger Kurrey's first published novel, the one that launched his writing career. Anthony already had this book in his collection, but his was a seventh edition reprint. The book Susan held was from one of the first print runs in 1974. Although Anthony had already read the book, several times in fact, he preferred to own the first editions. Anthony was too young to have bought the earlier books when they originally came out, but he felt that buying any of the first print runs he found was better than owning a watered-down, homogenized later edition. Anthony didn't trust whether the later printings had been re-edited, altering the original story in some fundamental way.

The cover of the book was very soft and worn with age. A testament to many years of being passed from reader to reader. Anthony didn't care. He liked the thought of a really good book accumulating plenty of *reader-miles*. Susan had discovered a diamond in the rough. A smile spread across Anthony's face as he rubbed his finger along the velvety worn cover.

Wearing a matching smile, she asked, "Do you have the original of this one?"

Anthony knew Susan enjoyed seeing him happy; this was one of the things that made him love her so much. She was selfless, always putting others first instead of herself. Sometimes, it made him feel a bit guilty because he was usually the opposite, but he loved her no matter what. Anthony was obsessed with realizing his dream of becoming a famous author and only wanted to succeed at that goal. That dream often dominated his thoughts. When Anthony looked inward and vowed that nothing would distract him from trying to achieve success, he also thought of Susan's selflessness. She was his number one fan, no matter if he succeeded or not. For that very reason, he cherished her for being there, supporting him in his endeavors.

"No, baby, I don't. Mine's a reprint. I've been hoping to get it, though." Anthony hadn't looked at her as he said any of this. Instead, he inspected the book in his hands, opening the cover, and scrutinizing the first few pages. He turned to the back cover and looked inside at the black-and-white photo of Roger Kurrey.

"I was hoping you didn't have it. I wanted to find something you'd be happy with since you came antique shopping with me. I know how much you hate it."

Her sentiment only fueled his guilt. "I don't *hate* it, really," Anthony lied, flipping through the pages of the book, his eyes scanning the pages. He stared at the picture of Roger again, wishing it were his picture in the book instead. If only he were a published author. In his daydreams, he imagined what it would be like to be famous, responsible for coming up with new story ideas, getting out of bed each morning to sit in front of a keyboard and work on a book, instead of commuting twice a day, every day, to a job he loathed.

Susan only smiled, with one of those smiles that says, *sure you don't hate it; you're just saying that to be nice*. "You ready to go?" she asked, knowing the answer before asking the question.

Written in black ink, the small, round, yellow sticker on the cover said the book was only fifty cents. Anthony looked up from it. "Yeah. I guess—" he stopped. Something over Susan's shoulder held his attention.

Susan turned to see what Anthony was staring at, but saw nothing other than a shelf laden with old office equipment. The shelf was a knot of tangled cords and wires, dot-matrix printers with pieces missing, tape recorders, desk lamps, calculators, and other assorted technology, most of which seemed out of place in an antique shop and more appropriate at a flea market. Susan turned her attention back to Anthony but found he was already moving toward whatever he had seen. He stepped past her and reached out to touch the keys of an old Royal typewriter in the middle of the mess.

"Wow, look at this," he said.

"It's just an old typewriter."

"Yeah, the kind writers used before they had computers."

Susan just watched him. Anthony suddenly seemed more interested in the typewriter than he was in the book. "Yeah, but you *have* a computer to write your stories."

"I know, but don't you understand, this is what *real* writers used before there were computers. They didn't have spell-check or grammar-check to rely on. They had to know the rules. Not like today, when you just type something and a computer program points out how ignorant you really are about grammar and punctuation." Anthony twisted the small white price tag hanging from the carriage return lever so he could see it. The typewriter was seventy-five dollars, which was more than Anthony could part with for nothing more than a novelty. "Too bad I don't have the cash or I'd get it."

He stood there for a moment, jabbing at some of the typewriter's keys, which surprisingly, were all there. As old as the typewriter appeared, Anthony had expected there to be a lot of parts missing from it. He turned to Susan and said, "Okay, I'm ready whenever you are."

They zig-zagged their way back through the narrow aisles toward the cash register. Anthony placed the book on the glass counter and the suspicious cashier folded his newspaper to ring up the sale. It was a whopping fifty cents. Anthony thought it was amazing the place stayed in business and wondered how the man paid the lease on the store, if there was one, let alone how he made a living. By the looks of it, Anthony doubted the store made enough money to even keep the doors open.

Anthony and Susan didn't attempt to engage the cashier in any small-talk. The man didn't seem like the chit-chatty type, just a "How y'all doin'?" from him and that was it. More of a rhetorical question really, which they both replied to by nodding and smiling. The man wore a yellow baseball cap—the CAT logo embroidered into it—atop greasy brown hair. Flecks of brown spittle rested in the right corner of his lips and, whenever he happened to talk, his yellowish-brown teeth became visible. A small Styrofoam cup filled with tobacco spit rested beside the cash register. When Anthony saw the cup, he turned to Susan and raised his eyebrows. She had also seen it because she crinkled her nose at Anthony indicating her repulsion. Her reaction made Anthony grin. He turned to accept his receipt and promptly stuffed it in the paper bag along with the book.

Once they were in the car, Anthony took the book out of the bag. Even though it was old, it was new to him, a first print run no less. Susan didn't say anything as she pulled out of the parking lot. She only glanced at Anthony, noticing that he was already engrossed in the first couple of pages. It was a long ride back to Oakwood from Moultrie, over an hour's drive down Highway 5. Anthony read for most of the trip. Finally, before arriving at his apartment, Anthony closed the battered paperback.

"You know," he said, "one day I'm going to be famous, too. If I can just get past this block I'm having."

"I know. Just give it some time. You were going strong there for a while."

"Yeah, but then it was like I hit a brick wall. I don't know why I can't think of anything to write about, but it's pissing me off." He dropped the book in his lap. "When I write a short story, it's easy. I don't have a problem coming up with something to write. But when I try to write a whole book, even if I can see the whole story arc in my head, I seem to lose track of it at some point. Everything just vanishes like a fart in the wind." Anthony became aware of his whininess.

"Don't worry, baby. Some inspiration will come that'll get you over the hump."

Anthony opened the back cover and stared at Kurrey's photo again. "God, I hate work and I hate traffic!" Anthony stopped, calmed down, and said, "It'd be nice to sleep in and not have to drive to work. To just walk from the bed to the computer, where I can sit and write." He sighed, relishing the visions of fame and fortune in his head.

On a Sunday afternoon two weeks later, Susan arrived at Anthony's apartment. She held a thin flat gift-wrapped box in her hand as she rang the doorbell. Anthony opened up the door and a smile spread across his face when he saw her holding the present.

Susan extended the gift toward him. "Happy birthday, baby!"

Anthony bent slightly, hugging her with one arm and accepted the package with the other. "You shouldn't have done this."

"Yeah, whatever. You know I can't resist seeing your smile. Go on, open it." Susan goosed his butt as they went inside.

"In a sec. Let me finish getting ready. I just have to brush my teeth and put on my shoes, okay. Where do you want to eat?" he asked, heading to the bathroom.

"I was in the mood for Mexican, but it's your birthday, so you decide."

"Okay, Mexican it is. We can try that new place over on Somerset, La Cozuela." He spit toothpaste into the sink and said, "A guy at work said it was really good."

"I've wanted to go there since it opened." Susan fiddled with the bow on the present, trying to straighten it.

Anthony returned to the living room, sat on the footstool, and began putting on his tennis shoes.

"Here" Susan said, extending the present to him again, "I can't wait any longer."

"All right." Anthony dropped his shoe and accepted the gift. He carefully removed the wrapping paper from the back. It was a self-editing book for fiction writers. "Cool, it'll come in handy when I finish my story," he said, opening the book and leafing through the pages.

"I thought you could use it. I saw it in the bookstore the other day and decided that's what I'd get for your birthday."

Anthony placed the book on the coffee table and continued tying his shoes. "Okay, let's go," he said, taking his keys out of his pocket.

Anthony locked the front door. Susan slid into the driver's seat and leaned over to unlock the passenger's side. Anthony pulled up the handle and swung open the door. When he saw what was waiting in the passenger seat, it rendered him speechless.

"Surprise!" Susan's face radiated happiness.

It was the old Royal typewriter with a red velvet ribbon tied around it.

"I can't believe you got this!" Anthony never would've expected Susan to drive all the way back to the antique store in Moultrie just to buy him the typewriter. Her selflessness knew no bounds, it seemed.

"The book on self-editing was just a red herring. I saw how much you liked this, so I decided to surprise you with it. Besides, it wasn't that expensive. I was able to haggle the guy down a little bit." Susan winked.

Anthony hefted the contraption from the seat and carried it into the house. Susan unlocked the door for him and Anthony set it down beside the book on the coffee table. Before leaving, Anthony ran his fingers over the round keys once again, enjoying the way they felt.

CHAPTER 2

That night, Anthony moved the typewriter to his desk in the den. He threaded some newly purchased reels of ink ribbon into it, and fed a blank sheet of paper around the drum by turning the knob. He placed the freshly opened ream of paper on the left side of the typewriter. He punched the keys, liking the mechanical click of the letterheads as they struck the platen. He continued typing nonsensically until the bell dinged, signaling that he had to reset the carriage.

Okay, enough playing around. It's time to get down to business, he thought and glanced at his watch. It was already five minutes after eleven. Susan had left only a half hour ago and Anthony was anxious to begin a new story using the typewriter. He thought for a few

The Old Royal

minutes about what he should write and an idea finally came to him about a bank-heist-gone-bad in the Depression. He started typing slowly, and his keystrokes gradually became faster.

Everything was coming together, the storyline unfolded so vividly in his imagination; it was like watching a movie in his head. A small group of gangsters entered the bank, their submachine guns discreetly tucked beneath their long trench coats. Anthony's fingers moved feverishly over and across the keys as he typed, relaying to the machine what he saw unfolding.

```
    "This is a stick-up! Do what you're
told and nobody'll get hurt!" gangster-
number-one yelled. He threw back the
lower half of his trench coat and
pulled a Tommy gun into view.
    Gangster-number-two was a hulking
man, about six feet five inches. He
held a sawed-off double barrel shotgun;
the barrels seemed large, big enough to
launch bricks. A "street sweeper" they
called it.
    A shot rang out as gangster-number-
three--a squat little Italian
brandishing another Tommy gun and a
snub-nosed .38--fired the pistol into
the bank's ceiling. He bellowed, "Yeah.
Keep ya trap shut, do what we tells ya,
and nobody gets hurt, see?"
    The three men trained their weapons
at the patrons, yelling for everyone to
lay face down on the floor. Gangster-
```

number-one unfurled a burlap sack and hopped over the counter. He stepped over the first prone teller and grabbed handfuls of cash from the open money drawer. He stuffed the bills into the sack and continued on to the next drawer and the next.

"Hurry it up! I think the cops're comin'," Italian-gangster said. His eyes kept darting around, ensuring that the customers were cooperating, but his actions made him appear fidgety and nervous.

Unlike the nervous Italian, hulking-gangster remained calm and collected, as if carved from stone. He surveyed the bank as though he were a guard watching over prisoners from a gun tower. His fedora was pulled low over the eyes, obscuring them in a shadow that outlined his enormous square jaw. He didn't talk. Not a single word the whole time.

He watched one of the customers, a pudgy balding man near the bank's front entrance, who was eyeing the doorway, probably thinking of making a run for it. The big guy said nothing, but, instead, kept his eyes on the man.

The pudgy man looked back toward the robbers, then slowly turned to study the door some more, calculating his chances. He wasn't far from the entrance. Maybe ten feet. If he could get to his feet fast enough, maybe he could make it. Sweat beaded on the fat man's forehead. This was probably the toughest challenge he'd ever faced. If he failed, he was as good as dead.

The quiet hulking robber only watched him. The man on the floor had his complete attention now. In the distance, the warble of sirens became vaguely audible.

Probably tipped off when the Eyetalian popped a round into the ceiling, thought hulking robber. *I should've plugged the little twerp back at the hideout.*

Hulking-gangster cast a quick glance over at Italian-gangster: he still appeared jumpy, trying to look everywhere at once. He's too high strung, too fidgety. If not for him, this would probably have been an easy gig.

Gangster-number-one was still busily throwing handfuls of cash from the teller drawers into the sack, which was quite full now. Plenty of large bills, too. Despite the Depression, there was enough loot inside to make each of them independently wealthy.

Hulking-gangster turned his head, fixing his gaze back on the pudgy bald man lying near the entrance. His street sweeper never wavered from its steady perch over the hostages. Pudgy-customer probably assumed hulking-gangster was unable to see him because of the banister that separated the teller's aisle from the lobby. He was wrong. The police sirens were much louder now. It wouldn't be long before the cops would have the place surrounded.

Anthony looked at his watch. It was now a couple of minutes past midnight. His eyelids felt heavy, his eyes dry. The food and beer from the restaurant were in his belly, making him sleepy, but he didn't want to stop just now, not in the middle of the action sequence. *Just a little bit longer*, he told himself.

"Hurry it up! The cops'll be here any minute!" Italian-gangster yelled at gangster-number-one, who was doing his best to hurry, but greed had settled in and he wanted to gather as much loot as he could get.

It didn't surprise hulking-gangster when the fat slug on the floor finally made an attempt for the door, the passageway to freedom. Once he had gotten to his feet, pudgy-bald-man dashed for the exit.

Hulking-gangster's street sweeper issued a flash. KABOOM! The shot nearly tore pudgy-bald-man in half. His tattered body fell against the front door. The limp corpse left a slick crimson trail as it slid down the glass.

A couple of women lying nearby screamed out. Just then, the cops pulled to a stop in front of the bank. They scrambled from their cars, using them as shields between themselves and the robbers holed up inside.

The words on the paper blurred. By now, Anthony's eyelids had grown too heavy and were losing the fight to stay open. He laid his head on the finished pages stacked to the right of the typewriter.

I'll just rest them for a little bit.

It was the last thought he had before he was sound asleep.

A police siren whizzed by outside the window. It seemed as if Anthony had rested his head on the desk only a moment ago. Pain streaked along his neck when he opened his bleary eyes. Bright light greeted him as he slowly and carefully straightened the aching crick in his neck. He rubbed the sore area and looked around. It took a moment for his sleepy mind to connect the dots and realize he was no longer in his den. The brilliant glare surrounding him gave the feeling of being in a dream. He was sitting on a crate. The Royal typewriter rested on another wooden crate in front of him. Light slanted in from a four-paned window on the brick wall across from where Anthony was sitting; it was sunshine. He couldn't tell if it was rising or setting, but knew it was low in the sky from the angle of the rays coming through the window.

Above him, a long steel rail ran along the ceiling with a block and tackle pulley system clinging to it.

A chain hung from the track system, a hook at one end. Anthony recognized that he was in some sort of warehouse. Luckily, not a busy warehouse because there was nobody currently around him. That was a good thing because when he looked down he discovered he wasn't wearing any clothes. The crate's coarse wood was poking his ass cheeks. He stood up carefully, hoping not to get a splinter.

The heat of embarrassment traveled up his neck into his face as he covered his groin. The ever-popular dream of waking up naked in class occurred to him. Only, this wasn't any classroom he'd ever seen and, luckily, no one was around to point and laugh at him. Everything felt surreal, out of place.

From outside came the sound of a passing car. Anthony hurried over to the four-pane window, which was open a few inches. As he neared the glass, he saw a neighboring brick building across the way with rows of windows running up the front. Anthony thought it looked like an old apartment building or maybe offices. He looked down and saw a hard-packed dirt street separating the warehouse—or whatever he was in—from the building on the other side. He reached the window just in time to see the car he had heard earlier pass out of his line of sight; it looked like a Model A, or maybe a Model T, Anthony wasn't quite sure what the difference was, just that they were both old.

An antique-looking delivery truck approached going in the opposite direction with a large Twenty Mule Team Borax logo plastered on the side.

Anthony recognized the brand from one of the metal signs that had been hanging in the antique store he and Susan had visited. The sign, he remembered, was weather-beaten and rust-pitted. The truck, on the other hand, appeared to be brand new. Anthony had no idea what was going on. Nothing seemed to make any sense. In his current naked condition, he didn't dare venture out to explore.

He turned and faced the typewriter. A sheet of paper rested in the carriage, curled over the platen. Anthony went over to look at the print on the page. It was his bank heist story; the one he was working on when he fell asleep.

As he reached for the paper, a sliding door somewhere in the next room screeched with a metal-on-metal sound. Footfalls echoed across the cavernous room. It sounded to Anthony like more than one person, and it sounded like they were heading for the room he was in. He looked around and saw some wooden crates stacked in the corner. He ducked behind them and, in his haste, scraped his knee on the edge of a box. He covered his groin with one hand and his mouth with the other. There was a reddening welt above his throbbing knee. Anthony whispered prayers that no one discovered him.

"Lenny, bring the swag over here and dump it. We gotta divvy it up."

Anthony's heart pistoned like a racecar. He peeked around the corner of the boxes and found a man in a long trench coat walking toward the same window he had peered out of only seconds before.

The man glanced out then turned. "Coast's clear!" The voice sounded nasally, with a northern accent, but familiar.

"Well, it won't be for long," the first voice said. "Not after shootin' that guy. They'll beat the bushes lookin' for us."

Something in Anthony's mind clicked, like two wires making contact that completed a circuit. Although he'd only seen one of them, the voices and the one man's appearance seemed oddly familiar. The gears in his head were turning, trying to identify why that was so, but he couldn't nail down the reason. It didn't help that he was naked in a strange place.

"What's this?" the nasally voice said.

Anthony thought he'd been seen and felt his bladder contract.

"Hey, fellas. There's a typewriter here with some paper in it."

More footsteps now, coming to join the first voice.

"What's it say?"

"I dunno. I didn't read it."

Anthony was doing his best to peek around the corner without being seen. They were gathered around his typewriter.

The circuit in his mind closed and he put his finger on what must be going on. He was on the movie set for some old gangster film! That was the only logical explanation he could think of for what was happening. Meanwhile, the beefy giant in the group reached for the paper in the typewriter and pinched the top of the sheet.

He yanked it. Just as the bottom of the page came free of the carriage…

———◆———

Anthony bolted upright in his office chair. A thin runner of drool hung from the left corner of his mouth. Anthony massaged the stiff knot in his neck from lying at such an awkward angle. He felt disoriented as he looked around at the familiar surroundings. He was once again sitting in his den. The Royal typewriter sat on the desktop, showing a devious grin. On the overturned page where his head had rested was a small wet spot. He clutched at his chest, felt his shirt, and looked down at it. It was the same t-shirt he had fallen asleep in while writing his story. Anthony turned his head from side to side, trying to work the kink out. He recalled the dream he had, which lingered in his mind so vibrantly, unlike most of his dreams that vaporized shortly after he awoke. Everything in the dream was strange yet wonderful. Well, everything except for the part of not having anything to wear.

I could smell the stale air, feel the wooden crate, and taste the dust in the air. It was like my story. My story!

The toothy typewriter just stared at him blankly.

What the hell happened to my story?

Anthony ran his fingers through his matted hair. The last thing he remembered was the big guy pulling the page from the carriage. He glanced over the right corner of his desk, between the wall and the desk where his wastebasket lived. A solitary sheet of paper lay beside the plastic bucket that Anthony used as a garbage can. He could see the Royal's typeface; courier letters stamped on the page. He reached down and picked up the discarded sheet, wondering how it had gotten there.

I must've done it while I was dreaming, like a sleepwalker.

He placed the paper on his desk and wiped away the lint.

When Anthony stood up, the sore spot on his leg throbbed. He ran his fingers over it and remembered banging it as he ducked behind the boxes. He dismissed it as something that might've happened while he was asleep, kicking around behind the desk perhaps.

Anthony went into the kitchen. He opened the refrigerator, grabbed the milk container from the first shelf, unscrewed the cap, and drank straight from the jug, taking a large gulp. Once his dry mouth was satisfied by something cold and wet, Anthony recapped the jug and placed it back in the refrigerator. The small digital window display on the microwave glowed 8:03 AM.

Shit, I'm going to be late for work!

CHAPTER 3

Anthony felt like freshly squeezed crap and his reflection in the mirror confirmed it. He didn't want to go to work without a quick shower. Steam clouded the bathroom as hot water pelted him from head to toe. As usual, Anthony lost himself in a daydream about being a professional author. How nice it would be to wake up in the morning, plop down at his computer, and churn out a few pages of his next blockbuster novel. Anthony indulged in fantasies as a way to cope with his lousy job, self-centered customers, and mindless, uncaring boss. He tried doing that in the shower, enjoying the thought of not having to deal with any of those annoyances again. However, the thought of rolling into work late made Anthony feel sick to his stomach.

If I called in sick, I could write all day.

He felt worse knowing that it was out of the question. He had already taken off too many days as it was. If he missed many more, they would surely fire him. He had recently received a warning from his boss about his tardiness. Anthony wondered what his boss would say if he came into work late this time. He had to stop thinking about it. If he didn't, he would actually make himself sick and he already felt queasy.

It was 8:45 AM. With his hair still slicked wet and his shirt untucked, Anthony pulled out of the driveway and began his 45-minute commute to work. Ten minutes later, he was rolling down the expressway entrance ramp. A sea of glowing red brake lights marked the lanes of Highway 5, but this wasn't unusual. Anthony was used to sitting in traffic. That's why his twenty-mile trip to work took so long to travel. Sometimes the drive took longer than the average 45 minutes, but that was usually when there was an accident or heavy rain. It was ridiculous; add a little water to the road and everyone drove as if they'd forgotten how. He merged into traffic and drifted into yet another daydream. Anthony loved to lose himself in his imagination to escape his mundane life; it was the only thing that kept him from going insane. He thought of what Roger Kurrey's life must be like. How great it must be to have so much free time to sit around writing. Kurrey's novels were already legendary. Many of his books had been made into movies. As with Kurrey's books, Anthony never missed any of the movies or mini-series adapted from his novels. Roger Kurrey was iconic and he lived a life that Anthony could only dream about.

During the past year, Anthony had written numerous short stories and submitted them to magazines. Unfortunately, his only responses were rejection letters. That didn't stop Anthony from trying though. He had read an interview in a literary magazine about Roger's early days, how he received his fair share of rejection letters, too. Roger Kurrey persevered, until he finally got his first acceptance letter for a novel. That resulting book deal had put him on the literary map.

Yeah, that's all I need, my first break. It'll be easier after that.

Anthony never stopped dreaming.

When he finally snapped out of his reverie, he found that the car in front of him had stopped. Anthony's car came to a screeching halt when he slammed his foot down on the brake. He reacted so quickly that he forgot to engage the clutch, leaving his car stalled in the middle lane while the car in front of him, the one he avoided rear-ending, sped away. Anthony's face flushed with embarrassment as he started his engine and drove away.

A half hour later, he jerked his car into a parking space outside of the six-story building where he worked and made a mad dash into the office where his small cubicle waited, piled with papers and a phone that would keep ringing all day with impatient—and often angry—customers wanting support. Anthony pulled the chair out from his cluttered desk and pressed the power button on his computer. When he turned in his chair, Anthony noticed a yellow sticky note posted on his computer screen. It read, *See me when you get in - Jim*. His ass puckered and his stomach clenched as that queasy feeling returned. The note was from his asshole boss. "Oh shit, he's already been looking for me," Anthony said under his breath. Sometimes Anthony wondered whether Jim enjoyed confrontations with him just to watch Anthony squirm. His previous warning from Jim was still fresh in his mind. Anthony hoped he wouldn't lose his job for being late again. He started toward Jim's office, preparing for the worst.

Anthony turned the corner at the end of the row of cubicles and looked at his boss's office at the opposite end. Upper and middle management were privileged enough to get real offices with sheetrock walls and a door they could close. If you had enough seniority there might even be a window in your office. The outer offices housed most of the executives and supervisors. Anthony and his colleagues referred to this area as *executive row*. These were the same people who hired temps with the promise of hiring them at the end of their trial period. Of course, that never happened, as far as Anthony knew. Instead, the temps were let go at the end of three months and a new batch were brought in under the same misconception that they would be hired as full time employees. This was just another example of the bad business practices his company employed.

As Anthony approached, he observed Jim giving his stress ball a workout, kneading it like dough between his pudgy fingers. Jim sat at his desk, his phone cradled between his shoulder and ear. When Jim saw Anthony, he beckoned Anthony inside.

Jim Bower was only two years older than Anthony, but projected the personality of someone much older. His build was like that of a squat tree stump, not in a muscular way, but chubby. Jim had a recessed chin and wore his hair shaved down to a little peach fuzz. Just his appearance alone rubbed Anthony the wrong way. In the beginning, he and Anthony seemed to get along fairly well. Whenever Jim mingled with his team, he often kidded, sometimes telling jokes that were inappropriate for work, but no one said anything because Jim was their boss. He was everyone's friend, or so Jim seemed to think. It didn't take Anthony long to learn that Jim wasn't what he appeared to be. Jim's moods swung between two extremes. One minute, he would joke around with you like he was your best friend, the next, after the shit had hit the fan, Jim was always looking for someone to pin the blame on.

Lately, it seemed like every one of Anthony's coworkers had learned how to pass the buck and did it frequently. If there was a problem with the software, the development team would say the implementation team incorrectly installed the product, or the implementation team would blame the developers when an installation hit a snag, saying that there was a bug that prevented their progress. Customers complained to Anthony and the other help desk technicians that the documentation was severely lacking or poorly written. Anthony had noticed over the past two months that the office politics was getting worse and making his workplace unbearable. Lately, it seemed like everyone was targeting someone to stab in the back in an effort to advance a rung on the corporate ladder or just keep their job. As a bottom-feeder on the totem pole, Anthony was always caught in the middle of a tug-of-war he couldn't do anything to fix.

"That doesn't sound like it's our problem," Jim said to whoever was on the phone. "I'll send an email to the guys in R&D for some feedback and let you know what they say." A pause, then, "Yeah, yeah. Okay, bye." Jim sighed and hung up just as Anthony was sitting down.

That's right, pass the buck.

"Go ahead and close the door," Jim said.

The knot in Anthony's stomach twisted tighter as he went over and shut the door.

This is it. He's gonna drop the ax.

Anthony sat in one of the two chairs facing Jim's desk. Anthony hated these talks. That's what they were, according to Jim, just talks.

"Did you just get in?" Jim asked, glancing at his watch.

"Yeah. Traffic was a mess."

"Your tardiness is becoming an increasing concern," Jim said in his usual condescending way. "I need someone who can be here on time to provide our customers with the quality support they need."

"I know, Jim, but—"Jim raised a hand, silencing Anthony.

Anthony hated when Jim acted cocky like this. To make himself feel better, Anthony recalled with fondness a time when Jim had taken it in the ass from the Director of Development after he tried accusing a developer of ruining a project deadline. The Director of Development didn't condone such behavior from the other departments and chewed Jim out for trying to offload the problem. Jim hadn't been so cocky then.

Jim was still blathering, "When you're continually late or absent, you're causing everyone else to pick up your workload. Imagine if your co-workers did that. How would you feel? I imagine you'd be fed up with it after a while. Is everything okay?"

Anthony fixated on that last question, wondering if, perhaps, he looked as sick as he felt and Jim was legitimately concerned about his health. He was wrong.

"Do you like working here, Anthony?"

Saying that Anthony *hated* his job was an understatement, but it paid the bills and left him with some spare time to write, what little of it he seemed to have. He was sure as hell not about to tell his boss the truth about how he felt. After all, tech support workers were easy to come by, a dime a dozen as they say. Anthony knew he was expendable; there was no denying it. As much as he might hate it, Anthony just needed to get through this confrontation with his job intact.

"Sure I do, but—"

Again, Jim interrupted him, "You've been tardy four times in the past two weeks. Two of those times, you were nearly an hour late. Just in the last month and a half, you've missed five days. That's not an acceptable track record, Anthony. I don't want to let you go; you've been here for almost three years. You were a really good employee, but lately your performance has started to taper off."

Jim paused looking at Anthony as if waiting for a response. Anthony had nothing to say. He didn't know *what* to say. Jim was right and Anthony knew it, but he couldn't tell Jim the truth: that he hated this fucking job and just wanted to write. Currently, Anthony's dream seemed ridiculous, but in his head, it was a comforting thought that he felt was absolutely attainable.

"I hope this is the last time we have to talk about this problem. We have two new accounts coming in and I need everyone's head in the game. One of these accounts is critical to our revenue. I need you to focus and give me a hundred and ten percent. We may have to work some overtime next month."

Jim bent his head forward, looking over his reading glasses at Anthony as a principal might eye an unruly student waiting for an answer.

"Yes sir," Anthony said, standing up, "I'm sorry. We won't have to have another one of these talks." Anthony left Jim's office, disgusted with his sudden yes-man attitude, but it made the problem go away. Anthony loathed kissing the ass of a man he didn't like or respect for a job he hated even more. Again, a daydream filled his head, allowing him to forget about his dipshit boss.

Anthony slunk back to his dismal gray cubicle. His phone was already lit up with people waiting to belittle him. He sat down in his chair, swiveled around, and thumbed through pages of addendums to the latest technical manual for the company's software. He positioned his headset over his ears and pushed one of the lit phone buttons.

"JSS Software, this is Anthony, how may I help you?" he asked. It was only 10 AM and already he knew it was going to be a long day.

Susan showed up at 12:20 PM to have lunch with Anthony. He was more than willing to get out of the office and the mere sight of her was a godsend.

"Let's go!" Anthony exclaimed. "I can't wait any longer."

"Where do you feel like eating?"

"I don't really care. I just have to get out of here."

Susan's smile faded as she trailed after Anthony through the building's lobby. Anthony's lack of enthusiasm for his job over the last couple of months was no secret, nor was it a sudden thing. In the beginning, Anthony's attitude toward his job was fine, but lately he really seemed to have little tolerance for it, complaining whenever the subject came up.

"What happened? Did your boss have another *talk* with you?"

"Yeah. I was late again. Traffic was shitty this morning." Anthony didn't want to tell Susan that he had stayed up to work on one of his stories and woke up late. It wasn't lying if he neglected to tell her, right? Besides, he didn't want her to be upset with him. If he told her that he had stayed up late writing, she'd clearly side with Jim. The thought of her siding with his boss was a slap to the face. He decided he could deal with his own issues without pulling her into them.

"Let's go to the mall," he said. "I want to go to the bookstore after we eat."

As Anthony followed Susan to an empty table on the outer fringe of the food court, he noticed that the mall was busier than normal with women and children. Did these people have jobs? What about school? He envied their freedom to roam the mall at their leisure.

The dream he'd had after he dozed off was still in his mind. Actually, Anthony was trying to determine whether it had indeed been a dream or if it had really happened.

Of course it was a dream, dumbass. You can't wake up in a completely different time! That's the stuff of science fiction.

Anthony kicked himself mentally for even entertaining the silly notion.

"I had the weirdest dream last night." He put his tray down on the table and took a seat across from Susan. "I started writing this cool story about a bank heist in the thirties that goes wrong. I typed up a few pages on that old typewriter you gave me. Only, I got sleepy and could barely keep my eyes open, so I laid my head down on the table for just a few minutes. I must've crashed."

"Let me guess, you fell asleep and had a dream about the story," she said and sipped her milkshake.

Anthony paused, thought about it. Yeah. It made sense, especially after hearing Susan verbalize it. That's why the men in his dream were so familiar. And to think he had chalked it up to being on a movie set! Well, he was asleep, after all. Things are usually wonky in dreams.

"Well, sort of. They were in it, but not at first. I fell asleep and dreamed I was in some kind of warehouse. I think I was back in the thirties. It seemed so weird, like I was really there. Oh yeah, and the weirdest part was that I was naked."

"Naked?" Susan covered her mouth as she laughed. "Yeah, I'd say that's weird. Sure you weren't in a classroom?"

Anthony felt that same sensation of humiliation from his dream creep up to his cheeks. "Ha. Ha."

"I had a dream like that before!" Susan said, "Only, I was dressed. I was walking in the woods. It was shady and peaceful, probably a pine forest because there was a blanket of pine needles on the ground and it was so quiet.

"Hills surrounded me. I remember there was one in front of me and two on either side. There was a large white boulder with green moss on it jutting from one of the hills and ferns all around. It was so beautiful."

"Damn, how do you remember all those details?" Anthony asked.

"I usually don't. Not all of them anyways, but, for some reason, those stuck with me.

"Anyway, I heard a growl in the distance to my left. I'm not sure how I knew this, but I could tell by the sound that it was a grizzly bear. It scared the heck out of me. I started to panic as I tried finding the bear through the trees. I looked for a nearby tree to climb in case I had to. It really freaked me out. I'm sure my heart was racing in my sleep.

"After that first growl, I heard another one somewhere behind me. That made me panic even more. I finally saw the first bear. I was a nervous wreck and kept searching for a tree to climb. I was surrounded by bears and they were closing in on me!" Susan's excitement became palpable as she recounted her nightmare.

"Yeah, sounds pretty scary, all right," Anthony said. "Do you remember the smell of the woods or whether the temperature was cold or hot?"

Susan's eyebrows furrowed at the question, as though it came from left field. She shook her head slowly and said, "No, I don't think I've ever experienced anything like that in any of my dreams. Why? Do *you* remember that kind of stuff?"

"No. Not usually, but that's what's so weird about this one. I've never remembered anything like that before. That's what I meant when I said it was so real and so…weird. Think about it. Did you ever wake up remembering such vivid details? I haven't. I don't even know if it's possible to feel or taste or smell anything in a dream," he said, wondering if there were any documented cases of such sensations. He was certain that his dream had been that vivid.

"I can't recall any dream I've had that I remembered *that* well," Susan said. "Of course, I forget most of them when I wake up, unless they're really disturbing like that bear dream."

"Somewhere, I heard that we never dream in color. I don't know for sure if that's true. I mean, I've had some really bizarre dreams, and I think I remember seeing certain colors, but I don't know if it was my conscious mind adding color to the memory or what. I definitely saw colors in my dream last night though, as well as sounds…," Anthony recalled the scrape on his leg after he had awakened. He could still *feel* his leg connecting with the edge of that wooden crate. "I'm telling you it was so real!"

Susan considered that and said, "Are you sure your conscious mind wasn't just filling in the blanks after you woke up?" She looked at her watch. "We've gotta go. It's been an hour and you don't want to be late getting back."

Anthony didn't want to be reminded about his meeting with Jim that morning, or about coming into work late. "Well, I don't know how to explain it, but it seemed very real. Maybe my mind filled in the gaps or whatever, but I've never experienced anything like that before in a dream. I even woke up with a scrape on my leg after dreaming about bumping my knee against a box in the warehouse." In the parking lot, he raised his pant leg and showed Susan the mark. She had no explanation to offer him.

At work, Anthony found it difficult to concentrate on his job. His mind kept drifting back to the story he had started writing and the dream that had followed. Maybe Susan was right; it was only his subconsciousness indulging in a world he had created while writing.

Maybe the dream was a result of me concentrating so hard on the setting.

It certainly made more sense than the silly conclusion he had jumped to while he was busy hiding behind the imaginary crates. The idea that he had awakened on a movie set made his cheeks flush with embarrassment.

Anthony was anxious to get home so he could work on his story. He still had a good feeling about it. If he could just get it out of his head and onto paper, he could clean and polish it during the editing process. After that, he would try submitting it to a publisher or an agent.

He glanced at his watch and saw that it was nearly time for him to go home; only fifteen more minutes remained in his workday. Fortunately, the support calls had tapered off. Knowing that Jim was in a meeting that would probably last another hour made Anthony consider skipping out early, but he decided against it when he remembered that morning's talk. Besides, he didn't want any of his coworkers to rat him out for doing so. He was already skating on thin ice; instead, Anthony browsed the Internet and answered another call before it was time to leave.

CHAPTER 4

Anthony didn't get home until 8 PM. He had stopped to grab a hamburger for dinner before he settled down to write. He planned to go to bed early so he wouldn't be late for work in the morning, which left him little time to write. He popped the top on a beer and sat down behind his desk. Picking up the last page he had typed the previous night, Anthony re-read what he had written. As he went back over the story, it felt like he was covering old ground that had already been trampled to death. The story was cliché.

I need something fresh—something that hasn't been done before. I'm never going to get published if I keep churning out the same old shit.

He didn't want to throw away what he had, even if it was cliché. He liked it and thought it was well-written. He placed the page on top of the stack and tucked it away into the desk drawer; next to a Roger Kurrey novel he'd recently finished reading. He stared at the book before shutting the drawer.

Now that was an awesome story.

He checked out the worn cover and broken spine.

It was original and gripping. *If I could just write like that!*

Anthony knew that if he wanted to make it into the ranks of authors like Kurrey, he would have to come up with a story just as original and compelling.

He sat for a little while, searching his mind for a story idea while sipping from the beer can. He turned ideas over, but nothing seemed to interest him. Finally, an idea began to form: the story of a traveling salesman on the verge of suicide.

In his mind's eye, he could see the main character's beat up car—a 1980 Cutlass maybe—pulling into a roadside motel. Anthony wasn't sure about all of the finer details just yet, but knew everything would eventually come together. He just had to be patient, let the story unfold in his head. Right now, he had the seed. The rest would gel; all he had to do was allow his imagination to stretch its legs.

He could see the whole story laid out in his mind, a series of rough still-frames. It had everything he needed: an antagonist, protagonist, a goal, obstacle, and the ability to hold the reader's attention, just as long as Anthony could maintain that tension and ominous setting.

That's it! This could be an awesome story.

Considering the story's potential motivated Anthony to start writing.

He took a blank piece of paper from the newly opened ream, rolled it into the typewriter, and adjusted the carriage. He began with the salesman pulling into the parking lot of a small roadside hotel. The rain shower he had been driving through was beginning to develop into a heavier storm.

```
     Stanley Pardin grabbed his briefcase
and threw open the squeaky door of his
Oldsmobile. He scrambled from the car's
warm, dry interior and made a half-
hearted run to room 139. The rain began
pelting his trench coat with quarter-
sized drops. Stanley's umbrella was in
the trunk. Thank God it's on the first
floor, he thought, noticing that there
was no cover over the stairs leading up
to the second floor. I'd be drenched if
I had to run up there.
     He reached his door beneath the
overhang, escaping the downpour, when
it occurred to him that it didn't
really matter if he got drenched, not
tonight anyway. This was going to be
his last night on Earth. He shoved the
key in the lock and gave it a twist.
The latch gave way, the knob turning
with the key, and he pushed the door
open into the stale darkness of the
```

room. He felt along the right side of the wall for the light switch and turned it on. A bulb hanging over a table beside a thick set of curtains flickered to life.

As Stanley stepped inside and closed the door he thought of his wife, Paula, and the last time he'd seen her--or more accurately, caught her. He had come home from a trip to Wisconsin earlier than expected. He had unlocked the front door to their second-floor apartment and set his briefcase on the dining room table as he went into the living room. He had thrown his trench coat over the back of their old blue sofa where they had spent many nights watching <u>The Late Show</u> following one of Stanley's long sales trips.

He heard a noise from their bedroom and crept down the hallway to surprise his wife. She didn't know he was coming home so soon. He thought she might be putting away some folded laundry, or was just getting out of the shower; it was only 8 PM after all.

The bedroom door was slightly ajar and Stanley sidled up next to it, ready to throw it open and surprise Paula. As he got closer, he heard the mattress creak as though someone were rolling over on it. <u>Was she taking a nap?</u> he wondered. <u>Did she hear me come in?</u>

Then he heard someone's voice from the other side of the door, one that clearly wasn't his wife's. It was a man's voice. Stanley's heart skipped in surprise and he felt as if he might lose control of his bladder. It was a nightmare coming true. The kind of nightmare that was so bad you never wished it upon anyone else. Heavy breathing and panting accompanied the deep voice, which said, "Yeah baby, right there." Rustling sheets and bedsprings. Kissing sounds.

Stanley's legs were unsteady, numb and distant, as though they were not his legs anymore. The moment seemed vaguely dream-like as images of his wife with another man materialized in Stanley's head. Sweat beaded on his brow and continued up to his receding hairline. His palms were already sweaty and his fingers felt fat and awkward.

Stanley had been afraid to move. Scared of letting them know he was there, listening. Then, Paula answered her lover with moans. "Oh God, yes! Fuck me! Yes!" she shrieked. The headboard began thumping against the wall.

Thinking of that night brought tears of shame and rage to Stanley's eyes. That had only been two nights ago. He'd had the scenario running through his mind ever since he had crept out of the apartment and sped away in his beat up Cutlass with its creaky doors and dented front fender.

His rage boiled over as he remembered finding his friend Dale's car parked across the road from his apartment. Dale lived six miles away in

Gloucester. _That double-crossing son-of-a-bitch! How long had this been going on?_

Dale was one of Stan's long-time buddies. They had worked together at the garment factory in town until Stanley took a sales job with Preston Carpet and Tile. There was more money in sales and Stanley was able to travel, see parts of the country that he'd never been to. Besides, Stanley found that he liked the Midwest and the open road. There was time for him to think and time to himself. _Obviously too much time,_ Stanley realized and found himself clenching his jaw and fists.

Stanley tossed his wet coat on the bed and laid the briefcase next to the mound of pillows covered by the floral-pattern bedspread. He opened the drawer of the nightstand between the beds and took out the Gideon Bible. Opening it randomly, he read the first verse his finger landed on: "Behold, I come as a thief in the night." He slammed the book, as the verse reminded him of Dan--that thief in the night--climbing on top of Paula on his bed.

Stanley felt cheated in more ways than one as he stood with the Bible in his hands. He looked toward the ceiling and said, "What've you done for _me_ lately, huh?" He dropped the Bible into the wastebasket beside the dresser.

Stanley opened the latches on his briefcase and removed the stainless steel Ruger .357 and dumped out the box of bullets he'd bought at a pawn shop when he stopped in Fargo. The bullets had spilled out of the box during the ride. Stanley opened the revolver's cylinder and carefully began filling each empty chamber with hollow point bullets. His hands grew shaky as he filled the last two holes.

<u>This is it,</u> he thought, placing the loaded pistol on the pillow as he considered one last time what it was he was about to do. A myriad of thoughts rushed through his head as he sat on the edge of the bed: Paula and how much he had loved her; his best friend, Dale, and all of the things they had done together over the years--card games and fishing trips; his career as a salesman. He thought about the finality of what was about to happen-- the last act of a broken man. What about the people who would find him? Would someone come running soon after they heard the gunshot? Stanley had already considered muffling the blast by putting a pillow between his head and the barrel. That would dampen the noise considerably, wouldn't it? But, what if it didn't?

He had read once that suicide victims often soiled themselves during the act, because their muscles loosened. He wondered if that was true. <u>More than likely,</u> he thought. <u>It made sense anyway.</u> He tried to imagine what people would say when they found him. He wondered how long it would take before anyone found him?

<u>What would Paula think when she hears about what I've done?</u> Thoughts of Paula and Dale together, in his apartment, came to the forefront. Stanley tried to think about the good times he and Paula had had together instead. But, it didn't work.

<u>Were there ever any signs? Any red flags?</u>

Of course, his imagination could convince him that there had been warnings. Dale had come over many times to hang out with them. Stanley was sure there were plenty of glances between them when he went to the bathroom or got up to get another beer. His imagination filled in the gaps, allowing him to believe the two were stealing kisses while he had his back turned for any length of time.

"STOP IT!" he yelled through clenched teeth. His fists were balled tight again and he wondered why he insisted on torturing himself further.

Thunder echoed in the distance, following a bright flicker of lightning. The sound of the rain coming down outside grew louder. <u>What a fitting night to make an exit,</u> he thought.

Stanley loved thunderstorms and couldn't resist the urge to walk over and part the drapes so he could watch the rain pummel the ground while lightning danced in the distance. When the next jagged flash occurred, Stanley glimpsed a dark silhouette moving quickly toward the hotel from the empty highway. The figure darted between parked cars and finally made a beeline toward the hotel.

<u>That poor guy's going to be drenched!</u> Stanley watched the person run up to the building, under the protection of the second floor walk way, and beyond his field of vision. Assuming that the person was entering a room further down, Stanley closed the curtain and turned to do what he had come there to do.

There was a knock at his door. A rush of adrenaline jump-started Stanley's heart. <u>No one knows I'm here,</u> he reminded himself. He stood, waiting, wondering who might be standing outside, especially in this weather. There was no follow-up knock, and when Stanley realized he was standing rigid, he relaxed his shoulders and let out a breath he didn't realize he had been holding. Just then, another knock came. Stanley tensed. He quickly shoved the pistol under the flap of blanket covering the pillows. He approached the door apprehensively, running his hands over his hair to smooth it.

"Who is it?" He stood close to the door gazing through the peephole, but was unable to see out into the dark stormy night.

The person knocked at the door a third time, but this time they spoke as well, "Please open the door, sir. It's raining out here and I can't get in my room. Can I use your phone?"

Stanley paused, wondering why this person wanted to use his phone. Why not go to another room? "Why not use the phone in the front office?" Stanley knew it was an asshole thing to say to someone caught out in the storm and he was almost never that way toward people, but this night was different. He was in the middle of something. Something big! He didn't want to be interrupted. Stanley started away from the door, thinking the person had finally gone away.

"Please, sir. The front office is closed and I'm locked out of my room. Can I just use your phone for a minute?" the voice pleaded over the pounding rain, punctuated by rolling thunder.

Stanley looked at his watch. It was 10:04 PM. Maybe the front office was closed. Stanley wasn't sure. He sighed and twisted the knob on the deadbolt. Before he opened the door, Stanley quickly glanced back over the room, making sure nothing was visible that shouldn't be.

He turned the knob and pulled the door open. The stranger hurried in from the dark night as Stanley stepped out of the way and took another quick survey of the room.

Satisfied that everything was safely concealed, Stanley pointed toward the phone sitting on the nightstand between the beds. The man shut the door and twisted the deadbolt before walking toward the phone. Stanley noticed that the visitor was tall. The black trench coat that he wore made him appear sinister. That wasn't what struck Stanley as strange, though. Despite coming in from a torrential downpour, the man was completely <u>dry</u>!

Stanley didn't know what to make of this. He had forgotten all about Dan and Paula. He wasn't even thinking of the business he came to conduct. He watched the man remove his coat and lay it casually across the bed. Stanley had no idea how wide his eyes were when he raised a finger toward the phone and said, "There's the phone." Suddenly, the room felt stuffy and much warmer than it had earlier.

The tall stranger sat on the edge of the bed closest to the door, the same bed where Stanley had hidden the revolver beneath the pillow. Stanley stared as the man sat and removed his black leather gloves by pulling on each finger, one at a time. The man placed the gloves on top of the trench coat and removed his hat, setting it atop the gloves neatly.

Stanley observed that the man's hair didn't have a hat ring. Instead, his shiny black hair bore fresh comb-tracks. His mustache and goatee were as meticulously groomed as the hair on his head. The stranger had a regal air about him that made Stanley uncomfortable.

Everything about the man's demeanor screamed "wrong". First, he walked in and sat casually on the bed while making himself comfortable instead of going directly to the phone. And then, there was what the man said...

"I was beginning to wonder if you were ever going to open the door, Stan."

How's this guy know my name? Stanley looked at the door. It was on the other side of the stranger. Stanley considered making a dash for it. Sweat stood out on his forehead. His mouth was dry and his tongue felt glued to the roof of his mouth.

The man sat patiently staring at Stanley as if waiting for a reply. When Stanley realized the man had not only cut off his route to the door but also the pistol, he felt trapped.

"How--" A lump rose in Stanley's throat. He swallowed."How do you know my name?" His voice sounded wafer thin, distant, only a whisper in the room.

The stranger smiled and stood. "Come. Sit, please. We should talk about some things." He stood and walked toward Stanley as though he was the gracious host and Stanley the visitor.

Stanley was still confused, but because the man spoke politely, and had a disarming graciousness about him, Stanley managed to relax a little. On a scale from one to ten, Stanley's anxiety had settled from a twelve to a nine. There was still something absolutely wrong about the whole situation. Stanley's brain tried to signal to his legs: SOMETHING'S WRONG...RUN, RUN! But, his heart knew he would never make it if he did try to escape.

The stranger guided Stanley toward the bed, leading him by his elbow. Stanley could feel how hot the man's touch was through his shirt sleeve. Stanley flopped down on the edge of the bed across from where the stranger first sat. Then the stranger took his seat again.

Anthony's vision blurred when he blinked and he realized that his eyes were beginning to burn. He was having a difficult time keeping them open. The small seed of a headache that had crept in earlier was starting to bloom. He glanced at his watch. It was 11:34 PM. He promised himself he was going to bed on time so he wouldn't be late for work in the morning, but that meant he should've been in bed an hour ago. Anthony was too wrapped up in his new story, loving how it flowed so effortlessly from his mind onto the page. It played out like a movie in his head; all he had to do was type what he saw. He didn't want to interrupt that Zen moment, but he had to, otherwise he would be late for work again and receive another ass-chewing from his boss. In the morning, he knew he would regret staying up even for an hour. He could already hear the dreaded alarm ringing. He hated mornings, absolutely despised them. It wasn't unusual for Anthony to sleep until 10:30 or later on the weekends or holidays.

Anthony stood, his knees popping, stretched out his arms, and yawned. When he saw that he had come to the end of the page, he pulled it out of the typewriter and placed it face down on the few pages that had already accumulated. He left the den and turned off the light.

Anthony arrived home around 6:30 the next evening, his usual time. He was anxious to get back to work on his story. He went to the refrigerator and grabbed a drink, then went to his desk and loaded a new sheet of paper into the typewriter. He had looked forward to this moment since his head hit the pillow the previous night. Anthony didn't want his story idea to grow stale before he could get it out of his head.

This is the one that's going to get me published. No more of this rat race shit after I get that book deal.

The thought made him giddy as he rolled a blank sheet into the carriage. Once everything was set, Anthony reread the last paragraph. When he was reoriented and his mental stage was set, Anthony began to type. The words came slowly at first, but then picked up speed as he slipped into his groove.

Stanley repeated his question to the stranger, "I asked how you know my name?" His voice was timid and weak. Stanley asked himself, why am I so scared? What's the worst he could do? Kill me? Isn't that why I came here? There was no talking himself around his fear, however. Even though he came to the hotel with the intention of ending his life, he was horrified by the thought of someone else doing it for him. He was prepared to chew the end of that pistol, but he sure as hell wasn't prepared to die at someone else's hands.

"How do I know your name?" the stranger asked with a smirk on his face. "Oh come now, Stanley. I've been watching you for some time." The man leaned forward, folding his hands over one another the way a ball player might sit on the edge of the bench in the dugout, spitting tobacco juice or sunflower seeds in the dirt.

Stanley's eyebrows rose in bewilderment. Did this guy know about Dale and Paula?

"I know all about your unfortunate circumstances."

At this, Stanley's heart rate switched into overdrive. Someone else knows about my dirty laundry?!

"I know about your wife, Paula, and your friend, Dale," the man confirmed as if reading Stanley's thoughts.

"Ex-friend!" Stanley corrected, surprising himself at his emotional bravado under the circumstances. He realized his fists were clenched again and he was gritting his teeth. His burst of rage overpowered the stranger's mystique and helped Stanley regain some of his composure. "Are you a private detective or something? Is that it?"

The man ignored the questions. "Well, well. I suppose you're right. I meant soon-to-be ex-wife and ex-friend. I also know that you intend to kill yourself, in this very room, tonight. And that is precisely why I'm here."

Stanley stood staring dumbly at the man, trying to understand how on Earth he could know any of that. Stanley had a knack for remembering faces, although names were a bit trickier. This man's face was as foreign to him as the surface of Mars. Then a thought occurred to Stanley: <u>He's an angel! Sent here to stop me.</u>

Stanley wasn't a religious man. He had only attended church when he was a kid and that was only when his mother made him go with her. What other explanation could there be? How could anyone know so much about him? Okay, knowing about Paula and Dale could probably be explained logically, but nobody knew Stanley's intention to commit suicide. The guy must be an angel!

"You see, Stanley, I'm here because I want your soul."

Stanley pointed a rigid finger at the man. "I knew it! You're an angel, aren't you?" he said, surprised that he was able to figure it out.

The man on the bed only smiled and said, "Well..." then paused.

Stanley walked slowly around him, toward the front of the room.

"You got me Stanley. I wasn't supposed to let the cat out of the bag, but you figured me out." He turned to watch Stanley studying him.

Stanley finished processing what the man had just said. <u>Wait a minute. Suicide's a sin. You don't go to heaven for it. You go to H...</u>Stanley gasped when he realized he wasn't talking to an angel, but instead he was talking to...what? Stanley stopped pacing. He glanced at the pillow covering the hidden pistol.

"Oh Stanley, are you actually thinking of shooting an angel?" the man asked, keeping up the charade. Yet he knew the jig was up. He could read Stanley's thoughts the whole time. He said he had been tuned in to Stanley for some time now.

"You're not an angel," Stanley said and began trembling. He pointed his finger at the man (or whatever) again, except now his finger was shaking. His stomach churned nervously. "I don't know what in hell you are, but..."

"You mean who in Hell I am, don't you? Stop being so goddamned obtuse, Stanley!"

The stranger stood up and faced Stanley straight on. His eyes glowed and Stanley could see the fires burning within them. The room suddenly grew much hotter and stuffier.

"Do you really mean to tell me you don't know who I am?"

A dark spot blossomed between Stanley's legs as he pissed himself before Satan. His legs felt as if they would collapse at any moment, but didn't. The Devil approached him and suddenly Stanley realized he didn't want to die after all, especially if it meant spending an eternity in Hell.

Anthony glanced at his watch, knowing it was getting late, but not wanting to stop writing. He was at a point where the words flowed freely from his brain to his fingertips. He was in the zone. This didn't happen very often but when it did, it was exhilarating. After staring at the black typeface against the white paper for so long, Anthony had to blink, forcing his eyes to focus on the hands of his watch.

Damn, it's almost ten.

He would have to quit now so he could shower before getting in bed. Again, he reveled in the venerating thoughts of writing for a living, thoughts that were his security blanket, insulating him from the cold world of reality.

Anthony got up, leaving the paper resting in the carriage of the typewriter so he wouldn't have to spend additional time setting up the following night. He went to his bedroom where he kicked off his shoes and undressed, dropping his clothes next to the bed, adding to the small pile of dirty laundry that accumulated until the weekend. He took a quick shower before crawling into bed.

Anthony woke up without the aid of his clock's annoying buzzer. He was groggy. Realizing he hadn't heard the alarm, Anthony panicked and reached for his lamp on the nightstand. There had been times when he mistakenly set the alarm for PM instead of AM. He hoped that this was not one of those times.

As he groped for the light, he knocked something onto the floor. He couldn't find the lamp so he threw the sheets off and stumbled out of bed in the darkness. He walked toward the light switch on the wall. In the dark, his toe struck the edge of what felt like the leg of a wooden chair. He cursed, bit his lip until some of the pain subsided, and took a few more shuffling steps until he felt the wall. Instead of the smooth painted sheetrock of his bedroom, he felt textured wallpaper.

What the...?

He moved his hand along the surface until he finally touched the switch and flipped it. The room lit up by way of two wall lamps on either side of a squat nightstand separating his bed from another bed of the same size.

Where the hell am I?

He surveyed the strange room he found himself in. It was obvious by the furnishings that it was a hotel room, but not just *any* hotel room. This was the room he had imagined while writing his story of the suicidal salesman.

Anthony jerked the blanket from the bed and wrapped it around himself after discovering for the second time he was naked in a strange place.

The thing he had knocked off the nightstand was the ashtray, but most hotels had banned smoking in the rooms. An old-fashioned Magnavox TV, with dials instead of a small infrared remote control window, occupied a space in the center of the bureau across from the bed. Beyond that was a doorway into what he could only assume was the bathroom. The light in there was off, but through the entryway, he saw his reflection in a large wall mirror over a sink. Above the bed hung a large print picture of a dog, probably a retriever of some sort, flushing game birds out of thick brush. He looked at the nightstand between the beds.

Hundred-to-one there's a Gideon Bible in the top drawer.

Anthony went over to the nightstand and pulled opened the top drawer. Just as he suspected, a

Gideon Bible was inside, along with a list of the TV channels. Of course, that didn't really prove anything. Anyone who's stayed in a roadside motel knows there's almost always a Gideon Bible in the nightstand drawer.

In the corner of the room, before a long stretch of drawn curtains, sat a circular table. A wooden chair stood beside it. The antique Royal typewriter was on top of that table. The last page of his story, *Stanley's Visitor*, protruded from the carriage.

Anthony plopped down on the edge of the bed, staring at the machine.

What the fuck's happening here? First, I wake up in a strange warehouse and now this.

He rested his head in his hands wondering how he would ever get home or to work. He looked around the room and saw the backside of what might be a clock-radio sitting on the nightstand on the opposite side of the bed. He ran to the other side and turned the clock around so he could see it. It was very early in the morning, 2:30 AM.

It dawned on Anthony that he could hear water dripping, but it wasn't coming from the bathroom. He went to the front door and looked through the peephole. He couldn't see much, except two cars parked outside. A streetlight cast its glow from somewhere off to the left, reflected by the grilles of the shiny wet cars. The sound he heard was falling rain. Just then, a jagged streak of lightning split the night sky, illuminating the outside world. In that brief flash, Anthony spied a road on the other side of the parking lot and what looked like a field beyond it. Thunder rolled through the night like falling bowling pins.

Anthony unlatched the security chain and twisted the deadbolt. He opened the door and peered outside. The night air was cool. Water dripped from the second floor overhang. His breath was a foggy vapor against the contrasting darkness. Another streak of lightning flickered but this time the thunder rumbled somewhere further in the distance. Anthony looked to his right. There appeared to be five or six rooms in that direction. A sign at the far end announced ICE and an arrow pointed toward the corner. To Anthony's left were more rooms, probably more than a dozen and then the front office. A neon sign indicating No Vacancies blinked in pinkish-red neon letters. Anthony stepped back into the room but not before reading the numbers on the door—138. He leaned out and looked to his right. The room next to his was 139. He ducked back inside.

This is the motel from my story.

Anthony made it a point to remember the smells, tastes, and sensations of things in this dream. Well, that's what Susan had called it anyway, a dream. How else would someone explain waking up in a strange place such as this? He could smell the stagnant air in the room—with the underlying hint of cigarette smoke, the cleansing-fresh smell of the rain as it came down, as well as its coolness. Not to mention, the fuzz of the carpet between his toes. It was all too vivid to be a dream. There was just no way this could not be real!

He remembered the big bank robber yanking the paper out of the typewriter the last time he was in this situation—in the warehouse—and how he had immediately awakened at home. Anthony approached the table where his Royal sat and looked at the paper. It was just as he had left it before he went to bed. He slowly reached out and grasped the top of the crisp white page with trembling fingers. When he jerked it out of the carriage…

CHAPTER 5

Anthony woke up in his bed in his own apartment. He looked around the room, realizing that it was not pitch dark. Weak sunlight filtered in through the drawn blinds letting in enough light for him to see his dresser. His wallet and keys still lay on top. The digital alarm clock beside his bed said it was 7:23 AM, seven minutes before the alarm was set to go off.

He threw back the sheets and climbed out of bed. His khaki work pants, pullover shirt, socks, and shoes were still in a pile where he'd left them. Anthony ambled down the hall and into the study where the Royal sat on the desk, staring at him with that toothy typeface grin, but now the carriage was empty.

The previously typed pages were still stacked neatly face down next to the typewriter as he'd put them. He picked up the topmost sheet and turned it over. It wasn't the one he'd left in the carriage overnight. Anthony went around the desk to his chair and saw the missing page lying face up on the carpet under the desk. "This isn't really happening," Anthony muttered to himself looking down at the paper, trying to get a handle on the moment.

Oh it's happening all right. How else do you explain the page winding up on the floor?

He searched his mind for some logical explanation for that mental question, but nothing came to him. Anthony knew damn well the wind didn't do it, as the saying goes.

Maybe someone else is doing this, playing a trick on me.

He couldn't help but think of a fairytale, the one about the shoemaker who would leave his work materials out at night, only to wake up and find shoes made in the morning. Later, the old shoemaker would discover that elves were creating the shoes while he slept. As soon as Anthony thought of it, he dismissed the notion just as quickly. That idea was beyond ludicrous, it was preposterous!

Not as silly as the other ideas I've come up with to explain it.

He was curious to hear what Susan had to say about this latest excursion but also hesitant because he didn't want her to think he was crazy.

The Old Royal

It was 12:20 PM when Anthony met Susan for lunch at a trendy gourmet sandwich shop. Anthony had hinted at the subject of his latest experience with the typewriter, testing Susan's reaction. When he realized she was just humoring him, he felt better about discussing the topic. They sat at a small table in the corner as he filled her in on the details of what had happened that night.

"I could *really* smell and feel everything in the dream. When I opened the hotel room door, the night air was cool on my skin and I could smell the wet ground. I even heard the thunder. The hotel room had a distinct odor, too; stale cigarette smoke. It was so damn weird! Just like the dream before, I could sense everything around me and feel it. It had depth. Not like any of my dreams in the past. After waking from one of those, I couldn't remember much of anything about them. No sounds, smells, or feelings ever stayed with me. But these last two were different, I tell ya. I can remember them just as well as I can describe eating with you now."

"Well I don't know what to say, Anthony. If you're so convinced they're real why don't you put your theory to the test?"

"What do you mean?" he asked.

"Are you kidding? Write a story about winning the lottery or something," Susan said.

He wondered why he hadn't thought of it earlier; probably because he had been focusing too hard on trying to explain it rather than think of ways to exploit it. "That's brilliant! Yeah, I'll go home and write about winning the lottery. What's it up to now?"

"I think it's at forty-four million."

"Okay. I'm going to do it." Anthony considered the possibilities. He was a giddy child with a magic lamp. The thought of being able to tell his boss to shove it so he could stay home renewed his excitement. "Can you imagine if I won the lottery?"

"Oh, you're just going to cut me out of it?" Susan crossed her arms with a look of disapproval. "It was my idea, you know. Don't I deserve something?"

"You know if I win I'll take care of you. You're my girl." He nudged her with his foot under the table knowing by the smirk on her face that she was just kidding around.

She made a kissy-face and then took another bite of her sandwich. Anthony didn't think she actually believed any of his nonsense anyway.

You'll see. When I win, you'll have to believe me.

"Oh I wanted to tell you," Susan said, "Roger Kurrey's going to be in Lauden this weekend for a book signing. They're opening a new Book Nook over there. He's the guest of honor for the grand opening. He'll be signing copies of his latest novel, uh…" She snapped her fingers as she thought.

"*Banshee*," Anthony said.

"Yeah. That's it."

"Oh, yeah? Where'd you hear this?" Anthony had been waiting four months for Roger's latest book to come out.

"It was in the Entertainment section of the paper yesterday. I knew you'd want to go because you don't have his newest book yet. I thought we could go together. Get the book, have it signed. You know, make a day of it. We can get something to eat after."

Anthony's get-rich-quick idea took a back seat to the news of the book signing. "Heck yeah, I want to go!" Anthony had never met Roger Kurrey in person, much less attended a book signing. The closest he had ever been to hearing or seeing his favorite author was through videos on the Internet where Roger read excerpts of his work to an audience or sat down for an interview.

They finished their lunches and left the sandwich shop to go back to work. Anthony spent the rest of the day thinking about the upcoming book signing and the lottery idea Susan had mentioned. Because of them, the last few hours of his workday were a little brighter. Anthony fantasized about having all the time he needed for his writing, but mostly he thought about winning the lottery. If the typewriter could fulfill what he wrote and make the stories real, then Anthony would be able to tell Jim where to shove his tech support job and spend the rest of his days writing like he wanted.

After work, Anthony rushed home to test his theory. On his way, he noticed a billboard beside the highway that displayed the updated lottery total. It was now up to fifty-six-million dollars. He stopped off at a convenience store near his house to purchase a ticket. He chose to let the machine randomly select the numbers for him.

The thought of coming into that much money lit a fire under Anthony's ass. He was even more anxious to get home than ever. He had the urge to jump up and down like an excited child at the thought of becoming filthy rich. His mind began to whirl with the plethora of possibilities for what he could, no *would*, do with all that money.

There was no doubt that he would quit his job; that was a given. That thought was the most intoxicating of all. He could finally buy a house where he and Susan could live comfortably. She could quit her job, too! They could get marr…

His thoughts were cut short right there as he remembered his father's vow, *That's it! I'll never marry again*, following his parents' nasty divorce when he was much younger. His mother had gotten practically everything; she had been a stay-at-home mom and never worked. Adding insult to injury, the female judge who heard the case ordered Anthony's father to pay alimony in addition to child support. His dad had insisted that "he was anatomically incorrect; he had a penis!" and that was the reason for the judge's decision. The years following the fallout of the divorce were rough for Anthony. His father's words always echoed in his head when he thought of marriage and the prospect of a costly divorce always left him with cold feet at the idea.

Well, we can still live together. And, she wouldn't have to work if she didn't want to.

When Anthony arrived home, he ran into his apartment and went straight into the study. Trying not to crease the fresh sheet of paper in his excited hands, he lined up the sheet in the mouth of the old Royal and cranked it into position. Then he typed:

```
I, Anthony Jessup, will wake up
tomorrow to learn that I have the
winning numbers in the state lottery. I
will be the sole winner of 56 million
dollars, which will allow me to quit my
job and live comfortably for the rest
of my life.
```

He sat back in his chair with his fingers interlaced behind his head and stared at his declaration on the page. A satisfied smile was plastered across his face.

Now all I've got to do is leave it there and go to sleep.

He looked at his watch. It was only 6:40 PM and he wasn't sleepy. Hell, how could he be with all of his pent up excitement. He would be lucky to fall asleep at all. He felt like a kid on Christmas Eve, too anxious to sleep in anticipation of Santa's arrival. All those presents!

Time didn't seem to be moving fast enough for him. Sure, when he was having fun doing something he enjoyed, it sped by. Now, that he was looking forward to something—a life-changing event, no less — time slowed to a crawl. It was as if the universe took enjoyment in torturing him.

It didn't matter though; Anthony knew that all he had to do was leave the paper in the typewriter. After all, time marched on. He would go to sleep eventually, no matter how anxious he was.

Before Anthony stood up from his chair, he glanced at the mounting pile of rejection slips from various magazines where he had submitted his stories. There were no handwritten messages on any of them, and Anthony took that as a bad sign. He liked to remind himself that the editors who read his manuscripts didn't hate him, nor did they think he was a bad person. They only rejected his stories because his and the editors' tastes differed.

Once I quit my job, I'll have more time to polish my stories.

He looked back at the paper in the typewriter once again. Despite the mound of rejection slips, Anthony was smiling.

He left the study and went into the kitchen where he grabbed a beer from the refrigerator. He paused, making a decision, put the beer back, and took out a can of soda. From the top of the refrigerator, he grabbed a bottle of vodka that had been sitting there and mixed a stronger drink.

What's this beer shit? I won't have to work tomorrow. All I have to do is cash in the ticket, call work, and tell 'em I quit.

That thought hadn't lost any of its thrills and Anthony enjoyed entertaining it, but at the same time, it only intensified his restlessness and anxiety. He found it difficult to sit still. Hopefully, the drink would mellow him out and a few would take his mind off of pretty much everything. He sat on the couch in the living room and tried watching television. He gulped the first drink down during an episode of Seinfeld, the one with the doll that looks like George's mother.

Anthony went into the kitchen, refilled his glass, nursing it in front of the TV. At 8:25, the alcohol finally began to affect him, making him more relaxed and encouraging him to have more. After his second, he began to nurse a third. He planned to go to bed at 10:00, but when that time came, hell, Anthony felt like staying up all night. At 11, they would draw the lottery numbers and he was eager to watch. Anthony wasn't worried about getting up early or being on time for work; the story in the typewriter would take care of all that. Anthony didn't make it to the lottery drawing though. By 10:40, he had passed out.

The next morning he took baby steps toward opening his eyes. The sunlight shining through the front window made it a painful process. His head felt like someone was inside of it, remodeling with a mallet. At first, Anthony wondered where he was, but then realized he was lying on his sofa, still dressed in his previous day's work clothes. Some early morning talk show played on the television. A half finished glass of vodka and soda rested on the coffee table. He looked at his watch. It was 9:20. Instinctively, Anthony panicked when he realized he was late for work. Then he remembered the lottery ticket and his story of winning millions. He attempted to hurry into his study on legs that refused to cooperate with a head that felt swollen. Once there, Anthony logged onto his computer. He navigated his way to the lottery website to verify his winning numbers. His heart beat like a triphammer from his excitement, and the smile on his face stretched from ear to ear. His hangover diminished because of the adrenaline in his system.

As he checked his numbers against those on the website, the smile on his face waned and finally disappeared. His heart was still racing, but not because he had won. Instead, it pounded because he realized he *was* late for work, and, with a hangover to boot.

On his ticket, Anthony only matched two of the six numbers. He had won nothing. He cursed the typewriter as he rushed into the bedroom to quickly change clothes and throw on some cologne to cover up the alcohol that reeked from his body. His head throbbed worse than ever now and the morning-after taste in his mouth reminded him of a truckstop toilet.

Anthony locked the front door and sprinted to his car. He knew he had to come up with a really good excuse for his tardiness.

A flat tire! Yeah. But a flat tire doesn't take more than an hour to change. It does if you realize you don't have a tire tool. Yeah, that's good!

He tried it on for size as he pulled out of the apartment complex, "Sorry I'm late, Jim. I had a flat tire and when I went to change it, I couldn't find the tire tool." He tried to imagine his boss's reaction. *Why didn't you call to let me know you had a flat and that you'd be late?* Of course, that's what Jim would say. He would catch Anthony in a lie with only a simple bit of reasoning.

What would I say then? I'll just tell him I forgot my cellphone at home. It's got to work. Damn, I can't get fired!

Anthony arrived at work, went inside, and gave Jim the rehearsed spiel. There was a tired scornful look on Jim's face, but, as lame as it was, he reluctantly accepted the excuse. Anthony went to his desk satisfied that there was no accompanying lecture. His phone blinked at him indicating there was a voicemail message waiting, but that wasn't uncommon in his line of work. While the computer was still coming to life, Anthony's email program opened, showing all of the unread messages in his inbox. He saw one from Susan; the subject read, "Well?"

He double-clicked to open it. The body of the email read:

So, did you win?! I'm going to assume if you're getting this at work, you didn't. But, if you're reading this at home I'm going to be pissed that you didn't call to tell me and I'm going to kick you in the ass when I see you. :)
Love Susan

It hurt when reality slapped him in the face, yet again. He had just known he was going to be the next lottery winner and all of his dreams would come true. Instead, here he sat in the depressing cubicle at a job he absolutely abhorred, not a penny richer. He typed out the sad news and suggested they go out for lunch so he could get away from the office. He'd only just arrived but already he sensed that the walls were closing in on him.

Susan and Anthony sat in their usual spot in the mall's food court. Anthony was eating a double cheeseburger, per his routine. Susan was eating teriyaki chicken and fried rice from one of the Asian places. Anthony always joked with her, calling it "terribly yucky" chicken.

He was hoping Susan might cheer him up after raising his hopes about winning the lottery. He had been sure the plan was foolproof since he had woken up twice in places he had written about. He couldn't help but wonder

Why the hell didn't it work?

"Okay, so you didn't win," she said. "That just proves that the dreams you've had are just that, dreams, nothing more."

"That's not it. I know it isn't. Like I said, those dreams were too real. I can still recall them vividly. Everything: the environment, the sounds, the *feel*. I just think…" he trailed off. Susan looked at him, her head cocked, waiting for him to continue. "Maybe it's not like a magic genie lamp where you make a wish for something and it's granted."

"Okay," Susan said, hesitantly, "then what do you suppose it is?"

"I don't know for sure what you call it," Anthony said and shook his head, "but I remember watching a show on TV where someone, no wait, it was a couple of people, had this thing that could do whatever they wanted as long as it wasn't for personal gain. They had, like, these powers or something. One of them could see the future. You know? Premonitions."

"Are you talking about that show, *Charmed*? They're witches. They can see the future and stop time and stuff. They can't do it for personal gain. I haven't watched much of it, but I've seen a few episodes. That's just Hollywood crap anyway, Anthony. It isn't real."

Anthony realized their conversation had derailed. Was he actually sitting here trying to convince Susan that he believed the typewriter was making his dreams come true? Yeah, it sounded pretty fucking retarded now that he thought seriously about it. "Maybe that's what I was thinking of, shit I don't know. What if there was a device that allowed you to travel through time though? I mean, wouldn't that be cool?" Anthony gave her a weak smile as he rubbed the back of his head. "My head still hurts and my stomach feels queasy," he confessed.

"You're not getting sick, are you?"

"No. I drank too much last night. Some vodka and soda, while I waited for the lottery drawing. I just knew I'd win. But, I passed out on the couch and missed it." He hated admitting any of that to her. It intensified his feelings of guilt, causing him to feel like he was an irresponsible child. "I just wanted to celebrate."

"You need to be careful. If you're late again, what do you think'll happen? You know Jim'll fire you. Also, it scares me to know you drink like that when you're by yourself."

"I know it does, but I was excited about becoming rich. I don't understand what happened."

"Now do you believe me, that they were just vivid dreams?" she asked, almost gloating. "Had you been drinking the nights you wrote any of the other stories?" Susan raised her eyebrows, looking at Anthony the way a mother will look at her child when she already knows the answer to the question, but wants to see if the response will be a lie.

Anthony just rolled his eyes at her for fixating on the fact that he had some alcohol. He didn't want the first, second, and third degree just because he had a few too many drinks.

"You shouldn't get that obsessed over them, they're *just* dreams. Stick to writing your stories. I'm sure if you keep editing and submitting, you'll eventually get published." She smiled and covered his hand with hers.

Anthony felt small at that moment. Here he was, hoping she wouldn't harp on him for indulging in something stronger than beer and she was showing him how much she believed in him. A big publishing house may not have validated his writing ambition, but Susan had. Whenever he felt low or depressed, Anthony knew she could turn all of that around. Despite her love, however, Anthony found that he still couldn't stop thinking about the dreams, or whatever they were. There seemed to be something more to them that he couldn't easily dismiss.

"You know, you're right. I'm just going to keep working on my stories. I'll never get published if I throw in the towel now."

That night, Anthony decided to experiment further with the typewriter. He sat in the chair in his study staring at the antiquated machine, wondering why or how he could experience the first two stories he had written, but not the lottery story.

Maybe I was right. It can't be used for personal gain.

When Anthony realized that the main difference between the stories had been their composition, content, and style, he began to scrutinize these aspects. The lottery story wasn't a story at all. In fact, it was merely a declaration. A couple of statements for something he wanted. Anthony decided to attack this in a different way and began pecking away at the keys. With a new idea, Anthony let his mind wander into the realms of his daydreams. He wrote that he and Susan lived in a large house purchased with money Anthony inherited from his parents. This time, Anthony was meticulous in his descriptions. After spending more than an hour establishing a grand, relaxing lifestyle on the page, he rubbed his tired eyes and shuffled off to bed, making sure to leave the paper in the carriage.

CHAPTER 6

Anthony woke up early on Saturday and waited for Susan to arrive so they could drive to the Book Nook in Lauden for the book signing. Normally, Anthony wouldn't wake until sometime between 11 AM and the crack of noon, but when Susan pulled into the parking lot at 9:20 he was waiting at the door. From his display of eagerness, one would think it was Christmas morning. He had already showered, dressed, and eaten breakfast. In fact, he had gotten up so early that he even spent a little while browsing the Internet as he waited for Susan to arrive.

The truth was Anthony had awakened early expecting a different, more lavish lifestyle awaiting him; the one that he meticulously transferred from his mind onto the page and left in the typewriter the previous night. What he discovered when he woke, however, was depressing, but not as unexpected as his lottery scheme had been. Nothing about his mundane life had changed. He decided to keep the experiment to himself in order to minimize his humiliation. He had crumpled the pages and tossed them in the wastebasket.

Susan stood next to the driver's door holding her car keys when Anthony came out, shut the door, and locked it. She waited, watching as he descended the steps and approached the car.

"Wow, I'm surprised you're ready to go!" she said, smiling. "I thought I was going to have to come roust you out of bed."

"Are you kidding? I got up at 7:30. Couldn't sleep. This is probably a first; waking up early on a Saturday." He smiled back. "I want to get there early before the lines get too long," he said. "Besides, they might run out of books if we wait and I don't want to miss getting one."

Susan maintained her smile but rolled her eyes. "I doubt they're going to run out of books." They got in the car and Susan drove to Lauden.

Lauden wasn't very far, only a fifteen-minute ride south on Highway 5. Susan pulled off the exit ramp and merged onto a four-lane road that was lined with shopping centers.

The town bustled with cars. People were shopping at Walmart and Home Depot, eating at Burger King, McDonalds, Applebees, Taco Bell, and Shoneys. Susan passed car lots, where Anthony saw people checking out the sticker prices of the latest models of Chevrolet trucks and cars. Balloons bobbed high in the sky and the Sale banners surrounding the property fluttered. Salesmen roamed the lot watching the customers like vultures circling a carcass, hoping to make a sale.

Orange construction cones blocked the right lane where workers had been paving the road in front of a newly built shopping plaza. For Lease signs occupied most of the retail store windows. Past the obstructed entrance to the parking lot was another entrance, already complete and accessible. Susan pulled in and turned left toward the newly constructed Book Nook, separate from the main building with its empty spaces for rent.

The parking area surrounding the book store was already full. Susan had to park several rows away. Large multicolored *Grand Opening* balloons danced overhead at the end of decorative streamers tethering them to the four corners of the store's roof. A marquee beside the front door announced Roger Kurrey's book signing and a line of attendees extended from the front door. At that time of day, the line wasn't as short as Anthony had hoped, but neither was it as long as he expected. Some visitors, obviously not there for the book signing, entered the store, bypassing the line of people. Anthony knew the line would most likely continue to grow longer as the day progressed. He and Susan hurried over to join the end and shuffled closer to the entrance as the lucky people inside had their turn meeting Mr. Kurrey.

The line moved faster than Anthony had anticipated. He kept hoping there would be plenty of books available so he could get a signed copy. When he and Susan entered the front door, the air-conditioning felt soothing as it enveloped them. Despite being the early part of autumn, the temperature outside was unseasonably hot. The sun shone bright from a cloudless sky and the lack of breeze felt more like early summer.

The line continued to inch forward. Anthony's gaze traveled down the line to the cordoned off area where Roger sat, tirelessly greeting his fans and scribbling his signature inside of the hard covers each person handed him. A couple of people ahead of Anthony blocked him from having a clear view of Roger, but it didn't matter because the line continued to grow shorter; Anthony would be there soon enough. A woman standing beside Roger gathered more copies of his latest novel from a freshly opened cardboard box and placed them on the diminishing stacks set out on the table. Anthony's face brightened with a grin when he saw Roger glance in Anthony's direction and survey the line after signing a book. A portly woman stepped forward and placed her book before Roger. He greeted her, opened it, and scrawled his signature as she said something Anthony couldn't make out. She was probably saying something trite about being his biggest fan, or that she loved all of his books.

They progressed closer to the front of the line and Anthony took a book from one of the stacks on the folding table.

"Hi, welcome to the Book Nook," the man behind the table said and rang up the total. "That'll be twenty-six dollars and thirty-four cents."

"I've got it," Susan said, digging a ten and a twenty from her purse.

While Susan paid, Anthony ran his finger along the glossy jacket cover. He looked at the picture of the screaming demoness and felt the beveled title, *BANSHEE*. Susan accepted her change and favored Anthony with a smile. He returned the smile with a kiss on the cheek. "You're awesome, baby," he said.

She put her arm around his waist as he flipped the book over to look at the back cover. Above the book's synopsis, blurbs from several critics informed the buyer that "Kurrey has simply outdone himself" and that this book was "Kurrey at his best". Anthony opened up the back cover and found a black-and-white photo of Roger sitting behind a desk with manuscript pages neatly stacked to one side. The bio under the picture said that he lived in Connecticut with his wife and their two cats. Of course, Anthony already knew this. Some of his previous novels were also mentioned. The moment was fast approaching when Anthony would finally get to meet Roger Kurrey, his idol, in person. Roger was the one living the life Anthony only dreamed about. Roger had it all and it made Anthony jealous to his core.

Finally, Anthony found himself standing across the table from the revered author. He handed Roger the book and said, "I'm one of your biggest fans."

Roger smiled and shook Anthony's hand. "I certainly appreciate it," Roger said and opened the cover. He scrawled his name quickly with a black Sharpie.

"I really love your books," Anthony said, glowing. "I've got all of them, even the out-of-print books, which I bought online."

Roger finished signing his name, handed the book back to Anthony, and said, "Well, if not for fans like you, my writing wouldn't matter. Thanks, I hope you enjoy this one."

Susan attempted to usher Anthony away from the table, but he didn't want to go. He wanted to talk some more. There were too many questions he wanted answers to. He wanted to hear Roger describe what it's like to write novels for a living, to have his books adapted into movies, the struggles when he first started his writing career. Anthony wanted some useful advice; to tell Roger that he, too, was a novelist. Anthony just wanted some encouragement from someone in the know. He wanted to talk shop, hear Roger's opinion of some of Anthony's work. Most of all, Anthony wanted validation.

Susan took Anthony by the elbow as they stepped out from behind the cordoned off area.

"So? How was it?" Susan asked. "Was it everything you thought it would be?"

The Old Royal

Anthony had finally met his idol face-to-face and the moment had passed by so...fast. Too fast, in fact. The whole encounter lasted only a minute at most, but that hadn't been long enough for Anthony. It was like experiencing a high and then dealing with the sudden crash of coming down in only a matter of seconds. Despite having fulfilled one of his dreams, Anthony felt a pang of disappointment. It was as though the universe had cheated him again by the too-brief encounter with Roger Kurrey. "I wish I could've talked to him more."

"What would you have said?"

"Well, I'd sure as hell think of something better than 'I'm your biggest fan' or 'I have all your books'..." Anthony's face screwed up into an idiotic expression as he made fun of himself by miming the silly gestures of a simpleton.

"Hey, look," Susan said, her laughter at his imbecile impression waning. She pointed to a cardboard cutout beside the wall. "He has another book coming out in the spring."

Anthony went over to check out the display. Across the top was a pumpkin-orange sunset. A long winding blacktop road divided the hills covered in a sea of barren skeletal trees. Letters at the top said, "The Long Journey by Roger Kurrey". In the lower right corner was a red circle. The text inside: "Available Spring 2011".

Susan waited until they were outside and, in an effort to placate Anthony's unhappiness, said, "Well, don't be too upset. He's just a person like everyone else. He still has to put his pants on one leg at a time."

Anthony hated that saying. Sure, Roger Kurrey *was* just like everyone else, but with two crucial differences: he was a creative genius and he was rich because of it! Roger Kurrey could sit around in his mansion and write all day if he chose to. Roger Kurrey didn't have to contend with assholes like Jim Bower breathing down his neck all the time, telling him when and how high to jump.

"Besides, you finally got to meet him and he signed your book. Now isn't that cool?"

"Yeah. It was pretty cool, I guess." Anthony flashed a quick smile. "I just wish I'd said something better than what I did. I mean, how many people does he meet at these book signings who say the same thing? I feel like a dork for being just another *biggest fan*." Anthony kissed Susan again, this time a lingering kiss on the lips as they stood behind her car in the parking lot. When they separated, Anthony thanked her again for buying the book and bringing him to the signing. Realizing his childish display, it occurred to Anthony that he was lucky to have a woman like Susan and her selfless love. He had meant it in the bookstore when he told her she was awesome, but he realized words couldn't express how much he actually did love her.

Susan never ceased to amaze Anthony with her unshakable tolerance of his selfishness. As of late, he had become cognizant of just how much he whined about how the world didn't seem fair because it didn't bend to his will. With his incessant complaining about work, how all he wanted to do was write, and his juvenile display in Roger's presence, Susan still loved him. Anthony felt small knowing that if the situation were reversed, he would've had enough by now and probably would have dumped Susan for being so negative all the time. He had to straighten out his attitude or possibly risk losing her. Nobody likes to be around a fun-sponge, the one who always dwells on the negative and wallows in their own self-pity.

"You know what, baby?" he said peering at her across the roof of the car.

Susan paused after opening her door and looked over at him.

"You really are awesome!" He winked and then he held up the book as though it was a trophy.

Susan smiled and said, "No, baby, you're awesome. I'm glad you had fun."

They left the parking lot, Anthony holding her hand in his on the center console. With the thumb of his other hand, Anthony stroked the raised letters of the book's title. Susan concentrated on driving from Lauden back to Oakwood while Anthony lost himself in yet another fantasy of being a famous author where he and Susan lived a luxurious life, happy and stress-free.

CHAPTER 7

Two weeks after the book signing, Anthony sat on the sofa in his apartment, not really watching the television so much as staring at it, trying to relax after another shitty day at work. *Sanford and Son* was on. Fred was trying to get into the *Guinness Book of World Records* by staying awake the longest. Anthony paid no attention to any of it, though. Instead, he sipped from a rum and Coke, his mind adrift with everything he had learned about the typewriter since he had begun using it.

During the past weeks, Anthony had verified that the typewriter could actually send him to other places in what appeared to be the past. Calling it a time machine seemed a misnomer because he had some influence over the environment he woke up in.

However, there were some rules involved that limited its ability. It was these rules that Anthony had to figure out, and he did so only by trial and error.

First, Anthony learned that he could in no way use the typewriter for immediate personal gain. He realized this not after writing the story of winning the lottery, but after writing the more lavish tale of inheriting money from his rich parents. His parents were neither rich nor lived a posh lifestyle, so after fabricating the story, Anthony awoke to find that his life had not been transformed. Nothing had changed.

Second, Anthony had learned that he could not travel ahead in time, but was limited only to the past. He remembered waking up in the warehouse sometime in the 30s and wanted to see what his life was like ten years from now, whether he would be a successful novelist. Again, he wrote a story that put him, not in an extravagant setting—he couldn't break the first rule about personal gain—but in a modest house where he worked from home doing what he dreamed about. When he woke, again, Anthony found that everything was the same. This was evidenced by the date on his computer and that day's newspaper. He was at a loss here, unable to fashion a decent story about the future because he wasn't sure what changes might occur between now and then.

He made another attempt to go into the future by writing a few stories at different intervals from the present. The first was a week into the future, then three days, and then twelve hours.

Again, nothing had changed.

During these experiments, however, Anthony learned new rules he hadn't even considered. Having watched popular movies that dealt with time travel, Anthony was aware of something called the Grandfather Paradox. The Grandfather Paradox was the belief that altering the past could dramatically change the future. For instance, if you could travel back in time to meet your grandfather—before he ever met your grandmother—and killed him, you would cease to exist. In theory, it made logical sense.

Anthony wanted to test this theory since he had a vehicle that afforded him the opportunity, but he was also intimidated by the prospect. The last thing he wanted to do was hurt someone through the process of experimenting. He decided to exercise caution and try something trivial.

Anthony had neglected to drop off his monthly car payment before the weekend. He decided to write a story that took him back to Saturday so he could. When Monday rolled around, he would call the little mom-and-pop dealership to verify that they had received his payment. Through his reasoning, if they said they had, then it would give credence to the Grandfather Paradox.

Sunday night, Anthony left the story in the typewriter. In the morning, he checked his computer. According to its calendar, it was 9:24 AM Saturday. Anthony showered, dressed, got his checkbook, and drove to the Car Corner used car lot where he had purchased his Honda Civic.

During his drive, Anthony remembered the last payment he had missed. It was the third payment since driving the car off the lot eleven months ago. With his embarrassingly low credit score, no other dealership was willing to finance him, but Car Corner was the exception. They advertised that they could finance anyone. Of course, that came with unadvertised consequences. If you were late or missed a payment, the nagging phone calls started immediately. Anthony wasn't sure what came after that. Obviously, repossession if the problem was never resolved, but he didn't let it get that far. After that first call, he had shown up with a check and smoothed everything over.

He pulled into the dealership's lot, went in, and wrote out a check. The secretary issued him a receipt and updated his account on her computer.

Anthony returned home and enjoyed the rest of his weekend, spent leisurely, of course. Monday, when he went to work, he called the dealership.

"Thank you for calling Car Corner, this is Melissa, how may I help you?"

"Hi, Melissa. This is Anthony Jessup. I was calling to verify that you received my payment this month."

Melissa asked him to wait a moment while she accessed his account. She asked for his account number. Anthony rattled it off. He could hear the keyboard clacking as she typed it into the computer.

A moment later, Melissa said, "Yes, sir. It says here that we received your payment on Saturday."

"Okay, thanks. Just wanted to make sure I hadn't forgot."

After he hung up, he considered the experiment and realized some things. First, he was able to milk another weekend out of the deal. While it was comforting to know that he could accomplish more in a single day thanks to the ability to squeeze in extra hours or days, they came at a cost. While he was able to do more things while the clock in the present was stopped, his body's internal clock continued to tick. If he didn't give himself time to rest, he became fatigued. Regardless, he considered this ability a double-plus that he might use somewhere down the line.

And, then there was the Grandfather Paradox, which seemed to be true. He had gone into his past and altered his future. There would be no irritating phone calls from the dealership due to him missing a payment.

That night, when Anthony arrived home from work, he had an idea for a story that had been in his head all day. This story took place around the turn of the century. It was about a black man on the run for a crime he didn't commit. Anthony thought it could be a spectacular crime caper with a southern gothic flare. He went into his study and saw a paper still in the carriage. It was the short story he used to make his late car payment.

He took hold of the page and yanked it out to begin working on this newest idea. As he wadded up the sheet, it dawned on Anthony that nothing had happened. Usually, when he removed the paper, he would jump back to a point in time soon after he had finished the story or shortly thereafter. But, this time, nothing occurred. Anthony sat back in his chair and pondered why he didn't find himself whisked back to Sunday, just after he had written the story.

He couldn't come up with an answer, only assumptions. The fact that he had already surpassed the story's point of creation and was in the future was the best logic he could come up with. He shrugged it off and fed a fresh sheet of paper into the Royal.

Anthony found himself staring at the blank sheet, searching for the best way to start his new tale. He didn't know shit about the turn of the century, other than what he saw in movies. He decided to just start slowly, using whatever came to mind and then go from there. If he needed to do any research, he figured the machine could take him back for that. Images began to form in his mind. He saw a black man running for his life at dusk. Anthony's fingers moved, hitting the keys.

```
   The   barking   dog   was   distant.  At
least, more distant than it had been.
Gordon bent over, resting his hands on
his  thighs  as  he  tried  catching  his
breath.  The  stitch  in  his  side  was  a
```

dull ache now, not the searing white-hot burn it had felt when he ran.

Gordon looked over his shoulder, across the rusty barbed-wire to the overgrown field he had just traveled. His knees and ankles prickled, itched, and stung from the saw briars that attempted to snare him during his escape. The sun was disappearing behind the woods across the pasture leaving behind its bloody crimson smudge in the blackening sky. Gordon couldn't see the torches that had been behind him. But, he knew they were somewhere back there. He couldn't wait around long or they would emerge from the darkness and catch him.

He hopped the shallow ditch and stepped onto the dirt road. That's what it was, although it was getting difficult to make out his surroundings with the daylight quickly fading. He felt the small pea gravel crunch together in the powdery dirt under his thin-soled shoes. When he looked side to side, he could see the road extend into the shadows cast by the trees flanking it. The trees seemed to form a dark tunnel which swallowed the road in each direction.

Gordon checked each direction, trying to regain his bearings. He turned to the left, but that felt wrong. His intuition told him so. That would be the direction he had come from. He shuffled around, facing the opposite direction, the pasture to his right.

Yeah, that felt better. His mental compass told him that was the direction into town. But, how far away was it? He didn't know. Gordon didn't care, all he knew was that he couldn't stay where he was. The dogs were coming. Their howling yelps were gradually getting louder.

He began staggering down the road, the muscles in his legs tight and full of blood from sprinting. He had outrun his pursuers. The images of them behind him were still very fresh in his mind. The men's torches looked like fireflies dancing above the broom sedge grass when he glanced over his shoulder to gauge his likelihood of escape.

When Gordon neared the trees growing beside the road, their branches reaching overhead to form a faux tunnel, he felt a sensation that the trees were closing in on him. Their shadows made it darker here and his eyes hadn't yet adjusted to the sudden darkness. He hesitated, fearful of what might be waiting in the dark. Maybe some more white men who were looking for him. His choices ran through his head. He couldn't go back the other way. Some of the white men had probably split off and made their way to the road. They would be looking for him there. The other men with the dogs would eventually follow his scent to the road where he now stood.

Gordon stared down the dim road that stretched out before him. His eyes were getting used to the low light. He could vaguely see the brighter shade of the road as it bent to the left ahead of him, around a curve. He swallowed and began walking in the direction he knew the town should be in.

When Gordon had rounded the bend, he heard something and stopped. It wasn't the dogs. It wasn't the sound of approaching men's footsteps. The sound was familiar, mechanical. Gordon recognized it as a car motor. He was torn between being excited about an approaching vehicle or scared that it was the white men. Maybe some of them had doubled back and brought their car out in search of him.

Gordon turned to look back and saw the telltale glow of headlights approaching the curve. He surveyed the sides of the dirt road. The gullies beside it were slightly wider and significantly deeper than they had been where he had crossed the fence. The bank to the left was steeper, too. Roots and tree stumps clung to the edge where the forest floor was at eye level. Gordon turned to his right. The pasture was in that direction, but farther from the road now as it curved away from the open grass. A thin copse of woods separated him from the field.

The car was growing closer. The engine louder and the headlight beams brighter. It hadn't arrived at the curve yet. Gordon licked his lips and rubbed his sweaty palms on his pant

The Old Royal

legs. Broken briars and hitchhikers clung to the fabric. He was unsure where to go. If he went right, he might be able to make it to the field before the car arrived, but he would have to get over the barbed-wire fence and then he would need to get through the sparse saplings. If he went left, he would have to scale the high dirt bank, hoping he could clear the top of it before the car arrived. Time was running out.

Gordon was exhausted following his earlier run. His body refused to give up another adrenaline boost to help him out. The car rounded the corner as Gordon moved to the right edge of the road. He adjusted his hat and shielded his eyes from the bright lights. He was anticipating the hoots and hollers of the white men he had left behind in the woods.

The car slowed as it neared. It was a four-door Nash. Gordon listened to the engine rattle and brakes squeak as it pulled to a stop beside him. Outwardly, Gordon simply tracked the vehicle with his eyes, watching carefully to see what the driver wanted. Inside, however, he was a bundle of nerves that waited for the other shoe to drop. He knew black men were lynched for petty reasons in this part of the country, especially in 1912. His heart thumped like a jack-rabbit on the run, but his legs were tired and nearly useless.

The passenger window lowered and an angelic voice spoke: "You wanna ride to town?" It was a girl. Gordon looked back down the road. No fiery torches were visible. He took a step closer to the car so he could see the vague features of the occupants. The girl looked like she might be young. Her voice sure sounded it, like maybe she was a teenager. The driver was a boy, probably around the same age as his passenger. He was wearing a tweed flat cap and Gordon could make out the dark stripe of suspenders against his white shirt.

Anthony stopped typing, enjoying where his mind had taken him and not wanting to stop now. He rubbed his weary eyes. His watch said it was getting late. Anthony stood up and arched his back. He walked around the desk, paused and looked at the paper hanging out of the carriage. He'd leave it there and see what the world was like back in 1912.

The following morning, Anthony awoke to find that he was still in the present, despite leaving the unfinished story in the carriage. When he arrived home from work that night, he examined the typewriter, turning it over until he found information about its production. A stamped metal plate was on the back, and Anthony learned his #10 Royal was manufactured in 1933; twenty one years after his story from last night was supposed to take place. Analyzing what had happened, Anthony learned another of the typewriter's rules: he was unable to travel to a time before the typewriter existed. It made some sort of weird logical sense that his vehicle couldn't visit a time before even it had existed. This was also the reason, he surmised, that he had found himself naked in the warehouse and the hotel room in the 80s; his clothes had not yet existed in either of those times and he had not explicitly written any clothes into his story.

These were the rules Anthony had discovered so far. He was happy to have learned them because they defined the machine's parameters. But, he wondered if he couldn't find some way to manipulate it to his benefit.

Anthony tipped up his glass, swallowing the remainder of his soda. He carried the empty glass into the kitchen to pour himself another, knowing that he really should go to bed. He knew that staying up late would make it harder for him to wake up early. He pictured Roger Kurrey at the book signing. His desire to have the life Roger lived drove him further into a funk. He realized that Roger was only human, just like everyone else, which made Anthony think that the possibility of becoming a novelist like his idol was very much within the realm of possibility. Anthony got another glass of soda and went back into the living room where he plopped down on the sofa.

One moment Anthony could convince himself that being published was within his grasp, that all he had to do was persevere, and that thought gave him the reassurance he needed. However, the next moment, even in his tired state of mind, he knew that his goal of becoming a career novelist was further away than he thought. This understanding was typically followed with him focusing on his mundane, pain-in-the-ass job, leaving Anthony to wallow in a quagmire of depression.

Different Strokes was playing on TV, the one where Arnold gets to meet "the Champ", Muhammad Ali. Seeing the boxer on the screen derailed Anthony's miserable thoughts. Anthony switched to another channel—he didn't like *Different Strokes* and had never cared for Gary Coleman's acting.

The channel he stopped on was showing the evening news. What got his attention was the mention of Roger Kurrey's name.

What's this about Roger?

He set the remote control on the coffee table after he turned up the volume. Apparently, Anthony's hero wasn't the affable person Anthony thought he was.

The news anchor read from the teleprompter: "...the famous author is accused of accosting a female fan during a book signing in Poughkeepsie, New York, yesterday after she charged around the table where Mr. Kurrey was seated.

"When asked about the incident, Kurrey's publicist, Norm Donoughue, said, 'Roger thought the woman was going to harm him and only acted in self-defense, which, under the circumstances, meant pushing her away and leaving the vicinity so the store's security team could intervene'."

Following the publicist's comments, the station aired earlier footage of the woman outside of the bookstore as medical technicians tended to her scrapes and bruises.

"I just wanted to hug him and tell him I was his biggest fan," the woman said "and the next thing I knew, he jumped out of his chair and shoved me. I don't remember anything after falling and hitting the edge of the table. Next thing I know, I'm sitting here in the ambulance and these guys are putting bandages on my head."

Anthony pressed the Power button on the remote, silencing the quacking box. He felt bad for the woman, knowing what it was like to be in the presence of someone as revered as Roger Kurrey. He could understand how a fan's actions could easily be misconstrued and recalled his own emotions as he stood in front of the man. He imagined what it must be like from Roger's perspective, too. As jealous as he was of Roger Kurrey, Anthony realized how exhausting is must be for a man in Roger's position, always in the public spotlight. After all, Roger was human, too, and not some god to be put on a pedestal.

In the silence, his mind turned to other things, mainly, the typewriter's rules. He was determined to find a way to use the typewriter's ability for his own purpose, much like a lawyer searching to exploit a loophole in the law. This was a difficult task, however. Anthony kept coming back to his disappointment with the lottery story. That had been too straightforward, too quickly executed. Too simple.

Anthony just wanted to be a writer and live a writer's life, or what he conceived was a writer's life. Kurrey's incident on the news was still fresh in his mind. It showed him a glimpse into Roger's life, a chink in the armor. Despite Kurrey's notoriety, he was susceptible to problems of his own. Anthony followed his thoughts down a rabbit hole. He was onto something.

After much thought, Anthony came up with an idea that struck him as brilliant. What if he wrote Roger's stories first? The idea's simplicity sounded too good to be true. Anthony decided to puzzle it out for flaws. He could write a story that took him back to the early seventies, before Roger Kurrey wrote his first break-through novel, and Anthony could pen the novel himself, beating Roger to the publisher.

If I can write the stories before he does, I'll become famous instead of him!

As with the lottery story's initial idea, Anthony felt the familiar streak of excitement course through him. With this new plan, he could fulfill his dream of becoming a famous novelist with certainty. This wouldn't be like the stupid lottery fiasco. Anthony was confident the plan would work because he didn't think it broke the rule of immediate personal gain. There was nothing immediate about it. He would have to allow himself time to write the story and do the work of submitting it to agents. It was all about timing. This seemed to be the loophole Anthony was looking for.

Hell, I pretty much know all of his stories by heart.

Enthusiasm. It flooded his body and wanted to spill out. He found himself pacing as he mulled the idea over. He tried poking holes in it, but none presented themselves because he knew the rules now. There was no instant gain involved. Mixed among his excitement, however, tinges of apprehension and guilt still lurked.

To carry through with the idea meant it would probably be the undoing of his hero. If he went back to take Roger's place as the author of those stories, writing the exact novels Roger was supposed to write, then Roger would not end up famous. It was essentially the Grandfather Paradox. Those twinges of apprehension grew stronger when Anthony realized this. He didn't want to hurt anyone.

Nah, that's ridiculous. Roger's a genius. He'll get famous with some other stories.

Although Anthony didn't want to do anything to adversely affect Roger, the opportunity to live the life Anthony had always dreamed of was too tempting, too overpowering. It was like the apple that taunted Eve. Anthony rationalized away his concerns.

It was already 11:30 PM, but his enthusiasm urged him on.

I wouldn't have to worry about my stupid job anymore. I have to start writing, my destiny is waiting!

Only it wasn't really *his* destiny, but Roger Kurrey's and Anthony was making plans to hijack it from him. He sat down in front of his typewriter and loaded a fresh sheet of paper. He rolled the drum knob, feeding in the sheet and lining it up.

He paused before striking any keys to put down that first word. He couldn't just jump into this. He needed to plan what he was doing.

Anthony thought about bringing his copies of Roger's books so he could just type them verbatim.

I don't know every word. Plus, they're already edited.

He went into his bedroom with a paper bag and began to put all of his Roger Kurrey novels inside. It was a good thing he owned a copy of every one.

This is fucking crazy. Me, writing Roger's stories.

Copying the books was a great plan because, even though Anthony would never admit it to anyone except himself, his own writing was always inferior to that of most published authors. In truth, Anthony told himself, his writing was pathetic. He was just deluding himself by thinking he was every bit as good as the other writers out there. Whenever he edited his stories, he discovered that he left huge plot holes, or his characters were one-dimensional and stilted. Despite those inadequacies, his natural gift was constructing sentences and dreaming up intriguing story concepts. It was when he tried to execute those ideas that he seemed to lose focus, fixate on being great, and everything fell apart.

Anthony had won nothing and published zilch. Yet, he was going to *rewrite* Roger Kurrey's stories, a man who taught college composition courses prior to becoming a career novelist and a household name. He was a prolific author of more than twenty books, numerous short stories, and the recipient of nearly every literary award imaginable.

Anthony had read every one of Roger's books. He knew the stories inside and out. But, it wasn't like he had a photographic memory or anything. Nevertheless, Anthony felt confident that he could sell them to a publisher. Despite his confidence level, he felt that taking the books with him was good insurance.

Deep down, acknowledging the fact that he was never going to be good enough to get a book deal, Anthony accepted that this was the only way he would ever fulfill his fantasy. He would finally get to live the lifestyle that his favorite author had enjoyed all these years.

CHAPTER 8

Anthony opened Roger Kurrey's first published book, *When the Clock Strikes Three,* and checked the printing date. It was June 1975. Anthony had educated himself about the publishing industry and knew the process of getting a book to print was slow and tedious. It usually took at least a year to get a novel out to bookstores. Anthony figured he would need to go back to early 1974 in order to type the manuscript and submit it to the publisher, Garfunkle Press, in time to beat Roger. Since Anthony already had the book, retyping it would be the quick and easy part, unlike creating the story from scratch.

Anthony took pride in knowing as much as he could about Roger's career and books, but he wasn't as knowledgeable about the details of Roger's first published book. He had read in Roger's memoir that Garfunkle Press published the book and doled out a fat advance of two hundred fifty thousand dollars, but aside from that, Roger hadn't elaborated on the rest of the details. Not his agent's name, nothing. In an effort to learn more about that first book, Anthony took to checking videos and interviews on the Internet, hoping Roger talked about them somewhere.

After nearly two hours of visiting several websites and watching plenty of videos of Roger speaking at engagements or reading to audiences, Anthony stumbled upon a site that contained details about debut books by authors dating back to 1968. Visitors could narrow the data down to a specific year, but then there was a laundry list of book titles by publishers in chronological order for the reader to sift through. Anthony clicked on 1975 and scrolled down the list. Three quarters of the way down the page, Anthony found the entry he was looking for.

Kurrey, Roger: *When the Clock Strikes Three*: Garfunkle Press.

Anthony clicked on the link and was taken to a page showing more details of that particular book. There was a date when the project was accepted, a synopsis of the manuscript, and several other details, but the one Anthony was interested in was near the top, Agent Representative. Next to that was the name he wanted, Stuart Bradshaw of Pembrooke and Stephens Literary Agency. Anthony took a pen and scribbled the information in the front cover of the book for later reference.

To be safe about the time aspect of his plan, Anthony set the date of his story to October 1973. He had no idea if anything might happen to interfere with his time table. Although he doubted it, Anthony decided to err on the side of caution and give himself a buffer. Since he was only a year old in 1973, he was vague about the fashions and minute details of the time. Relying on his memory was out of the question, so Anthony included things he had learned by listening to his parents reminiscing as well as from old photos taken during his early childhood.

Fueled by his growing excitement, images began forming in Anthony's mind and unfolding like a flipbook until, finally, his fantasy was playing like a movie. Anthony typed a story about a man working in a grocery store. This man rented a small apartment just a few blocks from where he worked. Anthony made an effort to construct the story in just such a way so that he would fit in easily if his plan worked and he found himself in the past. Anthony knew from previous experience that he didn't have to go into precise detail, but the more information he provided would minimize the need for improvisation by the old Royal. The way the missing gaps were filled in during the whole time travel experience was a gray area to Anthony. If he neglected to add a detail to his story that would affect his role in the past, the typewriter used some kind of voodoo to fill in that detail.

Anthony typed for quite a while until he began to get sleepy. He glanced at his watch, noticing that it was nearing 12:30. The stack of papers beside the typewriter had grown into a neat little pile of seven pages. Despite feeling sleepy, Anthony decided to press on. His eyes grew weary as he finished page nine. Anthony worried over his increasing drowsiness, because he didn't want to travel back in time to discover he had forgotten something important, although that was always a possibility. Before he learned the typewriter's secrets, he never paid much attention to the minutiae. Now that he knew he could visit a past influenced by what he wrote on the paper, that possibility seemed intimidating.

He thought of Susan, of leaving her behind, and his first inclination was to write her into the story. He stopped and recalled the night he had written her into a story with him, hoping to show her that what he had said about the typewriter was true. That was when he learned that the typewriter only worked its magic on the person who wrote the story. During that experiment, Anthony had composed a scene that took place in the 50s; he had visions of *Back to the Future* in his mind as he wrote it and set the stage for a sock-hop. Anthony woke up in a gymnasium decorated for a dance, but, Susan was nowhere to be found. Anthony sighed with frustration and turned his attention back to the current story, reviewing it for flaws.

The books! I almost forgot the damn books.

Anthony rationalized that copying the stories from the source would be faster and simpler, and assure him that they would be published so Anthony made it a point to include them in his story. He even went so far as to put the title of each of the books on the page so the typewriter's mojo didn't compromise them and derail his plan. Anthony had seen enough TV and read enough books to know that if a genie gave you three wishes you had better be specific to eliminate any loopholes. Anthony made sure to specify that the books were stacked neatly in a paper bag at the foot of the bed in the apartment.

He also included pertinent information for himself, including a tolerable work schedule; his character worked in the evenings, leaving him free to write during the day, as well as having the luxury to sleep in. With that final part out of the way, Anthony felt he could stop writing and go to sleep. His initial excitement had returned, but it was short lived. Worrying whether his plan would work began to plague his mind. He kept second-guessing what had gone wrong with the lottery story. Would this turn out to be in the same vein?

Another thought occurred to him, too. If he succeeded, what would it be like to live in the seventies? He had no idea. He was only an infant during that time. His thoughts turned on him, becoming depressing naysayers, so he pushed them aside and thought instead about what it would be like to walk in Roger's shoes, to be revered as a great writer, and have the money to buy whatever he wanted. Yeah, that was it; these new thoughts countered the negative ones and made him feel better. He had to believe in his story and give it a chance.

If he could just get to the past as he had written it, then he could manage the rest from there. With that, Anthony shuffled into his bedroom.

He undressed, leaving his clothes in a pile beside the bed as usual. He slid between the sheets and considered the possibility of waking up late for work. As a precaution, he set his alarm clock for an hour earlier than he normally woke. Just in case.

CHAPTER 9

When Anthony opened his eyes it was not very bright, but enough so that he could make out the room's features. The light bled in through closed blinds. He didn't get up with the enthusiasm he thought he might. Anthony felt sluggish and disoriented. His tired brain was to blame; staying up too late the night before. He was lying on his back, his hands stuffed under the pillow and his feet splayed out to the bottom corners of the mattress. An AC unit whirred in the window where more of the light seeped in. He rolled onto his side, blinking his eyes to break apart the sleep-glue that clung to them. A small nightstand with a clock radio on top stood beside his bed. The clock said it was 10:53 AM. It crossed Anthony's mind that he didn't remember turning off the alarm clock, nor did he remember hearing it go off. He lay there trying to wake up, watching the numbers go in and out of focus with every blink of his eyes.

He sat up in bed and threw his legs over the edge of the mattress. His mind was muddy and his eyelids didn't want to stay open. He rubbed his weary eyes and saw the Royal typewriter sitting on a small round table, much like the table he had seen when he awoke in the motel room. Against the platen rested the paper with the story that was supposed to whisk him back to 1973.

Did it work?

He rubbed the back of his stiff neck. Seeing the typewriter sitting on the table was a good indication that it had. He had left it in the study.

Anthony slowly stood up and staggered over to the window. He pried the blinds apart, letting in the morning light. He had to shield his eyes, and gradually, after letting them adjust, saw a parking lot with a few cars. There was a Volkswagen bus, a Vega, a Pacer, and a long Lincoln Continental. If the world outside the window wasn't the 70s, then the owners of those cars really needed to upgrade their wheels. Although Anthony perceived these cars as old, they were actually in very good condition, not worn with age as they should have been.

He removed his hand and let the blinds fall with a clatter over the window. When the room fell back into dim shadows, it felt better to his aching head. He moved with the careful slowness of someone who had taken several blows to the head from Mike Tyson. He didn't know why his head hurt. He had only drunk sodas during the night.

Anthony was experiencing mixed emotions, both excitement and trepidation; after all, he was taking a big leap of faith by executing his plan. It would not only affect his life but Roger's as well. He remembered the bag of paperbacks that was supposed to be waiting at the foot of the bed. He turned and looked. A brown paper sack sat where it was supposed to. Relief. His plan appeared to be working so far. Anthony moved closer and peered inside. But, there weren't any books.

no, No, NO!

He knelt beside the bag and ran his hand in it. The top edge crumpled around his elbow. There was nothing inside but empty space. Up until that point, it seemed as if everything from his setting was accurate, except for the books. It didn't take him long to figure out why the books were not there. He ticked off the rules in his head again. Anthony could have kicked himself for not remembering the rule about transporting anything before its creation date. He blamed his forgetfulness on staying up too late.

Anthony went to the typewriter. The paper hung out of the carriage as though the typewriter was sticking out its tongue, mocking him. Without removing the paper from the roller, Anthony read what he had written. He had been careful to include everything he thought he would need, everything he could think of anyway. He had included the books as he typed the last page and saw the lines where he mentioned them. Just as he thought, he had written that the books were in the bag at the foot of the bed. He had simply forgotten that they couldn't exist before they were created.

For a brief moment, Anthony considered jerking the paper from the machine, propelling himself back to the future in an instant. He didn't though. Instead, he let go of the paper, allowing it to fall limply over the carriage drum. He considered what to do before resorting to his contingency plan. Sure, he could just jerk the page out, return to the future, and come back once he figured a way around the problem. Or maybe he couldn't. What if the machine didn't have any more trips left in it? What if it ran out of gas or whatever caused it to do its magic? This idea hadn't occurred to him before, but now gave him pause. If that were the case, he would have wasted his chance to fulfill his dream.

I can remember the stories well enough to write them from memory.

Anthony tried to convince himself not to let his opportunity pass.

If the books wouldn't transport though, how would he be able to write the stories and submit them? Yes, he could try to rely on his memory, but even then, he couldn't be sure that he would include everything that gave the stories the same flair as Roger had. Nor could he be sure to convey the same feelings that Roger's word choices evoked. Under the surface, Anthony realized, there was more to writing than simply putting pen to paper and stringing together sentences. He had once seen a poster about the love of writing that said to write was to cut one's self and bleed onto the page. Anthony finally understood how accurate that sentiment was.

He sat on the edge of bed, not interested in exploring the world outside, racking his brain for a solution to get the books here with him. It occurred to him that at that very moment Roger was probably discovering the seed for *When the Clock Strikes Three* if not already writing it. Anthony's heart skipped a beat at the mere thought, as if he were in a race and his opponent had a substantial head start. Well, that was closest to the truth wasn't it? Roger could already be several pages into the story that would launch his career.

I could go back and copy the stories into a notebook or type them on the Royal.

Neither of those ideas was any good, he reasoned. If he did either, then their existence would be limited to that time and, therefore, would not translate to the past. No, those weren't good ideas at all. He continued attacking the problem from different angles, searching for yet another loophole.

He considered copying the books' text in longhand. First, he would have to set aside a few weeks of doing nothing but copying the story word by word into a notebook. That would be tedious, not to mention the time needed to copy just *one* book. Roger had written nearly twenty novels since the beginning of his career. If one book took Anthony two or three weeks to copy, then he would have to set aside several months devoted to the task of doing nothing but transcribing all the words. And then there were the few epic novels to consider, those with nearly a thousand pages. Anthony knew of three off the top of his head. No, copying the work would consume too much time. There had to be another way, but what?

He almost wanted to cry. He felt like Burgess Meredith in that Twilight Zone episode where he had all the time in the world to finally read, only to drop and break his glasses. Anthony was already here, in 1973, able to recall the stories Roger Kurrey had written, but was unsure of each book's sequence in Roger's career, and probably worse, unable to recall them as thoroughly as he thought he could.

As Anthony sat on the bed, on the verge of a deep depression, it came to him. Maybe it was the thought of copying everything down into a notebook. His mind turned to the medium. He considered a tape recorder. Anthony knew there was no such thing as digital media: no DVDs or CDs in the 70s, but there was analog tape. He wasn't that familiar with the media's history, but thought that the 90-minute cassettes he had seen in the 80s probably didn't exist yet and forget about micro-cassettes. In the 70s, Anthony knew there were 8-track tapes, but he had never used them to know if they were recordable like the later, smaller cassettes. However, he remembered that his mom and dad owned a reel-to-reel tape machine. Of course, Anthony had never used it, but knew that his dad had recorded some of Anthony's first words with it using a handheld microphone.

If Anthony could get his hands on that old tape recorder or find one for sale, then his plan might be salvageable. He thought about it, assuring himself that he could read the book onto a tape much faster than he could write it into a notebook. The only problem would be locating such a vintage piece of technology that still worked. And then he had to consider getting tapes for it, of course. Technology, Anthony chuckled at the word when he thought of it since he was considering such an antiquated piece of machinery. It almost seemed like an oxymoron when compared to micro-computers and mp3 players.

Now, it was time for Anthony to put up or shut up. If he was going to follow through, he realized he would have to remove the paper from the typewriter. He thought again of whether the typewriter had enough juice left in it to allow him to hop back and forth between the present and the past a couple more times. So far, he'd been lucky. Maybe the damned thing could keep transporting him back and forth forever. Anthony didn't know and sure as hell didn't want to gamble away his opportunity. But, neither did he want to risk wasting time writing from an erroneous memory.

He knew that if he was going to go through with his plan he had to be very calculating and conservative with pulling the page from the Royal. Putting faith in his revised plan, Anthony went to the typewriter and grasped the paper. He pulled gently at first, hearing the clicking of the drum as it turned, the paper loosening from its grip. Then, nervous and hesitant, Anthony stopped, still holding onto the paper. He ran his fingers through his hair, thinking about what it was he was doing. He could pull the paper and screw up his last chance. It was a fifty-fifty gamble and he didn't like the odds. Then he thought of Roger Kurrey, somewhere hundreds of miles away, typing his own version of the story and felt that lurch in his stomach again, that greed and pang of envy.

Anthony walked through the tiny apartment, not really looking at the furnishings or much else, but instead thinking, pacing. He returned to the bedroom, grabbed the paper between his thumb and forefinger and yanked…

CHAPTER 10

Anthony opened his eyes and abruptly sat up in bed. His surroundings almost appeared the same as when he woke up in 1973. The room was dimly lit as sunlight seeped in through the gaps in the closed window blinds. However, Anthony looked around at the room, noticing that the typewriter was missing from the table. He scrambled out of bed and ran to his study. The typewriter was sitting in its accustomed place on the desk, but there was no piece of paper protruding from the carriage.

Going back to the bedroom, Anthony noticed the time on the bedside alarm clock. It was 7:45 AM. He walked to the window and pulled aside the blinds. The cars in the parking lot were different, modern; none older than a '98 Toyota Camry. It worked. He had jumped to the future, or present, depending on your view. It was becoming difficult to keep his tenses straight at this point.

There was plenty of time for Anthony to jump in the shower and get ready for work. After being so close to fulfilling his dream, he hated the idea of returning to the job he dreaded so much. He knew it was wiser to go to work in case he couldn't make the leap back into the past. After all, finding himself stuck in the present without his job because of irresponsibility would be disastrous. Grudgingly, Anthony showered, toweled off, and dressed for work.

He had already paid his rent, car insurance, and utility bills with his last paycheck. All of these were good things because they were each one less concern to weigh on his mind. His new goal was to show up for work, go through the motions, and record the books on tape once he located a reel-to-reel recorder. He figured he could tolerate his job as long as he knew there was something worthwhile waiting for him.

The only difficult part of the plan would be finding an old recorder and some tapes, but he was sure he could find them somewhere. If collectors still sought vintage cars, record players, and such, then surely he could find a working reel-to-reel tape machine and tapes for it.

He had been fortunate to discover that one of his coworker's parents still had a reel-to-reel recorder in working order. Anthony asked if they would be willing to sell it. He was prepared to spend as much as a hundred and fifty dollars. He would even have gone as high as two-twenty-five, but was relieved to hear that they had no sentimental attachment to the damned thing and sold it to him for seventy-five bucks. All he needed now was some tapes for it.

When Anthony visited his mother, he asked about the old reel-to-reel, but learned that his dad had sold it during their divorce. Fortunately, his mom managed to hang onto the tape reels, now useless without the player.

"Can I have them?" Anthony asked. He figured his mom would probably be willing to part with them since she couldn't play them any longer.

"What do you want with those old things?"

"I came across an old recorder and thought it'd be neat to listen to them."

Anthony's mom shrugged and fetched the box of reels from the garage. When placed before him, Anthony pulled open the interlaced flaps and felt relieved to find a bunch of reels stacked inside.

"Is the tape with my first words in here?"

"Yeah, it should be," his mom said. "Look, if you find that one, hang onto it. I'd like to keep it."

"What for? It's not like you can listen to it."

His mom smirked. "Just do as I say, please. Who's to say I can't listen to it some time on the player you just got?"

Anthony carried the box out to his car and placed it in the trunk. He went back inside to enjoy dinner with his mother.

Three days later, Anthony arrived home from work, picked up Roger Kurrey's first novel, turned to the place he had bookmarked, and continued recording the story where he had left off.

The recording sessions were going well. Anthony had threaded the tapes into the recorder one after another as he taped over the old stuff with the new stuff he read aloud each night. In three days, Anthony was already nearing the end of the first book. It only took four tapes to hold the first story. There were plenty of tapes in the cardboard box and his progress was much faster than it would have been had he gone with his first idea and transcribed each of the stories into notebooks. Some of the longer books would definitely require more of the tapes, but Anthony figured he had enough to take care of all the recording he needed to do. If not, well, he decided to cross that bridge when he came to it.

Every night was the same: Anthony came home from work, got something to drink, and settled down to read into the microphone, picking up where he had left off previously. He read for several hours every night and labeled each reel with a magic marker.

That Thursday while eating lunch, Susan asked, "You want to go out and see a movie tomorrow night?"

"I better not. I'm in the middle of a new story."

"What's it about?"

Anthony stuffed some French fries in his mouth, hesitated, and said, "It's just a new idea I had about a guy that can travel back in time. It's coming along really well and I don't want to interrupt the creative flow."

"Okay. It's just that we haven't gone out in a while and I was hoping we could spend some time together."

Anthony took a large bite of his hamburger, feeling guilty about blowing off Susan's plans. This was just one of the many sacrifices he realized he would have to make if he wanted to see his dream become a reality. It hurt, but all he had to do was think of returning to his job and that helped quell the guilt.

Looking at Susan, knowing he was going to live in the past and therefore give up his relationship with her, Anthony tried to think of a plan to break it off easy between them. That guilt was like a lingering punch in the gut and there was nothing that could alleviate it.

She's been too good to screw over. I've gotta come up with an excuse for leaving that won't hurt her too bad.

Of course, Anthony knew that no matter what he told her, it was going to hurt. She was the best girl he had ever dated and deserved better treatment than being left empty-handed. If he could carry her back with him, he would do it in an instant, but he had already learned that the machine's magic only worked on one person at a time.

Anthony and Susan finished their lunches. Before returning to work, Anthony said, "Give me a few days to get the foundation of this story worked out and we'll go somewhere, okay?"

Susan smiled, kissed him on the cheek. "Okay. But, I'm going to miss you while you're locked away writing."

"I'm going to miss you, too," Anthony's eyes welled up at the thought, but he managed to hold back his tears.

Susan seemed to notice because she cocked her head, but didn't say anything.

Anthony finished with, "but it won't be that long. I love you, you know."

Susan squeezed his hand as they kissed before leaving the mall parking lot.

Back in his cubicle at JSS Software, Anthony's mind was occupied with trying to come up with a graceful departure. That was easier said than done, he learned. He thought about telling Susan that he was moving to another state because of a job opportunity he couldn't pass up, but realized that was no good.

What if she wants to come along? What if she says we should get married? What about my parents? They'll want to visit.

He could tell right away that a graceful exit was probably impossible to achieve.

Anthony looked at the red lights blinking on his phone, each one an impatient, puling customer. Anthony ran his fingers through his hair, trying to think. The lights continued to blink as the callers waited in call-center purgatory.

Anthony walked into his apartment at 6:45 PM and changed out of his work clothes into a pair of shorts. He took a can of beer from the refrigerator, opened it, and sat down in front of the tape machine. Before pressing the record button, Anthony took a long pull from the cold can. He hadn't been able to give much thought to how he would leave the present without upsetting anyone.

I'll just have to show Susan a good time before I leave. Damn, I sound like I'm about to commit suicide or something.

That was it! It sure as hell wasn't a *graceful* exit, but it would be tidy. The thought arrived whole and complete. He knew how he would do it. Before he departed, however, he decided to take Susan on a romantic date; something he hoped would show her how much she meant to him. With his mind more at ease, Anthony opened the novel to a dog-eared page, pressed the machine's Record button, and began reading.

A couple of months passed before Anthony made all of the arrangements he could think of. It was a Monday morning. He had put the original copy of the story that mapped out his past beside the typewriter for transcribing when he arrived home from work. The only modification he had to make to the story was to replace the books in the paper bag with the tape reels; he also had to add in the reel-to-reel player. Everything else, he thought, should be okay.

Now, his biggest consideration was what Susan's reaction would be.

Anthony had taken her to the mountains during the previous weekend where he had rented a cabin for both days. They enjoyed relaxing in a hot tub on the cabin's rear deck and gazed at the stars as they drank wine. Anthony wasn't a wine drinker, but he decided it would be more romantic than beer, so he compromised for Susan's sake. He had purchased an expensive bottle of imported French wine using money from his savings account. It's not like he was going to need it.

Afterward, he gave Susan a full-body massage in the bedroom. Following that, they made love and fell asleep, exhausted. Anthony had to agree with Susan: it was a marvelous and memorable weekend.

As he thought back on it, Anthony was glad he would always have that memory. If his plan worked out the way he wanted, he would never see her again. Since he was alone, Anthony let the warm tears slip from his eyes as he acknowledged that truth. After all, he could always remove the paper from the typewriter and return if he wanted, but his return might be permanent if the typewriter only had so many trips left in it.

CHAPTER 11

After brushing his teeth, Anthony left the bathroom. In his bedroom, he sprayed on some cologne and buttoned his shirt, grabbed his car keys and wallet. He looked at the paper bag resting at the foot of the bed. Inside, were the stacks of tapes, each one labeled with the section of book it contained.

Anthony stepped out his front door at 7:30 AM. He would arrive a little early for work, but that was according to plan. He pulled out of the apartment complex and made the drive to work without getting irritated at traffic or the asshole drivers.

Anthony parked, entered the office, and went straight to his cubicle. He resisted the temptation to go into Jim's office as he had imagined doing a thousand times to tell Jim to shove the job sideways up his fat ass. As much as Anthony wanted to do it, he knew it would most likely ruin his exit strategy, and he wasn't the type of person who typically burned his bridges. He just took pleasure in knowing that this was his last day working for JSS Software.

Anthony endured the workday without incident. He never succumbed to the temptation to tell off his boss and storm out, as difficult as it was to do. He met Susan for lunch and did his best to remain casual, as though everything was normal, but he did have to hide the act of wiping his eyes once or twice when they became watery. If she ever noticed anything unusual about him, she never said a word about it.

When Anthony arrived home that evening, he went around the apartment making last minute checks to ensure everything was as he wanted it. The tape reels were in the bag, the reel-to-reel was on top of the dresser where he'd placed it.

Anthony slid behind his desk in the study and rolled a fresh sheet of paper into the typewriter and began modifying the parts of his original story. Where he had previously written the detail of the bag of books at the foot of his bed, he changed it to be a bag of tape reels. Toward the end, he added that the tape recorder sat on the dresser in his bedroom.

"There," Anthony said, "that should do it."

He stood up from the desk and walked into the living room, remembering to leave the story in the typewriter.

Before turning in for bed, Anthony went into the kitchen, opened the refrigerator, and poured the milk and orange juice on the floor. He broke the glass coffee table in the living room and pulled his dresser drawers open, dumping his clothes on the floor and scattering them throughout the bedroom and hallway.

He had no idea what a real crime scene looked like, but after surveying the mess, he decided it would be sufficient to give anyone who discovered it the impression he had been abducted. He found it difficult to get into bed with the mess in his apartment; Anthony had to resist the urge to clean up the mess he had made. Instead, he managed to lay still and let a plethora of different emotion-invoking thoughts stream through his head.

Anthony knew he would be writing publishable stories. The books would sell thousands, even millions, of copies. They would be optioned for movies and sell just as well overseas. The possibilities of his success seemed endless. Anthony would be in a new social stratosphere.

Suddenly, his happy thoughts veered in another direction, somewhere unexpected; guilt. Anthony was on the brink of becoming rich and famous, like his idol, but only by stealing Roger's work, thus ruining the writer's career in the process. Now that Anthony was alone with his thoughts and able to give his plan and the consequences the consideration they were due, he realized it wasn't as trivial as taking an idea and shaping it into something new and different. No, the gravity of what Anthony planned to do weighed on him heavily. He was going to *steal* Roger Kurrey's ideas and pass them off as his own.

Anthony truly liked Roger, even if that admiration was distant, derived mostly from watching interviews on the Internet and reading the man's work. He believed that Roger was probably a decent, honest person. The thought of sabotaging the man's career, yanking the rug out from under him before he could even get started on the path to fame and fortune was almost too shameful to bear. Anthony considered removing the story from the typewriter before he fell asleep until a new train of thoughts derailed him.

In his mind's eye, Anthony imagined his dingy fuckhole of a cubicle, just one among a whole sea of cramped depressing spaces. The phone's perpetually blinking buttons, customers waiting to complain about their software woes. Anthony could hear the familiar buzzing of the phone, of all the phones in the office ringing at once with the unhappy, bitching clients, haunting him as he lay in his bed.

And then there was Jim and that smug smirk on his face whenever Anthony had to report to his office because of his work performance. Anthony doubted Jim had any qualms about firing him. Anthony knew he would never go anywhere in that company, never move up the ladder. His helpdesk job was a dead end. If Anthony was a programmer or salesman, he could potentially advance, but the sad fact was that as a help desk jockey, he was stuck on an endless treadmill.

Anthony thought about his small apartment, his arduous commute, never having enough money to do the things he wanted, of waking up way too early, sitting for eight excruciating hours in a tiny nook he hated every day. He felt his situation closely paralleled Winston Smith in *1984* and that JSS was too much like working for the Ministry of Truth. Anthony became acutely aware that he was clenching his fists and felt hot all over. He had worked himself into a frustrated rage. When he thought of Roger again and what he was doing, he got out of bed and ran to the typewriter.

"What the hell am I doing?" he asked himself, standing in front of the machine pinching the top of the paper. He stood at a crossroad. He could jerk out the sheet and probably never face this opportunity again, or he could follow it and walk down the path to fame and fortune. Unlike Winston, Anthony could do something about his situation.

Sorry, Roger.

Anthony dropped his hand. He decided to proceed as planned and went back to bed.

CHAPTER 12

Anthony awoke to the familiar dimly lit room he had experienced on his previous visit. He raised himself on one elbow and rubbed his eyes. He could see a corner of the reel-to-reel tape recorder on the dresser. If everything had gone according to plan, the sack of tapes would be at the foot of the bed. Anthony looked over at the floor. There were no clothes strewn about as there had been when he got in bed, which was good. It was a further indication he was in the past.

He threw his legs over the side of the mattress, stood, stretched, and then went out into the empty hallway. He peeked in the kitchen; no spilled milk or juice puddles soiled the linoleum. On his way back to the bedroom, Anthony glanced into the study. The

Royal typewriter was not on the desk. A bolt of panic struck him as he wondered if he was stranded in the past for good. Without the typewriter, he had no vehicle to return to the future.

He hurried back into the bedroom and saw the typewriter resting on the dresser behind the tape deck. It must have been obscured by the recorder when he looked the first time. The story still protruded from the carriage like a large white tongue. He let out a sigh of relief.

Anthony hefted the typewriter from the dresser and stowed it in the closet in the room he used as his study. He figured it would be safe in there and out of the way if anyone were to visit.

When the typewriter was safely put away, Anthony took a quick shower. He returned to the bedroom and found that his usual pile of clothes beside the bed were not the same items he had left there the night before. He picked up the shirt and held it out. It was a t-shirt, not the button-up he'd taken off. The pant legs flared, forming bell-bottoms and a white leather belt—the kind with double catches on the buckle—snaked through the belt loops.

Anthony opened the middle dresser drawer to discover it was filled with more bell-bottom pants. Some were corduroy; others were checkered plaid or regular denim. The drawer above it held a wide array of shirts with butterfly collars, turtlenecks, polyester, and more t-shirts. Three shirts sporting the butterfly collar, he noticed, were various colored plaids.

I better not wear those with the plaid pants. I'd be a Technicolor nightmare.

He pulled on the pants that had been lying on the floor and slipped the t-shirt over his head. The words printed on the shirt's front said, "What's your 20?"

"Great," he said and continued dressing. Next to a pair of high-top Converse was a pair of short black boots with a zipper running up one side.

These must be what they call Beatle boots.

Anthony opted for the sneakers.

Once he was dressed, and despite feeling awkward in the new clothes, he decided to check out his new environment. Anthony grabbed his wallet—a different version from his other—and keys and tucked them into his pockets. He stopped and rechecked the bag at the foot of the bed. The tape reels were resting inside with the book titles written on them so he could tell them apart.

He went into the living room where sunlight shone through the front window. His eyes hurt, not from the bright light spilling in, but because of the horrible color scheme in the apartment. The carpet was green shag. The sofa was an ugly brown. A console TV squatted against the wall with rabbit ear antenna on top. The front of the TV had only two dials instead of an array of buttons like Anthony was accustomed to, and in this new life, Anthony discovered there was no luxury of a remote control. He went over to the sofa and retrieved a copy of the

TV Guide that was wedged between the cushions. He looked at the cover. In bold black letters it said: Does TV Go Too Far? The date under the logo was October 13, 1973. He looked back at the TV with its dials and antenna, the lack of a remote, absence of a cable tuner box—Anthony wasn't sure whether cable TV had been invented yet—and became discouraged. These were things he had only briefly considered.

Well, here I am. Like it or not.

He walked out of the apartment and locked the door behind him.

Despite being an October day, the outside temperature was mild and pleasant as he walked along the sidewalk into town. The cars that passed him were all older models. Well, to Anthony they were old. In truth, the cars whizzing by were very modern. Some of them were brand new. A few were from the late 1960s. It was only 1973 after all. This was something Anthony would eventually get accustomed to, but at the moment he was experiencing culture shock. He was a resident of the past now, which was so fundamentally odd to him that a wave of anxiety threatened to overcome him if he dwelled on the thought too long.

Anthony felt silly as he walked down the sidewalk. He imagined the people passing him were staring like he had grown a second head. It was the clothes. They were so wildly different from what he normally wore that he felt conspicuous. His pant legs were too spacious, allowing the cuffs to swing freely and rub together as he walked. The t-shirt was a little too tight for his taste and the sleeves felt way too short. Although he felt odd wearing the clothes, his paranoia began to subside when he realized that people were not staring at him.

He stopped when he came to the main street that bisected Oakwood, looking first to the left and then the right. Despite being thirty years in the past, the landscape wasn't drastically different. He noticed many of the same buildings along the road to Highway 5; different businesses occupied some of the buildings, but that was to be expected.

To his left, Anthony saw nothing more than a two-lane road framed by field grass and a copse of trees. He thought it was weird that he could remember it branching out into four lanes surrounded by a host of retail businesses. In addition, a convenience store on the left-hand side of the road and a package store across from it that he was accustomed to seeing were not there. Instead, there was only more field grass and trees.

To his right, things looked more familiar, at first glance anyway. A few of the stores had changed owners in Anthony's time, but the buildings remained relatively the same. On the side where Anthony stood was a Color-Tile store, which, in the future, was a comic book store, and beside it, a Treasure Island. The Treasure Island had become a

Richway in the 80s, and then a Big Lots during the 90s.

The fast food chains were the same, other than the buildings' appearances and their signs. The McDonalds didn't have the play area out front as it did when Anthony had last seen it, and the sign out front didn't boast as many burgers sold. Kentucky Fried Chicken's sign was different, too. The other restaurants included a Wendy's and a Burger King. In the future, there were several more restaurants that were not here now.

Other buildings were homes to a bicycle shop, a dentist's office, swimming pool supply store, two hardware stores (in the future these had been replaced by a single Home Depot), a Nations Bank, and two grocery stores: Kroger and SuperValu. The SuperValu was across the street from the intersection where Anthony now stood.

This was the same grocery store where Anthony was supposed to be employed. He had written into his story that he worked there as a stock boy and on the truck crew, responsible for unloading the groceries delivered in freight trucks. Anthony remembered the SuperValu store from his childhood. His mother had shopped there regularly until it closed in the early 90s and finally became a Publix.

Anthony turned and walked toward the bank. He didn't have an account with Nation's Bank, but that didn't mean he couldn't withdraw money from their ATM. He passed a public phone booth along the way, noticing as he passed that it only cost a dime to make a call instead of thirty-five cents. As he crossed the bank's parking lot, he kept looking for the ATM machine. He paused outside the front door and removed his wallet. When he opened it, Anthony was surprised to discover he didn't even have a debit card, or any credit cards for that matter. However, there was a twenty and a five dollar bill folded in the bill compartment. He went into the lobby and looked around. There was no ATM in sight. He wasn't sure when they had been invented, but guessed they hadn't yet.

Anthony tucked the wallet back in his pocket and decided to check out the SuperValu before he was supposed to show up for work. In his story, Anthony had written that he worked from 6 PM to 1 AM, Monday through Friday. Since it was Wednesday he had to work. Looking at his watch, he learned it was a quarter after one. He had less than five hours before he had to be there.

Anthony waited for a Volkswagen Beetle to pass before he crossed the street. He was still experiencing culture shock as he went through the parking lot, seeing the cars' body styles and the shoppers' fashions.

As he neared the grocery store, Anthony saw that the adjacent building contained a ClothWorld store and a RadioShack. Anthony couldn't resist the urge to visit the electronics store, so he went inside. A man in a light blue button up shirt and a horrible paisley maroon tie greeted him. A pocket protector visibly poked out from his shirt pocket. His hair was neatly combed and parted on the side. He had mutton chop sideburns and thick black-rimmed glasses.

"Good afternoon," the man said. "Can I help you find anything?"

"No, thanks. Just browsing."

"Okay. Let me know if you need help with something."

Anthony looked around, amused by the obsolete gadgets on display: transistor radios; cassette tapes; CB radios; rotary dial telephones (none of the cordless or cellular variety); no sign of any videogame consoles he was used to. Anthony walked over to a display counter and looked at something that he at first mistook as a hand-held videogame (making an assumption based on his exposure to twenty-first century technology) and found that the item was a portable calculator. The price tag told him it was $129.95.

Other marvels of technology on the shelves included diodes, transistors, circuit boards, and a plethora of other parts for the hardcore geek who dabbled in building homemade radios or other electronic doodads. Anthony was left feeling disheartened and deflated. It dawned on him that he would have to wait many years before he could enjoy the videogames he was familiar with. Although Anthony wasn't a techno-geek or even a big video gamer, he understood how much he had taken those things for granted. Personal computers, the Internet, cell phones, ATMs, and so many other modern conveniences were either not yet invented or not a part of mainstream society. Anthony had only given brief consideration to this before committing to living in the past, but now he wished he'd given it more thought. Not having these luxuries was more shocking than he had anticipated.

Anthony left the RadioShack wondering whether he might have bitten off more than he could chew and went over to the grocery store. There were ten checkout lines at the front of the store; four of these were open, ringing up customers' sales. He walked by the service counter and looked at the pictures of the manager and assistant manager. The manager's name was Bill Hackney, a balding man that looked to be in his late forties. The assistant manager was Stewart Grimes. He looked slightly younger, with neatly combed dark hair and a crooked smile. Neither of the men in the photos appeared to be asskissing corporate drones like his former boss, but pictures could be deceiving.

He walked between the aisles toward the back of the store, thinking about earning a paycheck for keeping the shelves filled with products. There was definitely no complexity to the work. He also looked at some of the sticker prices as he went. He had a moment of clarity when he remembered the twenty-five bucks in his wallet, which he didn't think would stretch very far. After seeing the prices Anthony recognized that his money would go much further than he initially thought.

This'll be better than taking support calls.

Having looked at so much food, Anthony's stomach grumbled audibly. He decided to go to the McDonalds down the road and get something to eat, then come back to pick up a few items before returning to his apartment.

At McDonalds, Anthony spent a whopping two dollars and ate enough food to feel stuffed. He still couldn't get over how cheap everything was. Well, almost everything. The price of the calculator was oddly laughable, the complete opposite of what a simple calculator like it cost in the future.

When Anthony returned to SuperValu, he purchased a pound of ground beef, hamburger buns, condiments, a three-ring binder, a pack of loose-leaf notebook paper, and a box of pens. He carried everything to the front to checkout.

"You working tonight?" the cashier asked as though she knew him.

This caught Anthony by surprise. He remained calm and looked at her nametag. It said Lisa. She was a thin blonde with perky breasts. Very pleasing to the eyes.

"Uh, yeah. Same as usual," he answered, stymied.

"Oh, okay. I get off at five," she said as if they talked on a regular basis. She bagged the few items he had. "What about this weekend, you working?"

"I can't remember. Why?"

"I got a couple of tickets to see Rush but no one to go with. If you aren't working and want to come, you can."

"I'll have to double-check my schedule and let you know." He handed her the twenty and took his bag. She made change and handed it over.

"See you later, Lisa." Anthony appeared to be doing a good job of remaining casual.

She smiled, waved, and started ringing up the next person in line.

Anthony exited the store and set off for his apartment in a daze. The encounter with the cashier was too surreal. There was no doubt Anthony thought she was beautiful. And, apparently, she knew him! He'd only been in his new life for a few hours and already he had been invited to a rock concert. Anthony didn't give a shit for Rush, but if it meant going with a nice looking girl like Lisa, he didn't care who was playing. Although, he wished he could experience it with Susan instead. But, thinking of her still hurt and he found it difficult to get his mind off of her after he'd thought of Susan. He pictured Lisa again.

I don't know anything about her. What the hell am I doing?

When he got home, Anthony put away what he'd bought. It was a good thing he bought food, because there wasn't anything in the pantry to eat and he didn't think to check before leaving. The kitchen lacked the convenience of a microwave, but did have an electric stove, refrigerator, coffee maker, and plenty of cabinet space. There were already some glasses and a few dishes on the shelves. He pulled out a kitchen drawer and found a silverware tray that had only a few forks, spoons, and knives. Anthony discovered that there was no dishwasher and slapped his hand against his forehead for not having the foresight to add that detail to his story.

It was always the little things. If he had added all the finer details to the story, it would have been a novel in itself. Anthony had only concerned himself with the bigger picture: a place to live, a job to earn an income, and a schedule that would allow him time to copy from the tapes; although Anthony didn't like to think of it that way. Instead, he preferred to think of it as writing, even if he was just copying what he had recorded. Knowing that plagiarism was wrong, Anthony tried to justify in his mind what he was doing. However, the easiest thing to do was just to try and not think about it. He wondered if it was really plagiarism if he was writing something *before* it had even existed. He liked to think not.

Anthony carried the tape machine into the dining room and placed it on the table. He rummaged through the bag of reels and removed one, then took the notebook paper out of the plastic wrapping, secured the sheets in the new binder, and opened the pack of pens. Anthony inserted the tape reel on the spindle and carefully threaded the tape through the heads, connecting it to the receiving reel. After turning on the player, he spent his time before work writing the story in longhand.

CHAPTER 13

His first night at his new job turned out better than Anthony initially figured it would. He arrived at the SuperValu fifteen minutes early to orient himself with where everything was located. Anthony helped unload two trucks, putting plastic-wrapped pallets and cardboard boxes in categorized sections of the stock room. After the trucks were unloaded, Anthony maneuvered a pallet of breakfast cereals out into the aisle and began restocking the shelves. This wasn't a job for someone looking to climb the corporate ladder, but Anthony thought it was a hell of a lot better than working at a help desk. For one, there were no disgruntled shoppers lining up to tell him he had stacked cans of peas the wrong way, or they couldn't find a specific box of cereal they wanted. Also, with this job he could actually see the result of his labor, which made Anthony proud that he was contributing to something.

The other guys he worked with were teenagers or maybe slightly older, in their twenties anyway. Besides Anthony, the oldest member of the group was Steve. He and Anthony had hit if off better than Anthony had with the other guys, probably because Steve was older than the rest and appeared to have some real-world wisdom. It also helped that Steve attended college where he was majoring in Engineering. Steve was interested in technology, which Anthony knew something about.

While sitting in the break room after unloading the first truck, Steve addressed Anthony, asking, "You know anything about computers?"

You kidding? What do you want to know? I can probably tell you more than you'd expect.

"A little."

"What do you think of them so far?"

Anthony had to consider his answer carefully, because, for him, this was a loaded question. There was a time when he *did* like computers. It was the reason he'd gotten a job in technical support. But, what Anthony really wanted to do was program games like the ones he played when he had owned his first computer. Anthony learned that he didn't have the patience or aptitude for programming though so he decided to stick to tinkering with operating systems and hardware. Of course, he couldn't tell Steve any of this. So, he just said, "I think they're going to catch on one day and revolutionize the future."

Steve's face lit up at Anthony's response. Anthony continued, "I think that, one day, everyone'll have a computer in their home. It'll give them information about almost anything they want to know." Without meaning to, Anthony had opened a conversational can of worms with Steve.

"You sound like a true visionary," Steve said, "Have you ever heard of the Altair 8800?"

Anthony said he hadn't.

"Well, it's the first microcomputer developed for hobbyists that can be programmed by the user," Steve said, sounding more like a salesman for the manufacturer.

"So, what can it do?" Although Anthony knew a good deal about computers, he didn't know squat about the predecessors to the early IBM and Apple machines. Anthony's dad bought their first computer in the mid 80s. It had been a 386, which at that time was considered the latest technology. Anthony had worked with people through the years who liked to boast that they owned Commodore 64s back in the day, but Anthony thought it was mostly to appear knowledgeable among their coworkers, a form of boasting.

"Well, you can program it to play music," Steve said. "I watched a guy do a demo with it. He made it play specific frequencies and then held a speaker up to the box. Damn if it didn't play *Row Your Boat*."

"Do you have one of these Altairs?"

"No. But I'm going to buy one when I go back home. I'll probably use the money I make here to get it. My mom and dad, they'd never front me the money." Steve laughed. "They think computers are just a fad that'll eventually fizzle out."

Steve said the Altair could be purchased preassembled or as a kit and that the real enthusiasts bought the kit. It cost somewhere in the neighborhood of four hundred dollars and there were no peripheral input devices to feed it data. Instead, there were just toggle switches that the user had to flip on or off. By switching these levers, the user fed the machine instructions using a binary language. Anthony was disillusioned by how rudimentary the machine sounded, much too geeky. Without a monitor, keyboard, or mouse, Anthony didn't see any practical appeal for such a gadget. But, apparently, Steve did.

"I doubt they'll take off unless someone makes them easier to use," Anthony said, remembering the cryptic Linux operating system he had once used. "If they're going to revolutionize the world then they have to be a lot more user-friendly."

"User-friendly," Steve said, smiling and nodding. "I like that term."

Anthony had grown tired of their computer-talk. Of course, Anthony knew there were people like Steve who obsessed over computers and thought they would change the world, but Anthony's technical support job was still too fresh in his mind to feel passionate about computers the way Steve was.

Besides, Anthony's thoughts kept returning to the cute cashier he'd met earlier. He wondered if Steve knew anything about her.

"Hey, uh—what do you think about that cashier, Lisa?"

Steve looked up just as he bit into his sandwich and wiggled his eyebrows back and forth. As he chewed, Steve said, "Man, are you kidding? Lisa Stibbons is a fox!"

Stibbons! Finally, a last name.

Anthony nodded his agreement. "Yeah, tell me about it. She asked me to go to the Rush concert with her this weekend."

Surprised incredulity showed on Steve's face. "You've got to be shitting me!" He cast a quick glance over each shoulder, leaned in closer, and whispered. "You accepted, right?"

"Well, not yet. I told her I had to check my schedule. See if I was working or not."

"Screw that, man. Even if you're on the schedule, you need to talk to Stewart and get unscheduled! If that doesn't work, go talk to Bill."

Anthony didn't want to confront the managers about rearranging his hours. Thinking of Jim, he preferred to keep off their radars as much as possible.

"What do you know about her?" Anthony asked.

"Other than she's hot? Nothing really." Steve smirked. "She doesn't give guys like me the time of day."

"What do you mean, 'guys like you'?"

"She's clearly not into guys who're interested in computers and electronics. You know, nerds."

Anthony nodded. He knew what Steve meant, but Steve didn't look like a stereotypical nerd. Steve was clean-cut, intelligent, and—well, if Anthony was a girl, he'd admit it—handsome. Steve didn't show signs of having battled severe cases of acne, there was no pocket protector in evidence, and he didn't wear birth-control-glasses; what Anthony called glasses with white tape on the nose which prevented a guy from ever getting laid.

When finished with their break, Anthony and the other stock boys went back to work refilling the shelves with products and then finished by sweeping the aisles. Although the store had closed its doors to the public at 10 PM, Anthony's shift didn't end until one in the morning. This store wasn't like the Krogers and Wal-Marts of the future that stayed open for twenty-four hours, catering to insomniac shoppers.

Anthony went to the front of the store and climbed the stairs to the managers' offices. At the end of the hallway between the two office doors for the managers was a slotted timecard holder. Anthony found his card, removed it, and stuck it into the time clock's slot. The bulky gray machine issued a mechanical clunk as it stamped the current date and time. Anthony returned his card to the holder. On the opposite wall, he hung his smock on one of the many hooks where other aprons dangled. He walked outside into the cool night air—unlike the pleasant unseasonably warm air earlier in the day, it now felt as if December weather had settled in. Anthony would have to find a jacket in his apartment if the mercury continued to drop. Luckily, he didn't live too far from the grocery store. As he passed beneath the orange-yellow glow of the streetlights, Anthony marveled at how stress-free his new job was. He enjoyed not having someone breathing down his neck while he worked. Although the money wasn't even in the same ballpark as his last job (not by a long shot), Anthony didn't care. The reduction in stress was worth the cut in pay. Besides, it was an income, enough for him to live on, and his work schedule allowed him plenty of time to write.

The following morning, Anthony awoke at 8:30. He wanted to see if RadioShack sold typewriters, and if so, he wanted to know how much one would cost. He didn't have enough money yet to buy one—twenty bucks might go farther here than it did in the future, but he knew it wouldn't afford a typewriter. At least, he would know how much to set aside from his paycheck.

He showered, dressed, and ate a bowl of cereal before leaving. The weather was colder than it had been when he walked home from work; his breath vaporized in the frigid morning air. Anthony pulled the corduroy jacket's wool-lined collar tighter around his neck. He was thankful he had rummaged through his closet; otherwise the walk would've been miserable. When he arrived at the electronics store, the same man with the black-rimmed glasses and pork chop sideburns stood behind the counter helping a young man. Overhearing their discussion, Anthony learned the customer was asking about eight-track cassette players.

Anthony looked at the shelves around the store but didn't see any typewriters. He thought there might be a catalog behind the counter that he could use to order one. He milled about, looking at the various gizmos, waiting for the salesman to finish with the customer. After a moment, the employee door at the rear of the store opened and another salesman emerged. This guy looked less conservative than his counterpart. He had longer hair that was done up in a long ponytail with rubber bands, a bushy goatee, and wore a leather vest and moccasins. His appearance screamed hippie. When he walked behind the counter, the clean-cut salesman nodded in Anthony's direction and mumbled something.

"Can I help you?" the younger, long-haired clerk asked.

"Yeah. I was wondering if you sold typewriters."

"We don't have any typewriters in the store—"

"Do you have a catalog?" Anthony interrupted. He had already determined that when he didn't see any on display.

"I'm not sure if we offer typewriters," the man said doubtfully and bent behind the counter. He stood up with a thin booklet which he placed on the countertop. "Let's see what we've got."

Anthony looked on as the guy flipped through the pages. When they came to the last page, the man asked the other salesman if they sold typewriters.

"No," the first salesman said, shaking his head. "You can go to the mall in Lauden, though. The Service Merchandise carries them. So does Sears."

Anthony thanked them and left. Without a car, he would have to catch a bus to get to the mall in Lauden and he didn't want to waste too much of his writing time just trying to price typewriters. The arctic wind biting into his cheeks helped him make a decision. He would wait until Saturday, when he cashed his paycheck and had more time. Then he remembered Lisa's invitation to go to the concert. She had said *weekend* without mentioning which day, but more than likely that meant Saturday and Anthony already knew he didn't have to work that day. Since most concerts started late in the day, Anthony figured he could still go to the mall and have enough time to write before he and Lisa went to the show. Anthony walked home, his breath puffing out in steamy bursts.

Along the way, Anthony was imaging how Lisa would behave outside of work. He hoped he would get along with her as he had Susan. The thought of Susan made him wonder how she was holding up. It was only the second day following his vanishing act, and his guilt still felt like a leaden weight in his chest. Now that he didn't have her with him, Anthony couldn't shake the thought of how much he had taken Susan for granted; a void in his chest was begging to be filled. He wondered if she'd heard about his disappearance yet. If so, what was her reaction when she found out? Thoughts of Susan hurt too much, so his mind changed the mental channel. Anthony wondered whether his former boss knew about his disappearance yet and what he thought about it. Anthony wished he could've been a fly on the wall when Jim learned he had failed to show up for work. Mostly, though, his thoughts returned to Susan. How devastated she would be. He wondered if anyone had even discovered his ransacked apartment yet.

As he imagined Susan's reaction to his disappearance, his sense of guilt only worsened. He wished he could have brought her with him, but the typewriter only worked upon the person using it. Anthony smiled when he thought of what Susan might have to say about the hideous fashion and décor of the seventies.

At his apartment, Anthony gathered his pen and notebook, sat on the sofa with the binder in his lap, and opened it. He found the place he had left off transcribing the first few pages from the tapes. He switched on the player and resumed writing. After an hour of furious scribbling to keep up with his voice coming through the speaker, Anthony stopped the tape, put his pencil down, and went to get something to drink from the refrigerator.

Knowing he would eventually have to type the manuscript, Anthony verbalized his frustration, "I need a damn typewriter."

The act of composing long hand was just too tedious and hard on his hand. Anthony was more accustomed to working on his laptop, taking advantage of its various features: spell check, automatic indent, search-and-replace, and delete. Although the Royal typewriter didn't measure up to the conveniences of his laptop, Anthony would take it over composing long hand any day. At least with a laptop or typewriter he didn't develop writer's cramp. Anthony shook out his hand, flexing his fingers while he gulped a cold soda.

Anthony wondered again why he hadn't just waited to find a typewriter before beginning the story. Not only did his cramped hand ache, but he had to go back and retype the story anyway. All of the redundancy was precisely what he wanted to avoid. These were the actions of a moron. He knew he couldn't submit a hand-written manuscript to the publisher. Anthony wasn't sure whether it was acceptable in the seventies to submit hand-written work, but even if it was, his penmanship was atrocious. He might as well have written with the pen gripped between his two toes. It was as illegible as a doctor's prescription.

Anthony began to rethink whether he should wait until the weekend to go to the mall to look for a typewriter. Although he couldn't afford one right now, he could at least compare prices so he would know how much he needed to save. The muscles in his hand throbbed and his fingers felt arthritic. It was too painful to grip that damn pen any longer. He hated the idea of retyping what he had already written and, if he kept going, it would just be more to type later. All of that redundancy was insane.

He looked at his watch. It was 11:45 AM. He still had time to catch the bus to the mall. He put on his jacket, grabbed his keys, and left the apartment.

It felt like the mercury had dropped significantly since he had ventured to the RadioShack earlier that morning. Anthony rocked back and forth on his feet, watching his breath vanish in a steamy cloud while he waited at the bus stop. A woman dressed in a faux fur coat and pink Duncan Donuts outfit sat on the bench near Anthony. The bus squealed to a halt in front of them five minutes later. Stepping into the bus's heated air caused Anthony's cheeks and fingers to tingle.

Twenty five minutes later, after the bus had traversed its route from Oakwood to Lauden, delivering passengers along the way, it stopped outside the Cloverleaf Mall. Three people got off the bus with Anthony, but only two of them went to the mall. The odd man out made a beeline for the liquor store and from the way he staggered, Anthony figured it wasn't his first time there.

Anthony entered the double doors of Sears and set out searching for the typewriters. After walking around aimlessly for a while, he finally found what he was looking for. In one corner of the store, typewriters lined a narrow shelf along the wall. Small placards sitting beside the various models indicated their prices. None of them was even close to what Anthony thought a typewriter would cost. He looked at the electric models, and learned that a Selectric was nearly five hundred dollars; he decided a manual was probably more within his price range. He was wrong. If he wanted to buy a new typewriter, even a manual, he would have to save more than two paychecks, which was out of the question because he still had to consider paying his rent and buying groceries. He cringed at the thought of writing with a pen much longer.

Discouraged, Anthony left the mall and took the next bus back to Oakwood. There was no doubt he needed a typewriter. There was no way around it. He would just have to save his money and buy one later. As much as the thought of retyping the story pained him, Anthony wouldn't think of quitting. If push came to shove, he could probably ask someone if they had a typewriter he could borrow for a little while. When he remembered the things he had given up to chase this dream, he marveled at the irony of his situation.

Only a few days ago he had access to the Internet to do his research and a laptop at his disposal for writing. It felt that if he didn't laugh, he'd cry. Finally, it occurred to him: he didn't need a *new* typewriter; a used one would do just fine. He could probably find one at a yard sale or thrift store. The only problem was finding a yard sale where someone was trying to get rid of a typewriter, and he had no idea where any thrift stores were.

Anthony got off the bus when it stopped in Oakwood. He went to the nearest convenience store, a Stop-N-Go three blocks away. There was a row of newspaper dispensers out front where Anthony thought he might find advertisements for local yard sales.

One of the three dispensers was blue and sold *The New York Times*, which was useless for his purpose. An orange stand to the left carried the local *Oakwood Gazette*, and the other, a white stand on the right, contained free catalogs of local real estate listings; available homes and apartments which were also useless.

Anthony deposited a quarter into the orange box, pulled open the door, and withdrew a copy of the *Gazette*. He didn't pause to flip through the pages in front of the store because the temperature made it uncomfortable to linger outside. His jacket felt inadequate. Anthony folded the paper, stuffed it under his arm, and hurried home.

The walk afforded him time to consider returning to the future. He was cold, he missed Susan, he also missed the technologies he had taken for granted, and he was second-guessing his plan to pass off Roger's stories as his own. He seriously began to doubt whether he could actually pull off the stunt. With each reason for him to return, however, he thought of a better reason to stay. His job at the grocery store didn't pay what his previous job paid, but it was less stressful, freed up his schedule, and paid enough for him to make ends meet. His plan was simple. All he had to do was stick with it. His dream was finally within his grasp, so close to fulfillment.

Also, he reminded himself that if he pulled the sheet out now, there was no guarantee he could ever return. He had already considered this idea. He even thought that if he *could* go back and forth, that ability had the potential to end when the ink ribbon ran out or when the machine broke down. Sure, it was possible to replace the ribbon, but what if the machine's components as a whole provided the magic? This was something he hadn't thought to test earlier and now it was too late to experiment with. If he changed anything about the typewriter, cleaned it even, it might stop working. No. He wasn't about to chance it. He was here and he would have to give it his best effort.

In the end, Anthony decided to continue writing with the pen until he could afford a typewriter, then he would retype what he already had. Once each story was finished, he would do a quick edit and submit it to an agent. Not just any agent, but the same one that had discovered Roger. Anthony intended to pick up a copy of *Writer's Market* from the library so he could look up the agency's address. That wasn't important right now, though; finishing the manuscript was his top priority.

Having the completed story in his possession was a huge plus. He saw that his problems were not insurmountable. Dwelling on inevitably turning his dream into reality did wonders to cheer Anthony up.

When he got home, he unfolded the newspaper on the kitchen table and searched the want ads for sales. As expected, there were announcements for yard sales for the upcoming weekend. He read them carefully; circling a few that looked promising. None of the announcements mentioned typewriters specifically, but those that listed appliances sounded promising enough. When he finished with the paper, Anthony got out the yellow pages and searched for thrift stores. There were three: two in Lauden, the other in Acworth, on the other side of Oakwood. He wrote the addresses on a sheet of paper and set it aside. If the yard sales didn't pan out, he thought, he might check out the thrift stores.

CHAPTER 14

It was almost 4:30 PM when Anthony entered the grocery store. He was purposefully early so he could see Lisa. She worked the day shift and he didn't want to miss her before she left. He stopped inside the entrance and quickly observed the checkout rows. Only half of the ten lanes were in use and Lisa wasn't at any of them. Anthony's shoulders slumped when he didn't see her at any of the registers.

I must've just missed her.

Getting to work an hour and a half early and without anyone to talk to, Anthony decided to take a magazine from the book rack and sit in the break room to read until his shift started.

He looked over the various selections of magazines: *Guns & Ammo*, *Good Housekeeping*, *Life*,

Offroad, *Southern Living*, etc. None of them appealed to him. He went further down the aisle to the shelves of paperbacks and examined the many covers. Two books in particular caught his attention: *Bad Moon Rising* by Thomas Disch and *Among the Dead* by Edward Bryant. He turned over each and read the synopsis on the back. He settled on Disch's book because it was an anthology. Anthony didn't want to get engrossed in a book only to return it to the shelf when he had to work. At least with the anthology, he would be able to read a couple of the stories.

When Anthony entered the break room, he saw Lisa sitting at a table nursing a soda, an open bag of M&Ms beside her elbow. She was reading a magazine when he walked up to her.

"Hey," Anthony said.

She looked over her shoulder at him and perked up with a smile.

"I thought you'd already left for the day."

"I was waiting for you," she said, glancing at her watch. "I got off work a few minutes ago. I thought you wouldn't be here until six. You're early!"

"I wanted to ask about the concert this weekend, see what time it started, and when you wanted to leave. If you're still going," Anthony said.

"Yeah. I'm still going."

"Okay, let me rephrase that. I meant, if I was still invited." Anthony gave her a broad smile.

"I'm sorry. You never gave me a definite answer, so I asked Jeremy if he wanted to go instead," Lisa said.

Jeremy Hoffsteader was one of the younger guys on the truck crew. He was a loud-mouthed cocky braggart that no one got along with very well.

Anthony detected the teasing hint in her tone. "Really, you're taking Jeremy? You guys have fun." He smirked, calling her bluff. "So, why'd you wait around for me?"

She gave him a cunning grin and said, "Well, you never gave me a definite answer, so I figured I'd wait to find out for sure. If you don't want to, I can always get my friend Denise to go."

"I just had to make sure I wasn't working this weekend—"

"Well," Lisa interrupted, "are you?"

"No. But, I have to do something on Saturday. What time did you want to leave?"

"I was going to pick you up at five. The concert doesn't start until six-thirty," she said. "What do you have to do on Saturday?"

"I want to go to some yard sales or thrift stores to see if they had any typewriters for sale."

"If you need a ride, I can take you. I don't have anything planned."

Anthony was admiring how beautiful Lisa looked at that moment. He didn't need time to consider her offer. Besides, it would give him more time to get to know her better.

"Yeah, sure. If it's no trouble. That'd be great." Anthony couldn't hide the pleased look on his face. He wrote his address down on a slip of paper Lisa had taken out of her purse. She said she would see him Saturday morning at ten.

When Lisa left, Anthony leaned back in his chair and opened the borrowed book. However, he found it difficult to concentrate on reading because his mind was preoccupied with thoughts of Lisa. He couldn't help that he was beaming.

When Steve finally walked in and sat down across from him, Anthony was bursting with the news of his date with Lisa. As the two of them shuffled to the loading dock to begin working, Anthony told Steve everything he and Lisa had said.

Saturday morning, Anthony's alarm clock started its incessant buzzing at 8:30. He had awakened before the annoying alarm began, but remained in bed, waking up gradually. Although there were plenty of things he disliked about the seventies—the fashion, the music, and well, most everything else— Anthony was growing to love his work schedule. Sleeping past 7AM was one of his luxuries.

He rolled over and stopped the alarm, then pulled himself out of bed to shave and take a quick shower. It wouldn't be long before Lisa arrived. He wanted to look presentable and tidy up his apartment before then.

Once he was dressed, Anthony went through each room, emptying garbage cans, sweeping, picking up his dirty clothes, and then washing the few dishes that had been sitting in the kitchen sink.

It was ten minutes after ten when there was a knock at Anthony's front door. He opened it to find Lisa standing there looking better than ever, probably because she wasn't wearing the frumpy drab grocery store smock. Instead, she had on a black sweater and tight blue jeans. Before he could invite her in, she asked if he was ready to go. He said he was, locked the door, and followed her downstairs.

Lisa drove a red two-door Chevy Nova, which was parked beside the curb in front of Anthony's building.

"Nice car."

"Thanks. It was my brother's. He gave it to me when he and his wife bought a newer one."

"What'd they get?"

"A Gran Torino," Lisa said. "His wife wanted something with four doors because they're expecting another kid. They needed a bigger car, so they gave this one to me."

"They just gave it you?"

"Yeah. It pissed Emily off when Jeff did that instead of selling it cheap, but he always looks out for me." Lisa paused. "I'm going to give him some money for it though. They'll need it with another baby on the way, a new car, and the economy in the toilet."

Lisa went to Highway 5 and turned south toward Acworth where, according to Anthony's list, the closest yard sale was. When she pulled onto the street, Anthony saw about five or six cars parked along the curb in front of a little ranch-style house. Assorted items appeared to litter the front yard. People were milling about, rummaging through cardboard boxes and clothes lying on fold-out tables. A couple of kids were sifting through neglected toys in a nearby box.

Anthony stepped among the items for sale, searching for a typewriter. A woman wearing a beige pantsuit with long blonde hair parted in the middle approached him. "Looking for something in particular?" she asked.

"You got a typewriter for sale?"

"Sorry." The woman shook her head. "'Fraid not."

Anthony thanked her as he and Lisa went back to the car.

"One down," Anthony said, crossing the address off his list, "three more to go."

Lisa took him from yard sale to yard sale, exhausting Anthony's short list. There wasn't a single typewriter at any of them, which really didn't surprise Anthony. They weren't as ubiquitous as computers were in the future.

Around noon, they stopped at a Wendy's to grab some lunch. Anthony bought Lisa's meal and they sat down to eat. Anthony pulled the list from his front pocket and unfolded it.

"Do you know where the thrift store is in Acworth?" he asked.

"Not offhand. What road is it on?"

"I don't know," he said, consulting the address. "Butler Street?"

"I think I know where that is. If I'm right, Butler's off Broad Street. We'll find it," she assured him.

They finished their burgers and got back in Lisa's car. She was right; Butler Street crossed Broad Street. She made the turn onto Butler and soon they saw a sign for the thrift store near the end of the road.

There was a large parking lot with about a dozen cars gathered in front of a corrugated metal building. A sign over the front doors said it was the Acworth Community Thrift Store. Lisa found an empty space and they went inside. The floor was cement and there was one cash register beside the exit doors. To the left, rows of metal shelves formed aisles, stacked full of what looked like remnants from moving sales. The middle and right side of the store held rack upon rack of clothes beneath signs indicating sections for men, women, and children.

It appeared to Anthony that everything offered was the equivalent of Salvation Army donations; things people donated because they didn't have the heart to throw them away. Disheartened by his first impression of the place, Anthony went over to the metal shelves. There were roller skates, ice skates, miscellaneous dress shoes (both men and women's), toasters, radios, records, eight-track cassettes, little girls' dolls, glassware, books, grubby toys, and boxes of puzzles.

Anthony experienced a brief moment of déjà vu remembering the antique store in Moultrie he had visited with Susan, where they discovered the Royal typewriter. However, this store was much cleaner and the aisles were less crowded.

At the end of the aisles was a perpendicular walkway that separated the rows of shelves from the building's outer wall. When Anthony reached this path, he turned and looked to his left. In the corner of the store sat several floor-model television sets, rabbit-ear antennas, CB radios, clothes irons, a bag of golf clubs that was far from a full set, and not one, but three typewriters. Anthony couldn't believe his eyes nor his luck. He had been on the verge of giving up; thinking his search for a used typewriter was in vain.

Of the three, only one was not in acceptable working order. It was missing the A, S, N, O, and K strikers.

Well, I can't write with that.

Anthony remembered the main character in Roger's third book. A guy named Jason. With this typewriter, he'd only be able to type the J for the character's name.

I'd go insane having to back fill the missing letters.

Of the remaining two, one was electric. There was no outlet nearby, so Anthony couldn't plug it in to see if it even worked. He inspected the last typewriter carefully. It was a 1963 Smith-Corona Sterling. It looked heavily used, but in fairly good condition despite the wear. The price tag said it could be his for thirty-five dollars. Compared to the cost of a new typewriter, this was definitely a bargain. Luckily, Anthony had fifty dollars he could afford to part with. He lifted it from the shelf and carried it to the cashier where he paid the woman cash. He couldn't help but smile as he laid out the bills.

On the way back to Anthony's apartment, Lisa stopped off at an office supply store where Anthony purchased several reams of paper and a new ink ribbon. Once he had these items, Lisa drove them back to his apartment so Anthony could put "his toys" away. There were still a couple of hours before the concert, so Anthony invited Lisa in to relax before they had to leave.

"You want anything to drink?" Anthony asked from the kitchen. He held open the refrigerator door, looking inside at the sparse selection available. "All I got is tea and beer. I can make some Kool-Aid though, if you want."

"What kind of beer you got?"

"Pabst Blue Ribbon."

"That's fine. I'll have a beer."

Anthony removed two beers, popped open their tops, and settled on the opposite end of the couch after handing Lisa a can.

"So, what're you going to do with the typewriter?" Lisa asked. "Write your life story?"

"C'mon. I'm not that old." Anthony smiled at her sarcasm. "No. I'm writing a book." He pointed to the kitchen table where his notebook lay, took a swig from his beer, and said, "I'm already working on it. I've been writing with a pen in that stupid notebook.

But, I have to turn in a printed copy. So, I decided to get a typewriter. If you're like me and can't type, it's a tedious process." He mimed hunting and pecking the keys with his index fingers to illustrate his point. "Typing's slow when you're a member of the hunt-and-peck tribe."

"Are you kiddin'? You really writing a book?" She wore an incredulous smile.

"Yeah, I'm serious." Anthony stood up, went over and got the notebook. He handed it to her. She set her beer on the coffee table, opened the cover, and looked over the handwritten pages; there were sixty in all, single-spaced, front and back.

"Wow. How long've you been working on this?" She turned through a few of the pages, looking at all the scribbled words.

Anthony shrugged. He hadn't kept track of how long it'd been. He was just familiar with the routine of playing the tape while his hand transcribed the words.

"I don't know," he said, scratching his chin, "a few days, I guess."

"Have you written anything else? Any other books you haven't mentioned?"

"Yeah, I've written some other things. Not books though. Just some short stories, but I didn't do anything with them."

"What'd you do with them?" she asked. "You didn't send them to any magazines?"

Anthony shook his head. "Nah. I wanted to, but never got around to it. When I reread them, they just didn't sound right. Not like—" he stopped, catching himself. Out of habit, he almost said not like Roger Kurrey, but Lisa wouldn't have any idea who Roger Kurrey was. He wasn't famous yet and Anthony nearly painted himself into a corner by mentioning him like he was already a household name. If Anthony wasn't more careful, he would end up saying something stupid and have to lie his way out of it. He was tired of lying. It was like wandering around in the dark, and sooner or later, he knew he would run into a wall. "Not the way people really talk. Know what I mean?"

Lisa nodded, still staring at the page. "Well, this reads pretty good to me."

"Thanks," Anthony said, smiling. "That means a lot." Susan was the only other person to tell him how good she thought his writing was. Although it wasn't really Anthony's story, he liked hearing people's appreciation for it and enjoyed pretending it was his idea.

"So where are these short stories you wrote? Do you mind if I read one?"

"Oh. I threw those out. Like I said, they were pretty bad."

"Maybe you thought they were bad, but did you ever let anyone else read them?"

Anthony shook his head.

"You probably should've let someone else read them before you tossed them." She glanced back down at the page. "This looks really good. What's the name of it? Sorry. That was probably a little presumptuous."

"No. That's all right. It's called, When the Clock Strikes Three," he said.

"Ooh, that sounds cool. What's it about? Wait—you're not going to tell me I have to read it first, are you?"

Anthony shook his head. "No, but I'll definitely let you read it when I finish. I mean, if you still want to." His cheeks flushed a bit. Now, he felt like the one being presumptuous. "It's about this guy imprisoned in a futuristic compound. He's a political prisoner, except the crimes that he and the other inmates are charged with would be considered frivolous today. But, in the not-too-distant future, these crimes are considered serious because the government has become a ruthless oligarchy. All of the politicians are religious fanatics and they consider themselves the moral majority. They round up non-believers, homosexuals, prostitutes, people they consider riff-raff.

"At this compound, in the wing where the main character is held, all the prisoners have death sentences. Every day at 3 PM, a prisoner is executed. The prison kills them using one of three methods: hanging, firing squad, or electric chair. This guy's number is coming up, but he's found a way to escape and he's about to make his move."

"And?" Lisa asked, her intrigue was obvious.

Anthony shrugged. "And, that's it. I'm not going to tell you the whole thing."

"Does he escape?"

"You'll have to read—"

"Yeah, yeah. I know. I'll have to read it to find out." She was nodding as if she had expected as much. "Well, it sounds pretty cool. I definitely want to know what happens."

"Cool. I hope everyone feels the same way."

"Don't throw it away or anything before I get a chance to read it," she said. "You're probably your own worst critic. You could be writing something great and not even know it unless someone's here to tell you."

Lisa's enthusiasm about the story was contagious. With the accolades she was giving him, Anthony felt like he could sit down right then and hurry through the rest of the manuscript. Anthony was relieved to have met another person just as supportive of his endeavors. She was the first person since Susan who'd expressed a certainty about him getting published.

When Lisa was finished leafing through the notebook, Anthony put it away and turned on the TV. Lisa kicked off her shoes and nestled into the corner of the sofa. After spending more time with her, aside from the small talk they had shared at work, Anthony felt much more at ease with Lisa. He hoped to see their friendship eventually blossom into a deeper relationship.

As they waited, they talked about work. Their conversation eventually segued into a discussion of their childhood—Anthony remained vague about his, heavily censoring his stories for fear of giving away that he was from the future.

Lisa sat up and slipped her feet into her shoes just as the news was beginning.

"What time is it?" Anthony didn't bother looking at his watch.

She said, "It's five."

If they wanted to get close to the stage, they had to leave. They had talked for quite a while, longer than Anthony had with any one person in a long time. He and Susan had never talked for as long as he and Lisa had, and what's more, the conversation flowed. There hadn't been any awkward pauses to ruin its momentum. Anthony was glad that the two of them felt so casual with one another, but he also wanted there to be more to their relationship. Who knew? Maybe things were finally going his way. She seemed to feel comfortable in his apartment.

Anthony grabbed his jacket, locked the front door, and they went to the concert.

Despite the noise and throng of concert-goers in the arena, Anthony enjoyed being out with Lisa more than anything. Shortly after finding two relatively close seats, Journey opened with their first song. Lisa pulled a slender, tightly-wrapped cigarette from her purse. Anthony recognized that it wasn't a cigarette at all, but a joint and watched with uncertainty as she lit it and inhaled deeply. She held her breath for a stretch of seconds before exhaling the blue-white cloud. It had been a very long time since Anthony had smoked marijuana, but the smell of it burning was unique and, to him, fragrant. The last time he had indulged, he was a senior in high school. His first foray with smoking pot was the result of peer pressure, but he had enjoyed the experience nonetheless.

Lisa passed the smoldering joint to him and Anthony put it to his lips. He inhaled deeply, resisting the urge to cough. The smoke felt harsh as it filled his lungs.

Through the din of the crowd, she encouraged him to, "Hold it in."

He handed the joint back to her and pinched his nose. His cheeks puffed out like Dizzie Gillespie playing the horn. Anthony was sure he looked silly. Finally, after holding the smoke in for several seconds, he could take no more and gasped for air. When he did, a thick cloud of smoke poured out of his mouth.

Lisa smiled at him and took another drag.

They passed it back and forth until they had smoked it to a smoldering nub. Lisa rested her head against Anthony's shoulder. Anthony's mouth grew dry and cottony. He tried to slake his thirst with a beer purchased from the concession stand. The beer did nothing to satisfy him. After a couple of minutes, Anthony's hands began to tingle as though they had fallen asleep. Anthony felt the need to sit down while everyone around him stood, cheered, and swayed to the music. The sensation slowly spread up into Anthony's arms and he later realized that his feet tingled as well. When he closed his eyes and sat back in his seat, Anthony felt as though he was flipping head over heels through space. Accompanied by the music, the feeling was exhilarating and relaxing. Time seemed to have slowed down.

The concert had been loud and bustling. Anthony wasn't a Rush fan, but he thought their performance was okay. In his opinion, however, Journey sounded far better than Rush had. He wanted to tell Lisa what a kick-ass band Journey was, but thought better of it since they were still relatively new and not as popular as they would later become. The music at the concert, although loud, was merely background noise while Lisa and Anthony sat with their eyes closed, bobbing their heads to the rhythmic beat.

It was after 11 when Lisa stopped the car outside of Anthony's apartment. They got out into the cold night air and walked upstairs to his door. He opened it and she followed him inside.

Anthony sensed an opportunity and asked, "You want to stay here tonight? It's a little late to be driving."

She stepped closer and surprised him by kissing him on the mouth.

Anthony thought it was the best yes he'd ever received.

When Lisa ended the lip lock, she slipped off her jacket and tossed it on the couch. Anthony just watched her, feeling himself stiffen when he noticed how her sweater hugged her breasts.

"Do I have to sleep on the couch, or is that where you were planning to sleep?" she asked, flashing him a wicked smile.

Things were moving fast and the question seemed to come from out of nowhere. Anthony had no idea if she was serious about either of them sleeping on the couch.

"Uh...I guess I'll take the couch. You can have the bed," he said, hoping to conceal his true thoughts.

She went into the bedroom, not bothering to turn on the light. Anthony watched her disappear into the shadows. A moment later, her black sweater flew from the darkened doorway and fell to the floor. She had moved close enough to the opening that Anthony was able to see her perky breasts and the darkened triangle of hair between her legs.

"Well? Are you coming in here to keep me warm? It's cold, you know." Lisa abruptly turned, revealing her tight inverted heart-shaped ass before receding into the shadows.

The grin on Anthony's face got ever wider and nearly split it in half. He hurried into the bedroom after her. He peeled out of his clothes, letting them fall on the floor, and slid beneath the sheets. When they had finished having sex, Anthony moved to Lisa's side, where they spooned and drifted into sleep.

The Old Royal

Anthony's eyes fluttered against the bright sunlight spilling into the room. He lay on his back, sprawled across the mattress. His right arm reached across the bed where Lisa had slept, but she wasn't there. He turned his head and looked at the rumpled sheets. His mouth was as dry and scratchy as sandpaper. He worked his tongue back and forth trying to dredge up some saliva. The clock on the nightstand said it was 8:35 AM.

He raised his head and called out, "Lisa!"

There was no answer. He got out of bed and walked into the dining room. A sheet of notebook paper lay on the table with a pen resting on it. A woman's handwriting was neatly scrawled across the page.

Anthony,

Thanks for a wonderful time last night. It was heavenly. I hope we can go out again soon. I'm sorry I had to leave early, but I promised my mom I would go to church with her. She's been after me about going for two months. Today is her church's homecoming, and I promised I'd go. Sorry for not telling you sooner, but I forgot. Don't think that this is a date-and-dash. It's not. Call me: 458-4396

Lisa

After reading the note, Anthony felt better. Upon first glance, he had assumed the worst; that it was some kind of "Dear John" letter. He was happy to be wrong. He put the paper back down on the table and went to take a shower.

When Anthony was clean and dressed, and still able to harness the enthusiasm Lisa had fostered the previous day, he sat down to work on the novel. Now that he had a typewriter, he could type what he had already written. This, too, made him feel better because it would put him closer to submitting the story to an agent.

Since he didn't have to come up with the story from scratch, he thought it would be easy to just sit and copy the words back onto the page, but it was actually a little more difficult than that. He had to get his mind into a zone, and following the night he'd spent with Lisa, Anthony found it difficult to concentrate on typing what he had already written. Not to mention, he found it to be tediously boring.

Anthony set the typewriter up on the dining room table—he didn't have a desk in the study like he did in the future—and placed a fresh ream of paper to the right. Over to the left, Anthony situated his notebook. He got a sheet, rolled it into the machine, and centered the carriage. Then he typed the story's title, When the Clock Strikes Three, hit the carriage return twice, typed, By, hit the return twice more, and paused.

Anthony had almost typed his real name, but then thought better of it. He had no idea if that was a wise choice or not.

What would happen if I used my real name?

He had never given much thought to using a pseudonym before. Somewhere out there was another Anthony Jessup, an Anthony Jessup that was only one year old, his past self. Did his time-travel affect that other version of himself? Would his rise to fame, using his real name, cause problems for the other Anthony? He didn't know the answers to these questions, so Anthony erred on the side of caution and decided to use a pseudonym.

He considered this for a little while, writing down first names and last names that randomly came to mind. He mixed and matched them on a scrap of paper. None of them sounded right when he said them aloud. He wanted a name with pizzazz, one that sounded as though it belonged to a successful writer. The process was more frustrating than trying to devise a name for a character in one of his stories. He always hated the names he conceived, because none of them rang with the authenticity that other authors' characters did. After mulling over what he had written on the paper, a last name he had not written popped into his head: Beechum. Yeah! It had a definite ring to it. Excited, Anthony went down the list of first names, trying them out together. David? John? Jim or James? As he tried each one, none seemed to resonate like he wanted. To his ear, they sounded as phony as a used car salesman. The next name on his list was Robert.

Robert Beechum.

He liked the sound of it. It evoked the sort of feeling that Anthony was looking for: that of confidence and aptitude. It had authority. This was the name he typed on the title page.

Now that he had a name, Anthony pulled the sheet from the carriage and looked at it with appreciation. He set the page aside and began typing the handwritten text. Three and a half hours of feverish typing later, Anthony turned the page to discover that he had caught up to the end of the handwritten stuff. Like pulling a loose tooth, it wasn't as painful as he first thought.

He had reached a milestone. Anthony used it as an opportunity to take a break. By his watch it was nearly one o'clock. He went to the kitchen and poured some Kool-Aid from the refrigerator. He considered calling Lisa, but realized she might not be home yet if she and her mother went out to eat afterward. He decided to wait. The story's momentum was beginning to roll and now that he had typed all the handwritten parts a weight slid off his shoulders. He was free to let his fingers fly now and he didn't want to interrupt that creative flow. Anthony gulped from the glass, enjoying the coolness as it ran down his throat. He chugged the rest of it—a quasi-celebratory gesture for reaching a milestone, albeit a small one—and poured another glass from the fridge.

He plopped back down behind the typewriter, cracked his knuckles, and settled back into the process of writing, a task he took seriously. He picked up the previous page and looked it over. It was the part where Ron, the political prisoner and main character, was being shown to his cell for the first time. Anthony began playing the tape and resumed typing.

The walls in Block D were made of cinderblocks and painted an institutional gray; the floor was hard cement. Mesh-covered fluorescent lights hung from the ceiling in the lengthy corridor. Heavy iron doors leapfrogged one another down each side of the hall, giving way to cells that housed other inmates. Men and women incarcerated for crimes against the government, or as Ron liked to think of it, crimes against the regime.

After walking a considerable way down the hall, the guard escorting Ron stopped. He turned to face the metal door marked 634, unlocked it, and stepped aside. Ron, with his manacled hands hanging in front of his newly issued prison clothes, peered inside with the same curiosity as someone investigating a room rumored to be haunted. A second guard--one that had followed behind Ron, making him the center of a guard sandwich--nudged Ron with the end of his nightstick.

"Go on. Get in there!" the guard said.

The other guard who had walked ahead of him smiled as Ronald stumbled forward. "Home sweet home," he added.

Ronald Joseph Chambray, also known as inmate 265903, stumbled into the cold drab enclosure. This was his new residence at the Statesboro Detention Center, Cell Block D, which held all of the death row inmates. He, along with his associates, was charged with crimes that carried the penalty of death.

The last few weeks had been surreal for Ron, who had once been a Resource Manager with a successful engineering company. It seemed like only yesterday that he was sitting behind the desk at his cushy job. Then came the accusations, the charges, arrest, speedy kangaroo trials, and now, here he was.

After the shackles were removed, the steel door clanked shut. He listened to the clicking heels of the guards' shoes against the cold cement floor as they retreated down the hall. The cell's silence was deafening, broken only by a cough from a neighboring inmate. The sound amplified as it echoed off the walls and floor. When the sound faded, that overwhelming silence dropped on Ron again like a stifling stage curtain.

Ron hugged himself as he looked at the four walls that wanted to close in on him. A metal monstrosity sat in one corner. It was a toilet with a sink built into the top. A polished metal mirror was bolted into the cinder block wall above it. Opposite the toilet-sink was an uncomfortable-looking metal bunk, also bolted to the wall. A stained mattress was rolled into a bundle at one end. On the other, a thin pillow, mattress cover, sheet, and blanket. That was it as far as the furnishings.

A bare bulb behind a thick glass globe with wire mesh lit the center of the room. Aside from the bulb, the only other source of light came from one narrow window set into the thick wall opposite the door. Reinforced glass with embedded wire mesh closed off the world. Outside the window, another set of bars ensured that any prisoner could not escape should the glass be breached, which was a laugh because the width of the slit wasn't even wide enough to accommodate an adult's head much less their body. From his vantage point across the room, Ron could see gunmetal gray rain clouds hanging in the sky. He stepped closer to the window so he could see the world below.

The window looked out onto a courtyard, bare save for a distant brick wall. A maroon stain marked the wall's center and was encircled by a number of ragged pits. Ron wondered if that was where the firing squad dispatched the condemned.

He stepped over to his bunk and pulled the end of the small tie that bound the rolled mattress. When the string fell away, the mattress reluctantly unfurled. Ron smoothed out the piss-smelling cushion and made his bed. When finished, he sat upon the bunk with his back against the wall, hugging his knees to his chest as he remembered his comfortable job, spacious house, and freedom to come and go as he pleased. A tear escaped his eye and slid down his cheek.

When Anthony came to the end of the page, he paused the tape reel, removed the sheet and set it aside. He situated a new page in the typewriter, aligned it, resumed playing the tape, and began punching the keys.

CLACK! CLACK! CLACK!

He typed, immersed in the hypnotic zone that allowed him to concentrate on the words from the machine, watching the characters act out their imaginary lives in his head, and at the same time, filling page after page with the words of the novel.

The thing that brought Anthony out of his trance wasn't the phone or the doorbell; it was the pain in his hands. He had worked steadily for just over two hours—it was 3:15 now. He squeezed his eyes shut and reopened them, giving himself a kind of mental stretch, then looked around at his apartment. The light coming in through the windows had changed. The rays slanted at an angle through the blinds now that the sun was beginning its descent. A bit of lightheadedness also affected Anthony, as though he had quickly swilled several beers at once. As Anthony transitioned out of that zone, it felt as if he had just awakened from a nap.

He stood up and went into the kitchen where he got another glass of Kool-Aid and thought about calling Lisa. Surely, she must be home from church by now; it was after 3 PM. He looked down at her note on the table. *Call me*, it said.

He wanted to talk to her again, but that was putting it mildly. What Anthony really wanted was to have her with him again, physically. Last night had been exhilarating. Throughout the evening, he was comfortable with her, without any awkward moments. However, when he thought of calling her, butterflies fluttered in his stomach. His palms were sweaty and his heart pounded. It was like having a childhood crush and confronting the source of those emotions for the first time.

What would I say?

Although last night had gone so smoothly, Anthony could think of nothing clever to say if he called her. Everything he tried in his head sounded pathetic.

You're being ridiculous! Just call and ask how she is.

Anthony lifted the receiver with trembling fingers. Despite his mental pep talk, Anthony was still unsure of what to say. He wanted to strive for a casual tone. Consulting the paper Lisa had scribbled on, he dialed her number. Her phone rang three times. Anthony assumed she might not be home yet.

Just as he was taking the handset away from his ear, he heard someone.

"Hello?" the voice said.

Anthony's brow pinched together. It wasn't a woman's voice. It was deeper than that. He put the receiver back to his ear and asked, "Is Lisa there?"

Maybe it's her dad.

"Yeah, but she can't talk right now," the man said. "Who's this?"

Through the receiver, Anthony heard a female giggle in the background.

"Uh—" Anthony hung up.

Anthony looked at the phone in the cradle, wondering if he had dialed the wrong number.

No. He said she couldn't talk now.

Anthony examined the brief exchange and background noise in his head.

Maybe it was her brother?

She said she had a brother. Jack or something like that. That didn't seem right though. Something about the giggling he heard in the background raised doubts in his mind; they had sounded too playful.

Without wanting to chase his misbehaving mind down a rabbit hole, Anthony said, "I'll just call her later," and tried to forget about it.

The sun hovered above the treetops to the west. Anthony had spent the last several hours reading. He tried to watch TV and wasted several minutes cycling through the few available channels in search of something interesting. It seemed like everything was a rerun. Nothing appealed to him. He thought it might be a good time to call Lisa again. He no longer felt nervous about calling her because he wanted to hear her voice, if only to alleviate his suspicions.

Anthony dialed her number carefully, making sure he didn't make a mistake, although he was sure he had dialed it correctly the first time. The phone rang twice before a woman finally answered it. However, this voice didn't belong to Lisa either.

"Hello. Is Lisa there?"

"No, I'm sorry she isn't."

"Oh," Anthony said, glad to know he had the right number.

"She and Gary went to see a movie. I can take a message and give it to her when she comes in."

"No, really, that's okay," Anthony said suspiciously. "I'll talk with her later."

The woman said, "All right. Bye," and hung up.

Anthony hung up feeling numb. Who was this Gary she had gone to the movies with? She never mentioned anything about going to the movies, let alone with some guy. Anthony's subsiding jealousy erupted again in his chest, leaving behind an icy dagger wound.

Don't jump to conclusions. You have no idea who she's out with and you're already jealous. It might be her brother.

As he attempted to rationalize the situation, Anthony's jealousy began to settle once again until he thought about the guy who answered the phone previously and the woman's laughter in the background. He didn't want to assume the worst, but he also didn't want to act naïve and convince himself that she was just having a friend over to play on the swing set. Something didn't sit well with him about the whole situation. His gut instinct told him that something was up. He had had these intuitions before and learned to trust them because they usually turned out to be true. He decided to just confront her about it tomorrow at work.

CHAPTER 15

Anthony arrived at work earlier than normal. He'd spent most of his morning transcribing the story from tape and managed to get through several pages, spurred on by his jealousy at thoughts of Lisa getting friendly with another guy at the movies. He felt deceived, as if someone had stolen something from him. He doubted he would ever be able to properly articulate these emotions to another person.

When he entered the grocery store, he saw Lisa at the register in the fourth aisle. She was ringing up a large assortment of groceries for a hefty black woman.

Anthony walked by the checkout stand and tapped on the counter. Lisa took her eyes off of what she was doing to glance at him briefly. When she saw him, her face brightened with a large smile. The emotional tug-of-war waged on between Anthony's heart and mind at the mere sight of her. He just waved and continued walking toward the break room.

He deposited a quarter in the soda machine and selected a Dr. Pepper. He sat at a table in the employee lounge and looked at a newspaper someone had left behind, trying to ignore the multitude of thoughts vying for attention. None of the headlines held his interest, so he turned to the comic section and began reading Peanuts.

"Hey, you never called me," Lisa said, walking over to him.

"Yeah, I did."

"Really, when?"

"I called twice yesterday." Anthony felt that surge of jealousy bubble up, but he managed to put a lid on it. "Let me ask you something. What did you say your brother's name was?"

"Jeff. Why?"

"Because the first time I called, some guy answered. And the second time, a woman told me you had gone to the movies." Anthony paused, trying to gauge her reaction. He gave her a chance to say something. She didn't. "So, who's Gary?" By now, the jealousy and hurt was evident in Anthony's tone.

Lisa only stood looking at him in dismay. Anthony knew he had caught her in something. He figured she was trying to think of an excuse to explain her way out of it.

"Well?" Anthony asked.

"Okay. The truth is...Gary's my boyfriend."

"What?!" Anthony was glad there wasn't anyone else in the break room to witness this little scene. "You've got a boyfriend and you slept with *me*? What the hell's wrong with you, huh?"

"Calm down." Lisa sat down on the other side of the table. "I'm not really into Gary anymore. I just haven't told him yet. He came over yesterday and wanted to talk. We ended up going to the drive-in to see a double feature."

Anthony remembered the woman's laugh in the background during that first phone call. Something about Lisa's story still didn't seem to jibe. "Did you sleep with him, I mean, after the movie?"

Lisa hesitated and finally nodded as she stared at her hands.

"So you're not that into him, but you still sleep with him—"

"You don't understand, Anthony, it's not like you and I are that serious anyway."

"Well, I don't make it a habit of casually sleeping around. If I go to bed with someone, I figure we're beginning a relationship. You obviously don't."

"You don't want to see me anymore?"

The question caught Anthony off guard. Initially, he had convinced himself that Lisa just wasn't interested in him and would eventually break the news to him, not the other way around. Although he had no tolerance for infidelity, it pained him to be at this crossroads where he had to make a decision and possibly end up hurting her.

At that moment, he thought of his mother, who had cheated on his father when Anthony was much younger. Anthony had walked in on his dad, a man who rarely exhibited his emotions, as he sat in the living room of their house crying. Not one to beat around the bush, his dad had been blunt about the matter, explaining that Anthony's mother didn't love him anymore. She had found someone new. Although his parents had worked through some things and his mom didn't leave immediately, she didn't stop sneaking around either. After his mother had slept with a third man, Anthony's father had had enough and filed for divorce. Anthony remembered the court proceedings, the nasty accusations between his parents, their obscenities to one another. He vowed never to put up with a partner who wasn't monogamous. So, what was his answer? Did he not want to see her anymore?

"That's right," Anthony said, his tone quiet but stern. His eyes teared up. He desperately didn't want to cry in front of her. "I don't want to see you anymore."

Lisa wasn't crying when she stood up and left; another sign that Anthony had made the right decision. He figured that if she cared for him at all, she would have at least cried when she heard his answer.

Steve showed up five minutes before work and asked Anthony how his date with Lisa went.

Anthony said, "I don't want to talk about it."

"Oh, that good, huh?"

They left the break room and went to the loading dock.

Anthony looked over the sheet of paper resting in the carriage of the typewriter. He had done a lot of work today and decided to take a little break. Submersing himself in his work distracted him, keeping his mind from dwelling on Lisa. He sat down on the couch and, out of habit, looked around for the remote control. Anthony didn't know when the TV remote control would be invented, but it didn't matter, because he didn't have one. He sighed as he got up, walked over to the TV, and pulled the power knob. Sound came from the speaker before the picture fully appeared. It took a moment for the image to come into focus on the screen. Anthony squatted in front of the set, turning the dial hoping to find something interesting to watch.

Man, going back and forth to change the channel is bullshit.

There wasn't a lot to choose from, only five channels. Bored, he turned off the TV and got a soda from the fridge.

When he sat back down, Anthony reminisced about Susan. On the heels of the Lisa fiasco, he missed Susan more than ever and wondered if she missed him. Surely she did. He was curious about how she had reacted to news of his disappearance, how that scenario had played out. Were the cops involved? There was no doubt that they were. It had to be considered a missing person case by now. How were his parents coping with the news that their son had vanished?

I should've left them a note or something, telling them not to worry about me.

That would have eased their minds. Well, not completely, but at least they might suspect he wasn't dead. Thinking of his parents' anguish and Susan was too much to handle. Instead, he turned his thoughts to Jim, his former boss. How did Jim react to the news? Did he even know that Anthony was considered a missing person? Anthony enjoyed visualizing the pudgy asshole getting worked up over Anthony not showing up to work on time that first morning after his departure. Anthony liked to think that Jim might've gotten an ass chewing for being understaffed, but doubted that happened. He knew they would just hire some other flunky to fill the empty seat. Besides, he was only one person and he doubted that constituted being understaffed.

Thinking of his former job at JSS Software helped Anthony feel better about what he was doing. It was nice to be off the rat race's treadmill and when he thought of all those whiny clients calling for technical support and his superficial colleagues, Anthony was even more thankful that he didn't have to deal with them any longer.

Everything's so much simpler now.

If only the remote control had been invented. Anthony conceded that *some* technological advances were nice to have.

With nothing worth watching on TV and random thoughts in his head, Anthony chose to delve back into his work.

The rest of the week was uneventful other than the day Steve returned to California. The day after Steve left, Anthony found that he genuinely missed the guy, even if Steve only wanted to talk about technology. Without Lisa and Steve there to talk to, Anthony felt alone again, just as he had when he first arrived in the past.

Without the distractions of friends visiting or calling, Anthony concentrated on completing the book. It had taken just over a month to type the first story. Knowing that he had the final published version, Anthony didn't worry himself with making any major revisions. Only a cursory read through to make sure he hadn't introduced some typos or omitted any words, but that was basically it.

When he finished, Anthony rode the bus to the post office and sent a query letter and the first two chapters to Stuart Bradshaw at Pembrooke & Stephens Literary Agency in New York. Anthony found the address in a copy of *Writer's Market* at the local library.

Over the course of the next month, Anthony continued stocking shelves and unloading trucks at SuperValu. Although the pay was indeed small, it covered Anthony's rent and groceries and kept him off the street, while also affording him the opportunity to work on the books. But, the novelty of receiving such little pay for his efforts was wearing thin. He was ready for the fame and fortune to begin.

Anthony had expected to be more excited after finishing the first book. After all, this was the time a lot of writers looked forward to: celebrating finishing the writing process and shopping their manuscript around. For Anthony, there was no question whether the story would be accepted. Since there was no mystery and adventure in this part of the process, it dampened his enthusiasm. He was just going through the motions. The story would march toward publication, and a book deal would soon follow. There were still exciting moments Anthony had to look forward to, but the acceptance of the story wasn't one of them. The lack of fanfare saddened him.

While waiting for the response from the literary agent, Anthony tried his hand at some short stories. He rewrote a couple of his originals, thinking they might stand a better chance in the past when his ideas were not so clichéd.

The first story Anthony wrote was called *The Final Chapter*, about a woman named Dolores who had died following a car accident when she was a teenager. She was taken to the hospital where doctors revived her. One of her passions had always been writing, but since her accident, she was never able to finish a story. Before she could write the last chapter, Dolores would suffer writer's block. On a few occasions, she had blacked out before she could finish. Her doctor had told her that the blackouts were a side effect of the accident, a residual neurological effect that might possibly go away over time.

Anthony picked up the pages and began re-reading the story:

```
Dolores was sitting on the sofa, an
open photo album lying in her lap. She
had been strolling down memory lane,
looking at pictures of her husband,
their baby, Dolores's parents and
grandmother. Looking at snapshots of
the past rekindled old memories. She
remembered the car accident that had
changed her life. The recovery in the
hospital had been long and arduous.
When she was finally released to
return home, she thought the worst was
over. Then came the headaches, the
blackouts...the visions.
"What about this thing I saw, Dr.
Haber?" Dolores had asked. She was
referring to the sinister apparition
she had glimpsed soon after she
returned home from the hospital. During
```

that time, her grandmother was staying with them so she could be close to her granddaughter after the ordeal.

As Dolores sat in the living room with the album, that question echoed in her head. She was lost in reveries of her past. She could still picture that apparition when she closed her eyes and thought about it. It was like a shadow on the wall, a man, but there was no physical body that the shadow belonged to.

Dolores was in her room, putting away some clothes. As she lifted some shirts from her bed to put in her dresser, she glanced through her door into the hallway. The shadow was there, thin and tall. The arms held out in front as though it were creeping about. The long slender fingers were bent and crooked like talons. A top hat was on its head.

Dolores gasped, dropped the shirts, and...

That was it. She had blacked out. This was why she was seeing Dr. Haber again.

"The visions may just be a side effect from your accident," he said. "You suffered some severe neurological trauma. Side effects are to be expected. I'm actually impressed by your remarkable healing progress."

"What about the blackouts? Will these be commonplace?" Dolores asked.

"It's hard to tell. I'd expect you'll most likely have more. But, then again, they will probably subside as time goes by."

That had been an especially bad time for Dolores. Not only had she suffered her first blackout and been rushed to the hospital, but her grandmother had fallen down in the shower at the same time. Both of them were in the hospital, Dolores with a bump to the head, her grandmother in ICU with a fractured skull. Dolores's grandmother eventually succumbed to her injuries. The loss was a devastating blow to her family.

Dolores had seen the shadowy form several more times during her life. Two months after giving birth she had seen the figure in her and her husband, Terry's home. Again, she had blacked out. Four months later, still grieving the loss of their son, Dolores saw the figure in the living room. When she woke up from that blackout, she realized Terry hadn't returned home from work. She found him sprawled at the base of the steps leading to their front door. His neck was apparently broken due to falling down the stairs.

Now, Dolores sat in her house alone. Those memories hurt too much to think about any longer. To distract herself, Dolores put the photo album away and attempted to write again. She sat down with a pad and pen and contemplated what she would write about. Remnants of the tragic memories lingered. She decided to write a happy story, about herself, but opposite the events that happened in her life. What better therapy to cope with sadness than to express it through writing?

Her character Diane had a safe and memorable childhood. There were no car accidents that resulted in hospital stays, headaches, delusions, and black outs. Diane was married to a successful man working at an ad agency like her husband Terry had. They lived in a large house with a healthy child. Not a child who would die from S.I.D.S. as her little Dale had. Her character's husband wouldn't die young in a freak accident from falling down the stairs because they wouldn't have stairs in their house.

As Dolores wrote a fantastic life for her character, one that contradicted her own, her mind was busy connecting dots in the background, shedding light on some facts she had overlooked.

Dolores came to realize that every time she had seen the apparition, a blackout was sure to follow. But, not only did the apparition precede a blackout, a tragedy always followed.

Deep down inside, it became evident to Dolores that <u>she</u> was the cause of all of those previous tragedies. The ominous apparition who appeared in her pre-blackout visions was something that came back with her from beyond death's veil and it was using her as a vessel. Dolores figured the only way to stop the apparition was to continue writing her story to its conclusion.

   Dolores's hand began to cramp as she wrote. Her eyes were heavy and tired. She looked at the clock and saw that it was a quarter to midnight. She was nearly finished and hadn't suffered a blackout or writer's block. While her eyes were tired and her hand ached, her mind was finally clear.
   It felt good to get the truth down on paper. It became clear to Dolores the significance of the apparition, her blackouts, and the subsequent tragedies in her life. She just needed to write the story's ending, but she didn't know what it was.
   She rested her hand as she pondered where the story would end. Tears streamed down her cheeks as she realized she was the cause of her grandmother, husband, and son's deaths. It was only fitting that she confronted the entity that had used her.
   Dolores began writing again when an idea of how to end the story materialized whole and complete in her mind.
   When the big hand had caught up with the hour hand on the 12, Dolores dropped the pen. The notebook fell to the carpet and so did Dolores. She lay sprawled on the floor, looking up at the ceiling. One of her pupils was constricted, the other dilated. A small runner of blood trickled slowly from

her nose down her cheek. The tragedies in Dolores's life finally ended.

Anthony was thrilled with the story and submitted it to *Weird Tales Magazine*. Five weeks after placing it in the mailbox, he received a response from the editor. Excited, Anthony tore open the envelope and removed the folded letter from inside. It said:

Dear Contributor:

Thank you for submitting your story, but I'm going to pass on it. This tale didn't quite work for me, I'm afraid. Good luck placing your story elsewhere, and thanks again for sending it our way.

Sincerely,

Below the salutation was the scribbled signature of the editor. The cold rejection left a leaden weight in the pit of Anthony's stomach. He crumpled the paper and threw it across the room.

He had received stacks of rejection letters before, but prior to opening this envelope, he was convinced that streak of bad luck was over. He attributed this new confidence to the knowledge that he had finished a successful novel, one he was sure would be published. Through the course of copying that book, he thought *his* writing might have improved as a result. That elation dwindled when he remembered that the work he recently finished was not his own.

Frustrated by that understanding, Anthony decided he would quit trying to write any original material and stick to reproducing Kurrey's work.

A couple of days after receiving that rejection, another letter arrived in the mail. This time it was from the literary agency where he had submitted his query for the novel.

Looking at the stamped address on the front made Anthony's hands shake. The rejection letter was still too fresh in his mind and left him on edge. Anthony hurried into his apartment. He sat on the sofa as he stared at the envelope on the table. He picked it up with trembling fingers and inspected the outside as though trying to pick up a vibe from the contents.

This was it. It had to be good news or his whole plan was a bust. He'd have to yank the page out of the typewriter and return to the future. Back to the menial job in a cubicle where he would deal with the pieces of his broken dream.

Anthony ripped open the flap and took out the paper. His heart thudded with anticipation. He scanned the words on the page. When he glimpsed *a wonderful concept* and *would like to see the full manuscript*, he nearly hyperventilated. Those words were a stark contrast to anything he had ever received from someone in the publishing industry.

They want to read the whole thing! They're interested!

His hands were still quivering, but now it was from excitement. Without hesitation, Anthony gathered his manuscript along with the agent's letter and went straight to the bus stop where he intended to catch the next bus to the post office. He was determined to mail the story that day, fearful that the universe might change its mind and jerk the rug out from under him.

Anthony entered the post office thirty minutes later. Inside, he found five people waiting in line and two postal clerks tending the counter. With the passage of each minute he waited, Anthony imagined Roger sending off his manuscript at the same moment. In Anthony's mind, it was a final sprint to the finish line and he didn't know Roger's status. Anthony was impatient. All he could do was wait as he stood there holding the thick stack of loose pages.

When he finally approached the counter and stood before the weary clerk, Anthony plopped the manuscript down on the counter and said, "I need to mail this to New York, please." His words came out quick and excited.

The employee's eyes widened at the mound of paper. "Okay, let me see if I can find a box for that."

Not only was Anthony excited, he was nervous at the same time. This was the first novel he had ever mailed. He had sent off several short stories, but none of those had exceeded more than twenty-five printed pages. This was a behemoth compared to those, numbering three hundred-eighty pages. It had to weigh somewhere in the neighborhood of five pounds. While the clerk was locating a suitable box to put the manuscript in, Anthony looked back over his shoulder at the line. Six people were waiting as impatiently as Anthony had. He felt a twinge of guilt now that he was the hold up, but he also felt compelled to send the manuscript off as soon as possible. He hated to think that Roger's manuscript might reach the agent before his did.

When the clerk returned, she was carrying a thin cardboard box with a lid. She separated the lid from the bottom, placed the pages neatly inside, and set the lid securely on top. Without asking if that was all he wanted to include in the package, she began taping the edges of the box. Anxiety washed over Anthony before he remembered that the cover letter was already on top of the stack of papers.

"Go ahead and address it before I weigh it," she said, her eyes resuming that look of fatigue.

Anthony consulted the agent's letter in his pocket for the agency's address and, using the pen she handed him, wrote it and his return address on the box.

The woman placed the package on a spring-activated scale. "That'll be three dollars and fifteen cents."

Anthony fumbled for his wallet and gave her a five. He went back to the bus stop, feeling much better for sending the story as soon as possible and not waiting. It was out of his hands now. So far, it seemed like all the puzzle pieces were beginning to come together nicely.

When Anthony returned to his apartment, he thought he might begin work on the second novel, but found that he was too wound up to sit still.

Carrying a glass of tea, he paced back and forth through his apartment. His mind was abuzz with thoughts of selling that first novel. The agent's interest in reading more of the story was a very positive sign. Anthony was sure he would receive a contract agreement soon after the agent finished evaluating the story.

This calls for a celebration.

He was busting with good news, but there was no one around for him to tell. Before he let his loneliness bring him down, Anthony chose to go out to eat to celebrate his good fortune.

But, where?

The only places nearby were fast food chains, hardly an atmosphere conducive to celebrating such an occasion. Then he remembered that there was a Red Lobster in Lauden near the Book Nook. It had been a long time since he visited a Red Lobster; Anthony loved their all-you-can-eat shrimp. Afterward, he thought, he'd visit the bookstore and treat himself to a new book. It occurred to him, though, that the Book Nook hadn't been built. He reasoned that there had to be some bookstore nearby. If he didn't see one along the way, he could just ask someone.

Anthony got off the bus in Lauden at 5:30. As the sun settled behind the western horizon, the temperature was also dipping, nearing the freezing mark. Anthony tightened his collar with one hand and hurried to the restaurant. When he entered, he was happy to see that there was no long line. He had beaten the dinner rush.

When asked how many in his party, he told the maître'd that it was just him. She grabbed some silverware and a menu. "Follow me, please."

Anthony trailed behind the hostess to a table and noticed that the other patrons were more formally dressed than he was. He looked down at his sneakers and jeans and felt his cheeks flush.

The woman seated him in a booth near a window. Anthony opened his menu as she left. He skimmed the specials, hoping to see the all-you-can-eat shrimp. While Anthony was trying to decide what to eat, a waiter approached and opened a small wooden stand, which he placed a tray upon. On the tray were several plates with garlic shrimp scampi, lobster tail, popcorn shrimp, and a slab of salmon. The waiter began handing the plates to the guests across the aisle from Anthony. Smelling the food's wonderful aroma caused Anthony's stomach to rumble. He hadn't realized just how hungry he was until he smelled the food. The woman's shrimp scampi was still sizzling and steam wafted from the array of plates.

The last time Anthony had been to Red Lobster was with Susan shortly after they had begun dating. When he was a child, Anthony's mother used to order take-out from Red Lobster. His family always considered it a treat. His parents rarely went out to eat because his dad preferred sitting at home in front of the TV when he wasn't working.

A voice startled Anthony as he studied the menu, "Hi, my name's Debra. I'll be your waitress tonight."

Anthony looked up. The little nameplate on her lapel testified that her name was indeed Debra. She had blonde hair, sparkling blue eyes, a warm welcoming smile. She stood poised with a small notepad in her hand.

"Are you ready to order, sir, or do you need another minute to decide?"

"Uh." Anthony dropped his eyes back to the menu. There were so many choices and he hadn't selected anything. He really had his heart set on the shrimp special he enjoyed before. "Do you still have the all-you-can-eat shrimp?"

Debra reached over to a folded display on top of the napkin dispenser. "Yes, sir. It's right here." She opened the ad and handed it to him.

Anthony looked at his shrimp choices: garlic shrimp scampi, popcorn shrimp, or the fried gulf shrimp.

Anthony smiled and said, "I'd like the all-you-can-eat gulf shrimp, please."

Debra wrote it down and asked what sides he wanted. Anthony quickly picked two sides. Debra jotted it down and started to leave.

"Excuse me," Anthony said. "Can I get some bread, too?"

Debra looked at him quizzically and returned. "You want an appetizer, sir?"

Anthony was expecting the complimentary basket of garlic biscuits. When he asked the waitress, she didn't seem to know what he was referring to. Anthony picked up his menu and consulted the appetizer section. There was no mention of the garlic biscuits. He blushed and said, "I'll have the hushpuppies."

When she returned, she had five hushpuppies on a small saucer. "Your food should be out shortly."

Anthony thanked her and looked around at the other diners composed of couples or larger groups. He wished he had someone to join him, or had at least brought a book to read while he waited. Sitting alone made him conspicuous and uncomfortable.

A waiter finally arrived at Anthony's table. He opened a wooden stand and placed a tray on top.

"Here you are, sir," the waiter said, placing a hot plate on the table.

When the waiter left, Debra returned to make sure everything was okay. "Can I get you anything else?"

Anthony handed her his glass and she refilled it from a pitcher. He thought for a moment and asked, "Do you know of any book stores nearby?"

The question seemed to catch Debra off guard as she picked up his empty saucer. Her eyebrows furrowed as she considered it. "I think there's a Waldenbooks in that little plaza across the street."

Anthony thanked her before she left. He admired her smile. When he looked her in the eyes, they seemed to sparkle. He bit into a shrimp and studied her figure as she went to the kitchen. Debra wasn't as thin as Lisa or Susan, but somehow that only seemed to accentuate her attractiveness.

Anthony finished his shrimp and when Debra returned to check on him he asked for two more orders. She smiled, nodded, and went back to the kitchen.

By the time the check arrived, Anthony felt bloated. If it wasn't considered rude, he would've unfastened his belt to ease his discomfort. Anthony left a more-than-generous tip because he enjoyed Debra's attentiveness. It didn't hurt that he was strongly attracted to her. If he was more confident in his ability to carry on a conversation with strange women, he would have tried talking with her more. He figured the large tip would have to talk for him.

Anthony walked out of Red Lobster and looked up at the twilight sky where the moon was already beginning its nightly ascent. The last hint of sun remained to the west as a fading purple-maroon bruise. His breath billowed out in steamy clouds. Anthony hiked his collar up tighter around his neck and went across the street to the outlet mall. He scanned the store fronts and signs until he located the Waldenbooks. Anthony hurried across the street and the parking lot.

Roger Kurrey arrived home from his job at the foundry where he helped make transmission cases. His day had been long and he was glad to finally be home. It was warm inside the house and Roger went upstairs to wash his hands and change into some clean clothes before settling down to write.

His wife, Evelyn, was in the kitchen preparing dinner.

"Is that you, hon?" she called.

"Yeah, it's me."

"Dinner'll be ready soon."

"Okay. I'm just going to wash up and change."

Roger went upstairs to the bedroom he and Evelyn had shared for the past three years. Evelyn worked the day shift as a nurse at Mountainside Regional Hospital. Roger had been working at the foundry for two of those years. Prior to that, he had worked at a warehouse assembling windows and doors. The warehouse was never warm enough in the winter and always too hot during the summer. In addition to the horrible climate, Roger had spent ten hours a day standing at a workbench where he fastened together window frames nonstop. The foundry wasn't much better, but at least he didn't have to stand as long.

Roger married Evelyn in the summer of 1970. Her father was a foreman at the foundry and said he could get Roger a job there that paid more than he was making at the warehouse. Roger didn't hesitate to jump at the offer. He had toiled in the factory for two years and wrote every night during the last year. He worked hard on his first novel; one he hoped would get him out of the clutches of manual labor forever.

Roger entered the kitchen, straightening out his t-shirt. "What's for dinner?" He could smell something aromatic sizzling in the skillet.

"Your favorite," Evelyn said. "Sausage and peppers with rice." She turned to kiss him.

"How much longer before it's ready?"

"About ten minutes."

"Then I'm going to work on my book for a little bit." He disappeared into the den where his typewriter sat on the table. Beside the typewriter was a stack of papers Roger had been meticulously poring over with a red pencil, one he used to make editorial notes. Only eight pages remained for Roger to proofread.

He was nearing the end of his third revision cycle and had identified only minimal problems. He had addressed most of his plot holes, typos, and faux pas during the previous revisions. In this iteration, he discovered only a few pages with some misspellings and punctuation mistakes he had previously missed. He corrected those quickly.

"It's time to eat," Evelyn said. She looked in on him. "How's it coming?"

"I'm just about finished," he said, standing up from his chair. "I believe it's ready to submit." A smile of accomplishment stretched across his face. After a year spent writing the drafts and three painstaking revisions later, Roger had created what he hoped was his ticket to a better way of living; the start of a successful writing career.

It had been two months since he submitted the full manuscript and Anthony still hadn't heard anything from the agent at Pembrooke & Stephens Literary Agency. He was beginning to grow worried. His anxiety and impatience were already wearing him thin. After the first month had elapsed, Anthony realized he was drinking more than usual in an effort to divert his thoughts from the waiting game. In addition, he paced back and forth across the apartment until he was concerned he'd wear a path in the carpet. Finally, he decided to redirect his pent up energy and be productive by beginning work on the second novel. Although he had sped through the first book—all he had to do was copy the words, after all—the second book was progressing at a much slower pace. Because of his heightened anxiety over the first book, Anthony found he had lost much of the motivation he had while working on the second. The second book's pages would languish in the typewriter for days at a time without Anthony sitting down to add anything new to them. Whenever the mail arrived, he would run to the mailbox like a kid expecting a birthday present. Each day the mail contained nothing more than the typical junk or bills.

Anthony was growing tired of working at the grocery store. That job was only supposed to be a springboard, something to sustain him until the money from his book sales began to roll in. He had forgotten the long process involved to get a book published.

Also, Anthony had become lonely. His days consisted of writing in the morning—when he *could* write; in fact there was actually more beer drinking, reading, and watching television than writing—and working at the SuperValu until late at night. When his shift ended, Anthony would hurry home through the dark wintery night to crawl in his warm bed.

The second week in February, Anthony was sitting down to transcribe when his telephone rang. Since his spat with Lisa, Anthony hadn't received many calls, other than the occasional wrong number. Expecting another wrong number, Anthony stood and went to the phone. He missed not having caller ID.

He lifted the receiver. "Hello?"

"Hi. Is this Anthony Jessup?"

It wasn't a wrong number. Who could be calling? "Yes, this is Anthony."

"Hey, Anthony. My name's Stuart Bradshaw. I'm a literary agent with the Pembrooke and Stephens agency in New York. I was calling about the manuscript you sent me."

Anthony's legs suddenly felt like they might give out. He had to sit down. He developed a sudden case of the nerves the way many people do who are about to address an auditorium full of strangers. His future writing career hinged upon this call and Anthony didn't want to put his foot in his mouth.

"Yes," Anthony said. "I was hoping to hear from you."

"Well, Mr. Jessup, I've got to say, I really loved your story. If you're still in the market for literary representation, I'd like to extend you an offer."

Hearing this man's enthusiasm, Anthony's heart wanted to pop out of his chest. He resisted the urge to blurt, SURE, I ACCEPT! LET'S DO IT! Instead, he swallowed back his urgency and said, "I'd like that very much, Mr. Bradshaw."

"Please, call me Stuart. I'll mail you a contract agreement that I need you to look over, sign, and return to me."

"What's in it?"

Stuart laughed. "Just the usual stuff: agent commission, terms of agreement. Feel free to have an attorney look it over if you like, or you can call me with any questions you have. I know a publisher who'll more than likely be interested in your story."

"Yes sir, Mr.—uh, Stuart. I'll be waiting for the contract." Anthony's face was beaming like a Halloween jack-o-lantern. He doubted the smile on his face would ever diminish.

"All right, Mr. Jessup—"

"Oh, you can call me Anthony. No need for the formalities."

"Okay, Anthony," Stuart said, chuckling. "I'll send the contract out today."

Anthony thanked him a few more times before they hung up. After he put the phone down, Anthony skipped and jumped around in his apartment as though he'd just won the lottery. In a sense, he had. Another piece of the puzzle had just fallen into place.

Four days later, Stuart Bradshaw's parcel arrived in the mail. Anthony ran in his apartment and tore open the envelope. Inside were several folded sheets of paper that detailed the agency's agreement. Anthony straightened the pages on the kitchen table and read over them slowly, trying to digest all the legalese. Anthony was as ignorant as any layman when it came to legal-speak, but he was able to decipher enough of it to understand that it sounded like pretty straight forward stuff. Basically, it specified that the agent would not submit Anthony's work to any publisher without his client's express approval and it specified that, as Anthony's agent, Stuart would receive a ten percent commission on paperback sales and twenty percent of any hardcover sales. All of this seemed fine to Anthony.

He sat back in his chair and wondered for a moment if Roger had accepted all of the contract's terms or whether he had haggled over anything. Anthony doubted it. All of these terms were just for the agent, not the publisher. From Anthony's understanding, the agent was on his side. He represented Anthony to the best of his ability, because the more money Anthony earned, the more money the agent also earned. The only thing Anthony knew to beware of were agents that wanted author's to pay them a reading fee. Stuart's contract didn't mention any such fees, so Anthony signed in the appropriate places and stuffed the documents into the return envelope Stuart had provided. Anthony went back out to his mailbox and inserted the letter.

Time was beginning to pass at its usual rate of speed now, or so it seemed to Anthony, now that he had obtained his agent. He hoped Stuart would call him with good news sooner rather than several months later if he was ever to quit his job at the grocery store. Anthony was eager to start making some real money.

Roger Kurrey arrived home from work and turned to hang up his coat. "I'm home!" The air was redolent of cooking fish. He walked into the kitchen, hugged Evelyn from behind and kissed her neck.

She turned her head and kissed him back. When she resumed cooking their meal, she said, "You got some mail today. I think it's from an agent."

Roger's face lit up. His excitement peaked. "Where is it?"

Evelyn pointed toward the dining room with a wooden spatula. "There, on the table."

Everything in the land of Kurrey seemed to be looking up.

Roger picked up the envelope. It felt thin. Never having had an agent, Roger wasn't sure if that was a good or bad sign. He tore it open at one end, blew apart the ragged seam, and fished out the paper.

Roger's shoulders slumped. The excitement on his face withered. It wasn't good news. He had received yet another rejection letter.

Without turning away from the skillet, Evelyn asked, "What's it say? Is it good?"

"No," Roger said. "Another rejection."

His wife scooped the golden filets out of the hot oil and placed them on a bed of paper towels. She moved the pan off the burner, put down the spatula, and went over to Roger. He was still looking at the rejection letter from Pembrooke & Stephens Literary Agency. She hugged him around the waist from behind.

"Everything'll be okay, hon. Just keep sending out queries. Someone's bound to represent you sooner or later."

"That's the fifteenth rejection already," he said with a sigh. "My list of agents is running out."

"Well, maybe you should start on another book and try selling this one later." Evelyn didn't know how or what to say to cheer him up. "You ready to eat?"

"Well," Roger said, hesitantly, "I'm not really that hungry now."

He dropped the rejection letter onto the table and kissed the top of his wife's head.

It was March twenty-seventh when Stuart called to give Anthony some news.

"Are you sitting down?" Stuart asked.

"Why? Is it bad?"

"Only if you consider a twenty-five hundred dollar advance bad news."

"Get out of here! Who bought it?"

"Garfunkle Press. They want to get the book on store shelves by December." Stuart paused. "But, I'm guessing it'll really be January, at the earliest. I'll send out the check tomorrow."

"That's great news, Stuart."

"Congratulations, Anthony. I'll keep you in the loop about anything else I hear. I'm still shopping around the paperback rights."

When the call was over, Anthony decided that another night at Red Lobster was in order. This time, he thought, he would try to muster the nerve to ask out the cute waitress, if she wasn't already seeing anyone.

Anthony looked at the kitchen clock. It was a few minutes after four, perfect time to beat the dinner crowd. Before leaving the house, he changed into some nicer clothes and sprayed on a little cologne. He didn't care about what the other diners thought, he only wanted to impress Debra.

Anthony locked the front door and went down the stairs. The air was cold and crisp; it nipped at his face and hands. Anthony shoved his hands inside his wool-lined pockets and hurried to the bus stop.

When he stepped aboard the bus, the hot air stung his reddened cheeks. It had taken him five minutes to walk to the bus stop and another ten minutes of waiting before the bus arrived. He dropped into a seat midway down the aisle.

During the ride, Anthony entertained thoughts of his book sale. Stuart had mentioned he'd mail the check tomorrow. It was for twenty-five hundred dollars, but Anthony had expected it to be much more although he didn't know why and figured it didn't really matter. In the 70s, that amount would stretch farther than it would in the future. He knew that amount was just the tip of the financial iceberg. He had already planned to open a savings account with the money. It was difficult not to dwell on his dream materializing, but Anthony began thinking of Debra. He hoped she was working tonight. Then he realized he had no idea what to say to her if she was. He would think of something.

The bus stopped in front of the Color Tile store and Anthony stepped off. The bus belched and wheezed diesel fumes as it lurched back into traffic. Anthony headed for the restaurant next door.

"Just one?" the hostess asked.

Anthony nodded, unbuttoning his coat.

The hostess gathered his silverware and menu. Anthony followed her. Seeing that she was taking him to the opposite side of the restaurant from his last visit, Anthony said, "Excuse me. Is Debra working tonight?"

The hostess paused and said that she was.

"Do you mind seating me in her section? If there's a space available, I mean."

The hostess looked across the dining room. "I don't think that'll be a problem, sir."

She led Anthony to a table near the window. An elderly man and woman were sitting at the table beside his. The man spooned soup into his mouth as the woman bit into a hushpuppy. The maître'd placed the silverware and menu in front of Anthony and walked away.

While Anthony was studying the menu, Debra passed him to check on the elderly couple. She removed some of their empty plates. Passing Anthony once again, she said, "I'll be back in a minute, sir."

Anthony nodded and stared over the top of the menu to watch her. When she emerged from the kitchen, Anthony's eyes darted back to the open menu. He didn't want her to catch him staring.

"Okay," Debra said, removing the pad and pen from her apron pocket. "What can I get you to drink?" Her face brightened when she vaguely recognized him.

"What beer've you got on tap?"

Smiling, Debra rattled off his choices. Anthony ordered a Michelob.

"Also," he said before she left, "I already know what I want. Can I go ahead and order?"

"Sure," Debra said. "You want the all-you-can-eat shrimp again?"

Anthony's eyebrows rose in surprise.

She remembered!

"No." Anthony's smile brightened. "Not this time. Instead, I want to get the lobster."

She scribbled on her pad. "Okay. I'll bring you out some bread, too."

"Thanks," Anthony said. She went away and Anthony tried thinking of a way to break the ice with her, something that would lead to small talk. If he was lucky, he would have the nerve to ask her on a date.

Debra returned and set a frosty mug of Michelob on the table and went over to the old couple.

Anthony didn't know if he'd have the confidence to ask her out. The thought made him suddenly self-conscious. His hands were sweaty and his mouth dry, as if all of his fluids were leaking out through his palms. He drank some of his beer.

Before his food arrived, Anthony had emptied the mug and had nothing else to drink with his meal.

"You want another beer?" Debra asked.

Anthony shook his head. "I'll have some water though," he said.

Anthony forked some of the lobster tail into his mouth. It was buttery and succulent. Debra returned and put the glass of water on the table. Anthony was still trying to think of a way to spark some small talk, but fortunately, Debra saved him the trouble.

"Do you live nearby?" she asked.

"Yeah, in Oakwood," Anthony said. "What about you? You live here in Lauden?"

She nodded. "Yeah, not too far. So what do you do in Oakwood, if you don't mind me asking?"

"No. Not at all," Anthony said, wiping his mouth with the napkin. "Right now, I'm a stockboy at SuperValu, but I'm trying to break into writing. I just sold my first book."

"Really?" Debra's eyes went wide, as if to say well-look-at-you. "What kind of book?"

Anthony gesticulated and said, "A sort of horror-slash-science-fiction story. That's why I'm here tonight. Treating myself. My agent called me to say he sold it. Last time I was in here, I was celebrating getting an agent."

"What's the name of your book? I'll have to buy a copy and read it."

"It's called *When the Clock Strikes Three*. It probably won't be available until early next year though."

"Wow, that's a long way off."

"Yeah," Anthony said. "Sometimes it feels *too* long. I'm ready to give up my job at the grocery store. I'm working on a second book now."

Debra glanced around and excused herself to check on some of the other customers. She returned later with a pitcher of water, refilled Anthony's glass, and they resumed talking. Through intermittent bouts of this type of conversation, Anthony learned that Debra was a divorcee. She had no children and lived in an apartment complex several blocks away from the restaurant. Learning that she was unattached and not dating, Anthony felt his confidence level rise and considered asking her on a date.

"Hey, I hope you don't take this the wrong way," he said when she returned, "but would you care to go see a movie with me sometime?"

She picked up his empty plate and looked around quickly. "Sure." She gave him a wry grin. "That sounds nice."

She had to leave and circulate among the other tables. Anthony continued nursing his glass of water. The icy hand of fear had dissolved from inside his chest. He'd done it. He had asked. She'd accepted. Everything seemed right with the world.

A moment later, Debra returned. "I just want you to know that I don't make it a habit of hitting on my customers."

"Oh, I didn't think that you did," Anthony assured her.

Her smile returned. "What movie did you have in mind?"

"There's a double feature playing this weekend at the Buford Drive-in. The only problem is I don't own a car. I take the bus everywhere." Anthony's cheeks flushed. He reminded her, "Being a stockboy in a grocery store doesn't pay very well."

"That's okay. I don't mind driving. What's playing?"

"Do you like horror movies?"

"Yeah, they're not my favorite, but I can watch them."

"Well, they're both horror movies. The first film is *Don't Look in the Basement* and *Last House on the Left* is the second. Someone at work said *Last House on the*

Left was really good. Scary, because it could happen!"

Incredulity peeked out from Debra's smile. She glanced around quickly. "Here," she said and began biting her lip. She placed her pad and pen on the table. "Write down your address and phone number. I'll call you so we can work out the details for this weekend." She hesitated as she looked at him. Her cheeks had reddened. "You did mean *this* weekend, right?"

"Oh, yeah." He wanted to add, *The sooner the better*, but knew that would make him sound too desperate. It's not like there was a line of people beating down his door to do things.

When Anthony left the restaurant, he was on top of the world.

CHAPTER 16

During the remainder of that week, Anthony and Debra talked on the phone for several hours. Their conversations seemed to flow gracefully, without awkward pauses, which Anthony deemed a blessing. He learned a lot about Debra but felt guilty that he hadn't divulged much about himself, there wasn't much for him to tell or that he could tell without giving away his secret. Aside from that, with only his job and writing to discuss, Anthony thought he was leading a fairly boring existence. He told her about his dream to become a famous novelist. Debra told Anthony that she dreamed of starting her own business one day. When asked what kind of business she wanted to open, Debra had said, "I don't know.

So far, coming up with a good idea seems to be the hardest part."

Anthony went about his normal routine that Friday. He shaved, showered, and dressed. After eating a bowl of cereal, he sat down to write. He didn't have to worry about work because he had swapped shifts with one of the other guys and had the day off. The second book, called *The Black Talon*, was progressing nicely. There were more than fifty pages of typed manuscript stacked neatly beside the typewriter.

With the first book scheduled to hit bookshelves in the coming months, Anthony knew he was ahead of schedule with the second story, so he didn't hurry himself through it as he had the first. That sensation of racing against time had moved to the background. Instead of spending all of his mornings sitting down to copy the story, Anthony found himself reading more and occasionally watching television, although the shows still didn't hold his interest most of the time. Anthony found that he preferred the special-presentation movies over the regular network shows, although he was developing a list of favorite programs, which included *The Carol Burnett Show, Dean Martin's Comedy Hour, The Flip Wilson Show,* and finally, *M*A*S*H*. Then there were the shows he absolutely hated and avoided like the plague. Among these were *Mary Tyler Moore, The Bob Newhart Show, Love Story, Maude,* and the one he loathed the most, *The Waltons*. Anthony would consult the *TV Guide* at work to see if there were any movies he wanted to watch during the days he didn't have to go to work. On some evenings, he would switch over to a network that was airing a movie he was interested in. With all of the horrible programming on only a handful of channels, Anthony was left with plenty of time to read.

Knowing that his first book was marching ever closer to publication and his agent was shopping around the paperback rights, Anthony felt naturally motivated to work on the second book. He sat down behind the typewriter and hesitated before pressing the PLAY button on the tape player.

He picked up the few typed pages beside the typewriter and riffled through them, recalling the story. Although Anthony considered himself Roger's greatest advocate, he didn't care as much for this book as he did the later books. The name of this one was *The Black Talon*, a book composed of four novellas Roger had published, which took its name from the first story. This story was about a public official named Blake Duchamp, who alienates an elderly woman during a public hearing to discuss zoning issues. Unbeknownst to Blake, the woman, Margaret Kitteridge, practices witchcraft and makes it her mission to knock Blake off his high and mighty perch.

Anthony put the pages back down, started the tape and began typing. This business of typing the words as he listened to the tapes had become so habitual that Anthony had stopped paying attention to the actual plots. He simply pecked at the keys like an automaton, stringing the words together, which he did now.

Blake found himself alone at home on Saturday while his wife was visiting her sister. After lunch, he decided to walk out to the mailbox. It was a beautiful spring day: cloudless and not too hot. Blake pulled open the mailbox door and saw a bundled paper towel on top of the envelopes. The ends were drawn up and tied with a red strand of silk ribbon.

He removed the paper bundle, feeling how light it was in his hand, and looked up and down the street. No one was around. Blake unfastened the loose strand and let the towel unfold in his hand. In the center was a severed raven's foot. It was black as crude oil and curled into a gnarly fist. Strange nonsensical symbols were written on the inside of the folded paper.

Being a city councilman with plenty of enemies, Blake had seen a lot of strange things in his day. He carried the mail and the "gift" inside where he promptly tossed the mess into the wastebasket.

<u>Probably some loony neighbor's idea of revenge,</u> he thought.

Blake knew that most residents took the passive aggressive approach to voicing their disapproval. He had received other such items in his mailbox. On two separate occasions he had received handwritten notes from some pissed off resident who cursed enough to make a sailor blush. Another time, someone had left a bag of dog shit in his mailbox. Blake didn't waste his time with such people and considered them beneath him.

Since it was such a beautiful day out and he had the house to himself, Blake decided to settle himself on the back deck overlooking his yard to read a book. It would be a nice opportunity to relax and work on his tan at the same time. He carried a cold glass of lemonade out with him and sat at the patio table.

Blake opened his book to the dog-eared page and began reading. Yes, this was how to spend a peaceful and relaxing day. Blake sipped from his glass and continued reading. The main character was about to confront a nasty villain when…

CAW! CAW! CAW!

Blake's concentration was broken, as was the peace and quiet, when a large crow flew over his roof into a tall elm tree beside the deck. It settled on a limb high up in the tree and began bellowing.

CAW! CAW! CAW!

When the bird stopped, Blake attempted to pick up where he had been interrupted. No sooner had he found his place and read three words that the bird began squawking again. Frustrated, Blake snapped the book closed and set it on the table. He stood up from his chair and looked up at the black bird.

"Shut up!" Blake said. "Get out of here!" He waved his arms, trying to shoo the bird away, but the bird ignored him.

The crow's head moved left and right. Its big oil drop eye trained on the insignificant man below. It crowed several more times. Blake went down the steps to the yard and gathered a handful of pebbles from his wife's garden bed. He marched back up the steps and went to the rail. The bird was about twenty feet away. Blake hurled the rocks at the top of the tree. The projectiles flew apart like buckshot and struck the limbs. They ricocheted around and fell, bouncing off limbs as they dropped. None of them struck the bird, who only watched from its perch, amused.

Blake's attempt to run the bird off was unsuccessful.

<u>Stupid fucking bird!</u>

Blake was determined not to let the bird ruin his tranquil day outside. Now that he had thrown the rocks, the bird had stopped its incessant crowing. Satisfied, Blake took his seat and opened his book once again.

As Blake neared the end of the chapter, the main character found himself in a particularly tricky spot with the villain. They were in a standoff, guns raised at one another…

CAW!

> Blake tried to ignore the noise and get to the end of the chapter.
> CAW! CAW!
> Each time the bird squawked, it sent a shudder through Blake, like raking a fingernail across a cheese grater. He held his place in the book with his thumb, sat back, and looked up at the tree. The bird was quiet, looking with those obsidian eyes.
> Two more crows sailed over the rooftop and lighted on branches in the tall elm. Blake's anger rose when the birds became a chorus, a cacophony of caws. One was bad enough, but now he had to contend with three of the bastards!

After spending two hours at the typewriter, lost in that zone of zombie-like concentration, Anthony's train of thought was broken when his phone rang. He looked over at it as though it had snuck up behind him, and debated whether he should answer it. He was on fire and didn't want to stop. He found himself longing for a caller ID display like he was used to. He wasn't in the mood to talk to anyone. Reluctantly, he stopped the tape, lifted the handset, and put it to his ear.

"Hello?"

"Hey. Anthony?"

He recognized the voice and his mood quickly changed. He sat up straighter in his chair. "Hey, Debra. What's happening?"

"I was just thinking about the movies tomorrow. We still on?"

"Sure we are."

"What time should I pick you up?" Debra asked.

Anthony suddenly wished he had a car. It made him feel inferior because he didn't own one. He didn't like to rely on his dates to drive when they went somewhere. He decided to make it up by paying for everything. "Can you be here at seven?"

"Sure. No problem. What're you up to?"

Anthony told her he was working on the next book and despite Debra's apology for interrupting him, Anthony kept her on the phone for several minutes talking about other mundane things. When Anthony hung up, he was glad that he had answered the phone. Listening to Debra's voice made him perk up and sent a tingle through his body. He looked forward to their date tomorrow night and his mind wanted to wander off to think of the fun they'd have.

Anthony stood up and stretched as he looked over the pages that had accumulated beside the typewriter. He was nearly finished with the first story in *The Black Talon* and didn't want to stop so close to the end. He sat back down, started the tape, and resumed typing.

```
  Blake  looked  up  at  the  tree,  now
filled with crows who seemed satisfied
mocking  him  from  their  lofty perches.
Their    cavalier    stares    only   fueled
Blake's  anger  and  began  to  drive  him
```

mad. Their chorus sounded more and more like lunatics cackling.

Blake stormed back into his house and headed for the bedroom closet. He rummaged through the suit jackets and shoes until he found his air rifle propped in the back corner. He located a box of copper B-Bs stored on the top shelf and returned to the deck.

<u>Now, we'll see who laughs last, you sorry little shits.</u>

Blake poured some ammunition into the gun, loaded, and cocked it as he stared skyward gritting his teeth. He took aim at the closest bird, the first one, sitting serenely on a fat limb. As Blake's finger tightened on the trigger, the gun coughed out its shot and the black bird's wings fluttered in a spasm. It dropped dead from the tree.

The other birds became animated as they hopped around on the limbs. Their crowing became increasingly loud and belligerent.

Blake laughed in triumph. "What do you think of that, you bastards?!"

He inserted another B-B and began pumping the gun for another shot. As he took aim at another bird, the group began flapping their wings. Because of their fluttering, he found it difficult to keep any one of them in his sights. Then, they took wing and swooped from the tree flying straight toward him.

Blake waved his arms, trying to swat at the onslaught of black wings flapping near his head. In his frenzy,

Blake lost his grip on the rifle. It fell and clattered on the deck. The rifle discharged, sending a B-B hurtling toward Blake's ankle. The pain caused him to lose his balance and stumble toward the banister.

#

Carol returned home from visiting her sister. When she entered the front door, she saw the sliding glass door standing open.

"Blake, I'm home."

No one answered. Carol saw the pellet rifle lying on the deck outside. She went closer to the sliding door. It was quiet. As she neared the deck, she saw a sweaty glass sitting on the patio table. A book was lying beside it. She looked over at the gun again and noticed that the banister was cracked. When she ran over to it and peered over the edge, she found her husband lying on the ground below.

Blake was very pale. His neck was twisted at a funny angle. Carol began screaming.

Anthony sighed. He had finished a quarter of the book. He removed the last page and placed it on top of the others, then straightened the stack. When he stood, his knees popped. He got a soda out of the refrigerator and sat on the sofa to think about his and Debra's upcoming date.

Friday evening, Roger arrived home from work and went into the house where he found the mail waiting for him on the dining room table. Among the envelopes was one with his address written in familiar handwriting. It was familiar because the handwriting was his. The return address was from Tippany Literary Agency, the last agency on Roger's list; his last hope for representation.

Roger's heart rate doubled with that understanding. He disregarded the rest of the mail and lifted the envelope with his handwriting. It was thin. Too thin, he thought, to contain good news. He opened it and hesitated, questioning whether he should be so eager to look inside. He didn't want to think of the bad news it may contain.

He drew the folded paper out and straightened it. His stomach dropped as he read the words. Another rejection. Just like all of the previous responses. This one said that their agents were busy representing a full list of clients already and encouraged him to try again later.

Fuck later!

The only thing on Roger's mind was the time he'd wasted writing and polishing his manuscript. And now the time he'd spent waiting for rejections. All for nothing.

He went into the kitchen where Liz was preparing some kind of sauce in a pan.

She looked at him when he walked in. "Hey, hon. How was your day?"

"Eh. Same as usual."

"What's the matter?"

"Another rejection."

"I was going to tell you that there was a letter in the mail for you."

"Yeah, I saw it."

Elizabeth turned the burner down and set the wooden spoon on the stove. Roger sat in a chair staring at the letter in his hand. Liz leaned over, kissed his cheek, and rubbed his shoulders. "Are there no other agencies you can query?"

"I already exhausted my list," he said solemnly.

"Well, what are you going to do now?"

"The only thing I can do, start working on the next story."

"Have you got something in mind?"

"Yeah. I have an idea." Roger stood up. "I better get started." He went toward the door into the den where he had written *When the Clock Strikes Three*.

Elizabeth watched him leave and went back to the stove to cook their dinner.

CHAPTER 17

Anthony was busy typing when there was a knock at his door. He went over and opened it. Debra stood outside with a big grin on her face. It was contagious. At the mere sight of her, Anthony's face lit up too.

"Hey. Come in."

Debra stepped inside as Anthony glanced at his watch. It was ten minutes to seven. Time had gotten away from him as he immersed himself in his work.

"You ready to go?" she asked.

Anthony patted his pants pockets. "Yeah. I just need to grab my wallet and keys."

He went into the bedroom and returned to find Debra looking at the paper in the typewriter. "This one of your books?"

"Yeah. The second one."

"What's with the tape machine?"

"Oh, that. I, uh, like to record the stories before I sit down to type them. It's easier to record what I see in my head instead of trying to type it out first. Less mistakes that way and I can work faster."

Debra nodded. "Makes sense, I guess."

"Okay. You ready?"

They left the apartment and Anthony followed Debra to her car in the parking lot. She led him to a beige '69 Buick Skylark. When Anthony noticed that it was a Gran Sport, he wanted to tell her he had a friend who had one that he'd fixed up and painted black to look real slick. He thought better of it when he realized it might lead to questions he couldn't easily avoid. Questions that might make him slip up in his lies about where (or better yet, *when*) he had come from. Instead, he said, "Nice car."

Debra smirked as she got in and reached over to unlock Anthony's door. "I got it in the divorce settlement. My ex wanted it, but he had to choose between this or the Camaro?"

Anthony nodded. "A Camaro, huh? What year?"

"I don't know. It was older than this. '67 I think."

Anthony pictured a '67 Camaro. Probably a Super Sport. Yeah. He would've chosen the Camaro, too.

"I wanted the newer car. Let him have the older one. He can work on it when it starts having problems."

The conversation transitioned through several topics during their ride to the drive-in. Like the conversations he had had with Lisa, there were no clumsy pauses. Debra said she wanted to go back to school to get a degree. She hadn't made up her mind in what area, maybe biology or business. She said she was growing tired of waiting tables.

Anthony said he understood and expressed his desire to become a famous author. "I want Hollywood to make movies based on my books," he said.

"That's pretty ambitious," she said. "It's good to know what you want and go after it. People like you usually have the determination to follow through with their dreams."

If she only knew the truth.

It still hurt when Anthony considered that he was getting recognition for art that wasn't his. He appreciated her insight, though. "I think it can happen." Not wanting to sound like an arrogant blowhard, he added, "Several people have said my ideas are interesting and wouldn't be surprised if it actually happened." Of course, that was a lie, but Debra didn't know it and Anthony was positive it would happen. Eight of Roger's novels had wound up on the big screen and four had been adapted into mini-series. Anthony had to keep all of this to himself, though.

When they pulled up to the ticket booth, Anthony paid for their tickets. After they settled into a parking spot, he went to the concession stand and purchased their food, too.

Anthony hadn't been to a drive-in since he was a young boy. So young in fact, that his recollection of the experience was no more than a series of out-of-focus snapshots. It was a novelty listening to the movie through a speaker you lifted from a pole and hung on your window. They talked right up until the movie's title shown on screen and settled into quietness. It was nice not having anyone shush them for talking.

They sat munching popcorn and funnel cakes and washed it down with large cups of soda. Compared to movie concession prices in the future, Anthony considered what he had paid a real bargain.

After enduring the horrible first fifteen minutes of *Don't Look in the Basement*, Anthony wanted to strike up a conversation, but Debra sat with her eyes glued to the screen. Although he considered it extremely cheesy and poorly acted, Anthony chose not to interrupt the movie for her. While it may have entertained Debra, it didn't live up to the standards set by movies that would later follow.

An hour and a half later, when the movie had ended and the intermission was being announced by a line of dancing snacks singing "Let's all go to the lobby", Anthony asked, "What'd you think?"

Debra held up a finger. "Hold that thought," she said and opened the door. Anthony watched her hurry toward the lady's room.

When Debra returned, she shut the car door and shrugged. "I've seen better."

Me, too.

"I've heard the next one's supposed to be a lot better."

Debra said, "Yeah. I heard that, too."

When the next feature started, they both sat quietly watching the screen. Anthony had seen the original before. Even with a lower budget, Wes Craven managed to direct a much better film. During the rape scene, Debra looked uneasy. Anthony was unsure of how to handle the situation and hesitantly put his arm around her. Doing so felt uncomfortable so Anthony removed his arm.

"Sorry," he said.

Debra smiled and blushed, but there was some tension showing through it. "That's okay."

Horror movies at the drive-in were usually conducive to romantic behavior, but watching a violent rape scene on a first date only magnified the awkwardness of their situation.

It had been a long time since Anthony had seen this movie. As the conclusion neared and Anthony recalled the ending, he watched for Debra's reaction. When it was over, he said, "Well, what'd you think?"

Debra sat wide-eyed. "It wasn't what I expected. That's for sure."

They drove back to Anthony's apartment and sat in the parking lot for a moment.

"You want to come in?"

"I'm not sure," Debra said. "What time is it?"

Anthony checked his watch. "11:20."

"It's kinda late."

"I don't mind. You don't have to work tomorrow, do you?"

"Yeah, but not until noon."

"Well, why don't you come up for a little bit? We can talk some more."

Debra smiled and considered it briefly. She was more hesitant than Lisa had been. Eventually, she said, "Okay. Why not?"

Inside, Anthony went to the refrigerator. "You want something to drink?"

"Do you have any wine?"

Anthony shook his head and mentally kicked himself. Debra was more refined than Lisa and her tastes showed it. "Sorry. All I have is beer, tea, and water."

"I'll have a beer then."

Anthony removed a can for her, opened it, and handed it to her. They sat on the sofa and talked more about Anthony's future plans.

"I'm going to quit working at the grocery store if my book takes off," Anthony said.

"Must be nice. I want to quit waitressing, but I've got to finish school first."

"How much longer do you have left?"

"Another two years."

"How'd you get into waitressing?"

Debra looked down at the can between her hands. "I met David my senior year in high school. We started dating and got real serious. Just after graduation, I learned I was pregnant, so college was out. I couldn't go to school and raise a family."

"Why not?"

"Well, okay. What I should've said was *I* wasn't going to do that. It would've been too much."

"I thought you said you didn't have any kids." Anthony said.

"I don't." Debra focused on her hands again. "I miscarried two months later."

Now there was a moment of that dreaded awkward silence. But, thankfully, Debra broke it. "I was devastated. I think it affected David too, but in a different way. We started to grow apart. Over the following years, we grew more and more distant. Three years ago, I found out he was cheating on me. So, I filed for divorce."

Anthony stared at her eyes as she recounted the bitter end of her marriage. Her blue eyes looked beautiful when the light struck them, even at such a sad time. He couldn't imagine why anyone would deceive and hurt her. "I know how bad it feels to be cheated on." He told her about Lisa, saying she was "a girl I felt a strong connection to", and how Lisa had secretly harbored a boyfriend.

"It tore me up inside to know she was seeing someone else. I thought we had made a connection and then, when I found out she was cheating on someone else with me, I felt really bad. If we had ended up dating, I just knew she would end up cheating on me, too."

They sat there for a minute, each contemplating how things might've been, could still be perhaps, if things had gone differently. Anthony looked at Debra, admired her natural beauty. She didn't wear a lot of makeup the way Lisa had. There was something safe and innocent about Debra that Anthony couldn't put his finger on.

He wanted to lean in and kiss her, but didn't because it could go one of two ways: she would allow it, meeting him in the middle, or she would deny him because his advance might offend her. Anthony wasn't good at interpreting women's subtle signals. He needed neon lights and arrows, signals to guide him in this area.

He took a chance and gradually eased forward as he stared at her. She didn't back away. But, she didn't advance either. Anthony didn't know it, but her heart was beating just as fast, if not faster, than his. When his face was within six inches of hers, Anthony looked into her eyes, and saw that they were focused on his. The tension in the air seemed to crackle. Both of their breathing was rapid. Gradually, she leaned in to meet his lips with hers. She parted them slightly.

The feel of Debra's lips against his was warm and soft, sensual and arousing, but Anthony's mind was focused on something else, a conundrum. He realized Debra was in her early thirties. In 1973, Anthony was only one year old. This knowledge forced open the door for a series of considerations that trailed through his mind rather quickly. Debra was at least thirty years older than Anthony was in this time. Why hadn't he thought about this when he was with Lisa? The age difference caused him to imagine his mother. Anthony kicked himself for it, forced out the mental picture and tried instead to concentrate on the feel of Debra's lips.

When Anthony finally got his mind right, they shared a wonderful kiss before Debra eased away. Her face was flushed. She looked at her watch. It was nearly midnight. She stood up and gave him a polite and conservative smile.

"I had a great time tonight, but I've got to—"

Her actions seemed hurried and caught Anthony by surprise. He stood up. "Do you really have to go *now*?"

Debra took his hand loosely in hers and rubbed her fingers across his knuckles. "It's getting late, Anthony."

He glanced toward his bedroom door then back to her. "You could stay here, if you want."

Debra shook her head. "I wouldn't feel right doing that."

Anthony was perplexed. He had anticipated an evening with Debra much like the one spent with Lisa. Despite the great first date he and Debra had, her reluctance to stay was like two and two adding up to five. He blamed the thoughts he had during their kiss and wondered if Debra somehow picked up on that vibe. But, that was ridiculous. "Was it something I said? Or, something I did?"

Debra shook her head. "No. Nothing like that. You didn't do anything wrong. It's just—I don't want to rush into anything."

She released his hand, smiled, grabbed her coat and went to the door. When she opened it, she hesitated and looked back at him. Her face was shy and warm. "I'll call you later. Okay?"

Anthony returned the smile, but wished she would change her mind. "Okay. Yeah, call me."

Debra pulled the door shut. Anthony went over and engaged the deadbolt then tucked his hands into his back pockets and looked around at his empty apartment. Debra was nothing like Lisa, which, considering Lisa's promiscuity was probably a good thing. It made Anthony want to be with Debra even more, to learn what made her tick and discover her deeper feelings. Anthony hadn't been with many women, so his basis for how they acted and behaved was gained through hearsay and whatever was popularly portrayed in the media. Susan and Debra were enigmas, stark contrasts to what he had learned vicariously.

He attempted to analyze his earlier thoughts. Why the hell had he thought of his mother, for Christ's sake? Maybe because Debra was older, more mature than Lisa was. Debra's interest in him seemed genuine. Anthony really liked her and felt comfortable around her. Remembering his mother's face during the kiss left him feeling icky. He hoped it wouldn't happen again, the thought, not the kiss. He really felt that there was some deep connection between him and Debra.

———◆———

When Anthony woke up, he tried recounting the dream he'd had. The fleeting fragments he retained were nice. Susan was in it, but somewhere along the way she had turned into Debra. The details were already fuzzy and only becoming more obscure as he rubbed the sleep from his eyes and let the morning light burn away the recollection. He missed Susan and realized he also missed not being with Debra. In this time, she was the equivalent of Susan.

Anthony showered, dressed, and sat down to type. He was lacking the motivation, however. Although he didn't have to concentrate on the mechanics of writing a book, such as dealing with character development or creating settings, Anthony found that his mind wasn't prepared to concentrate on the words to copy them down. Instead, he was preoccupied with Susan, Debra, and his recent book sale.

It was Sunday, so there would be no mail today. Anthony had checked his mailbox each day since speaking to his agent, anxiously awaiting the arrival of his advance payment. It wasn't a life-changing amount, but it sure as hell would help with the bills.

Things were looking up for Anthony, but he didn't exactly know what the immediate future held for him. Pondering his recent good fortune, he wondered what Roger was doing.

Roger sat behind the desk in his study rereading the acceptance letter he'd received Friday from a magazine where he'd sent a short story. The editor expressed great interest in publishing *Less Than Perfect* in an upcoming issue.

While the money he'd receive for the story was meager—only twenty-five dollars—it was nonetheless another publishing credit to put on his resume. He enjoyed reading the words "Absolutely loved it!" at the beginning of the letter. It gave him a rush to know someone out there recognized good writing when they saw it. It was a validation of his talent. Unlike the rejections he'd received from agents he had queried with his recently finished first novel, this acceptance letter fueled his ambition to persevere.

All Roger had to do was keep plugging away at his typewriter, churning out more novels and short stories, submitting them until, eventually, he received a book deal. At least, that was the plan. He knew this was the same routine his predecessors had to endure. Roger had to pay his dues like them, working his way up the ladder while he honed his writing skills and perfected his craft. He'd been doing it for seven years already. This first stage, he'd read, was not predictable. But how long must he suffer, toiling in the trenches with the rest of the undiscovered authors? The number of years each writer spent in this purgatory wasn't set in stone. The amount of time it took for a writer to reach a book deal was as much a mystery as the meaning of life.

When that big break came, it was invariably a different experience from writer to writer.

He'd read about debut authors in *Writer's Digest* who'd been trying to break into the industry for a decade or more. Some had been at it for only a couple of years before they'd gotten lucky and received a huge advance for a novel the publisher wagered would be a mega-bestseller.

As but one example, Roger read in a recent issue about Margaret Muirez. She was the author of the crime novel, *Dia de Muertos*, where a Mexican family learns that their murdered son actually died at the hands of his father instead of another man who had been charged with the crime. According to the article, Mrs. Muirez's publisher, Blake Publishing Group, paid her a four-hundred-thousand dollar advance. Roger had to read the number again to make sure he hadn't mistaken the amount. This was her debut novel and Mrs. Muirez had only been writing for four years, the first three of those as a journalist for a newspaper in Arizona.

Roger often savored these stories of new authors hitting a rich vein of luck in the publishing industry. He fantasized about it happening to him. However, he knew it was a matter of being in the right place at the right time. Roger had tried to hedge his bets by attending college, where he obtained a bachelor's in English. But, he didn't stop there. He went on to get his masters and finally a PhD from the University of Delaware. He had worked at a newspaper and a magazine after college, but learned quickly that working as an editorial assistant didn't leave him with the time to devote to his own writing. Nor, was he interested in teaching, another logical career choice for someone with an English doctorate. This last realization came from observing his professors who had to maintain publications and grade essays and term papers in what little spare time they had. Roger tried his hand at teaching creative writing courses but found that grading papers and devoting time to students after class cut into his writing time too much. Teaching simply wasn't something he wanted to do.

Like most college graduates, Roger went into a career field unrelated to his major. Roger hated working at the foundry, but his father-in-law had worked there and got him a job before retiring. The economy wasn't exactly thriving and jobs were in short supply. Roger was happy for the opportunity at the time and it afforded him a decent income in addition to time to devote to his writing. Of course, in the face of all the rejections he was receiving and the back-breaking work, Roger's motivation waned and depression threatened to settle in and crush his ambition. Roger was determined not to let that happen.

In the publishing industry, there were many things outside of the writer's control. Giving up without trying, however, was not one of them and Roger was not about to give up without a fight.

He opened his top drawer and removed a silver flask, a gift on his and Elizabeth's third wedding anniversary, and took a swig of whisky. He expected it would help settle his nerves after letting himself get worked up thinking about the rejections, and it would serve as a celebratory gesture after selling the short story.

After recapping the flask, Roger shut the drawer and turned to his typewriter. In it was his current work-in-progress, a second book, a collection of novellas called *The Black Talon*.

CHAPTER 18

On Tuesday, Anthony returned to his apartment after a quick bite of lunch at a nearby fast food restaurant. A package was waiting for him outside of his front door. His curiosity was piqued by the sight of the cardboard box sitting there. He bent, picked it up, and went inside, anxious to see what it was.

It wasn't exactly a mystery. During their last phone conversation, Stuart had mentioned that he was sending a proof copy of the book for Anthony to inspect for any mistakes.

Anthony tore open the flap and riffled through the Styrofoam packing peanuts until his hand touched the hard edges of the book's cover. He fished it out and surveyed the artwork. A looming clock tower with the hands indicating three o'clock.

His heart swelled with pride when he read his penname beneath the title.

Anthony sat on the sofa with the book, first turning it over in his hands to examine the exterior. He opened it and thumbed the pages then held it close to his nose and inhaled the scent of newly printed pages. He loved the smell and feel of a book. He thought the smell was even sweeter when it was a book with *his* name on it, even if it was a pseudonym.

Anthony turned to the beginning and read everything, even the front matter. Three hours and ninety-seven pages later, he dog-eared the corner and put the book aside. He had to go to work.

Anthony was a slow reader, but he managed to get through the three-hundred-eighty-four page proof copy in just three days. He'd found only four mistakes, typos, probably introduced by the typesetters. He made note of them and set the book aside.

His phone rang at 11:30 that morning.

"Hello?"

"Anthony?" the voice was familiar, a man's.

"Stuart?"

"Yeah. I was—"

Anthony interrupted. "I just finished going through the proof. Man, it's such a rush to hold your own book!" His ear-to-ear grin couldn't be helped.

"Well, I'm glad you like it. Did you see any problems with it?"

Anthony told him about the four typos.

"Okay," Stuart said, "just make a note of where they are and we'll take care of them before it goes to press. That wasn't why I called though. You sitting down?"

Sitting down?

"No. Why?"

"You might want to. I just got off the phone with Simon and Shuster. They want to buy the paperback rights and sign you to a two-book deal."

"That's great news."

"That's not all of it." When those words came over the phone, Anthony thought of the old TV commercials peddling junk products. *But wait, there's more!* Stuart continued, "They went as high as two-hundred-fifty grand."

Anthony's legs went weak, but he remained standing.

Two-hundred-fifty thousand? A quarter of a million dollars!

Anthony stood in his living room, staring off into space. There was no reaction from him at that moment. His mind flooded with the possibilities all of those zeroes had to offer.

Should I quit my job? What do I do now? I need to call Debra.

"Hello? Anthony, you there?"

Anthony felt disconnected from himself, almost as though he was witnessing the scene as a fly on the wall. He managed to find his voice again.

"Yeah...Stuart, I'm here." His voice sounded faint, to his own ears anyway. "Sorry. I don't know what to say." It was like coming out of a dream and finally realizing where he was. If he died right then, it would be with a stunned expression on his face. "Two-hundred-fifty thousand? I—"

"Yeah, two-hundred-and-fifty thousand dollars. Congratulations, Anthony!" The excitement in Stuart's voice was evident.

Anthony felt strange, like he was swimming in molasses. He thought he should sound more enthusiastic like Stuart instead of this hushed recipient of such good news. He was still dealing with the shock, but he was beginning to come around. "I just can't believe it."

Anthony and Stuart talked for several minutes, but Anthony couldn't really recall what they had said to one another. Stuart would probably understand. It wasn't every day that he delivered news to someone that they were getting such a substantial, life-changing sum of money.

When Anthony replaced the phone in the cradle, he went into the kitchen and took a beer out of the refrigerator. He chugged a good deal of it before returning to the living room where he picked up the phone again and dialed Debra's number. He hoped she was at home. She answered on the third ring.

"Hello?"

"OhmygodI'msogladIgotyou!" Once out, Anthony inhaled and realized he had to slow down.

"What? Anthony, is that you?"

"Sorry," he said, still grinning. The news made him feel like bursting if he didn't share it. "My agent just called. He sold the paperback rights for my book! The publisher wants to sign me to a two-book deal."

There was a slight pause on the other end of the line. He could hear her take in a breath. "Ohmygod! That's great news. I'm so happy for you."

"I want to see you again. When're you off?"

Debra hesitated. "I don't go back in till tomorrow afternoon. Don't you have to work tonight?"

"Are you kidding? I'm turning in my resignation as soon as we get off the phone. My calendar just opened up."

He made plans to see Debra that evening, insisting that they should go somewhere nice to celebrate. He'd cashed the first advance check a day earlier and said he'd use it to take her somewhere nice, a five-star restaurant. She agreed, and said she knew of a great place.

Elizabeth walked into the study where Roger had been spending all of his free time lately. She paused in the doorway and stared at him as he typed.

CLACK, CLACK, CLACK!

He was so deep in concentration he hadn't noticed her standing there. He was close to finishing the first draft of his second novel. The story's dramatic conclusion was nearing its peak and Roger's mind was caught up in the tangle.

CLACK! CLACK! CLACK! CLACK!

"Hon?" Liz said tentatively.

When Roger didn't answer, she tried again, only louder, clearing her throat to get his attention. "Hon? You at a stopping place?"

The frantic rhythm of levers striking the paper diminished and finally stopped. Roger looked up at his wife standing in the door. His concentration ceased with the noise.

"Sorry to disturb your work," Elizabeth said, "but you've been in here every day for the past week. Don't you want to take a break? Maybe go out to eat or see a movie?" Elizabeth's smile faltered.

"No. I don't want to go out or see a movie. I'm almost finished with this draft, Liz. Once I do that, I can start on the revisions."

Elizabeth's smile vanished. His recent withdrawal had become increasingly more noticeable. The only time they'd spent together had been earlier in the week when Roger sat down only briefly to eat and then retreated to his desk in the study where he stayed until bedtime. In the days since, he'd begun eating his dinner at his desk and coming to bed well after Elizabeth had fallen asleep. It wasn't good for him to remain up so late during the week when he had to wake early for work, but Roger was doing it nonetheless.

"Now, honey, if you'll excuse me, I need to get back to it. I don't have much more to go before I'm finished." Seeing the smile vanish from his wife's face, Roger added, "I promise, we'll go out tomorrow, after I'm finished." He smiled, hoping to diffuse the sting of his agitation. He was unaware of how much his recent coldness was affecting her.

Elizabeth turned and went back into the kitchen.

Roger looked at the words he had typed last, hoping to salvage the fading momentum of his hot streak. Once his mind was back in the zone, the steady rhythm of hammering keys resumed.

CLACK! CLACK! CLACK! CLACK!

Moments later, while Roger was still happily lost in his story, Elizabeth walked by the door of his study. She was wearing makeup, her coat, and her purse. "I'm going out. I'll be back later." Her words were succinct and to the point.

Roger didn't acknowledge her departure, but simply kept typing as she pulled the door shut behind her.

CLACK! CLACK! CLACK!

Debra knocked on Anthony's door at 7 PM. He opened it, dressed in khaki slacks, a red button-down shirt, and a corduroy jacket. His cologne wafted faintly in the air when he greeted Debra.

"Wow, you look gorgeous!" he said.

Her smile widened and her cheeks flushed. She was wearing a black evening dress beneath a navy blue wool jacket. She had on a hint of makeup that accentuated her face's natural beauty. "You ready to go?"

Anthony turned to lock the door then offered her his arm as they walked down the steps to the car. "So, what's the name of this place?"

"Dante's," Debra answered. "It's a dressy steakhouse in Acworth. I went there for a friend's wedding reception and always wanted to go back, but David and I couldn't afford it."

It was 7:45 when they entered Dante's. Anthony held the door and followed Debra up to the podium where the maître'd waited.

The maître'd smiled as he looked up at them from the registration book. "Name, please?"

"Uh," Anthony stammered. He hadn't made any reservations.

Debra rescued him. "Wilkens. Party of two." It was a good thing Debra worked in the restaurant industry and had the foresight Anthony lacked.

The host consulted his book. "Ah, yes. Right this way, please."

Anthony and Debra followed, soaking in and admiring the atmosphere. All of the tables were covered in clean white linen; the other diners wore elegant suits and dresses; the wait-staff's uniforms were crisp and clean. This was not the type of place where you could get away with jeans and sneakers. Everyone looked dressed to the nines. As they passed other tables, Anthony peeked at the various dishes people were enjoying. He began to salivate at the sight of steak, salmon, lobster, the aroma of onions and succulent vegetables. The presentation of the dishes made them look like works of art and all that more enticing. Thankfully, the portions were large because Anthony's stomach was grumbling.

They slid into a booth at the far side of the restaurant, beneath a sconce light that shed enough light to illuminate just their booth. Somewhere orchestral music played faintly in the background, lending to the romantic atmosphere.

As soon as the maître'd left them alone, Anthony leaned toward Debra and said, "I have to admit, this place is definitely fancy." He was also curious about the prices.

This is going to cost me a small fortune.

Debra nodded, smiling. A waiter placed menus before them and recited the specials. He asked if they would like to look at the wine list, to which Debra nodded.

Anthony told her to get whatever she wanted. Tonight was on him, regardless of price. He enjoyed feeling like a big shot, knowing that this was just the tip of the iceberg. Soon money wouldn't be a concern. He opened his menu and looked at the prices. His eyes widened with shock. Under the appetizers was escargot in garlic butter with a splash of cognac. It was ten dollars. An *appetizer* that cost *ten bucks*! Never had he eaten in a place this expensive. He was hesitant to turn to the main entrees.

When the waiter returned, Debra ordered a glass of French Pinot Grigio and, feeling a bit crass at the thought, Anthony ordered a Long Island Ice Tea. So what? He wasn't a wine connoisseur.

"Wow. Going for the heavy artillery, huh?" Debra said when they were alone again.

"Well, I don't care much for wine and somehow I figure beer's too unrefined for a place like this. Besides, we're celebrating and I don't drink mixed drinks that often."

They ordered, talked, dined, and enjoyed themselves and each other's company. Anthony decided to try the escargot in addition to his rib eye. Knowing it was cooked snails, Debra passed when he offered her one. "What's it taste like?" she asked, wrinkling her nose at it.

"Like butter and garlic."

Debra made a grimace and continued eating her lamb chops.

"So, did you really quit your job today?" Debra asked.

Anthony nodded, chewing the escargot. When finished, he said, "Yeah. I wasn't joking."

"What're you going to do now?"

"What do you mean? I'm going to keep writing. I have a two-book deal, so I'm on the hook for the other two books. A quarter million'll go a long way."

"Yeah, but the IRS'll take their share. It won't last forever." Like Susan, Debra was the voice of reason.

"I know."

"Sorry," Debra said. "I'm not trying to be a wet blanket, but I just don't want to see you get in a bind or fritter it away."

Anthony winked and smiled. "I know. Believe me, I've got plenty of books left to write. Also, my agent's working to sell the foreign rights. Things are beginning to take off."

The candle on their table had burned down considerably; wax congealed at the base of the holder. Following dessert, the waiter presented Anthony with the bill.

With a little stab of pain in his chest, Anthony paid and they went back to his place for a nightcap.

CHAPTER 19

It was almost a year before Anthony and Debra returned to Dante's restaurant. This was to celebrate the release of his second book, *The Black Talon*. They were there not only to celebrate the second book's release, but also to rejoice over the sale of the movie rights for *When the Clock Strikes Three*.

Anthony's agent had said a studio in Hollywood was thinking of optioning the book for film, but the deal had fallen through. Anthony had been disappointed, but it wasn't for long. Shortly after, another studio, United Artists, had stepped up to the plate and considered the deal. They offered four-hundred-thousand for the rights.

When Stuart called to discuss it with Anthony, there was no hesitation on Anthony's part. Four-hundred grand was sweet music to his ears. Sold! The money was as good as in Anthony's account.

He and Debra were dressed in their most fashionable when they entered Dante's again to celebrate. The two had been dating seriously since their last visit to this restaurant. This time, however, Debra had Anthony's second hardcover secretly tucked away in her purse. She wanted to have him sign it for her because she knew he got a kick out of it. While waiting for the waiter to bring their appetizers, Debra recognized her opportunity and removed the book from her purse along with a black felt tip pen. "Will you sign my copy?" She asked, grinning sheepishly.

Anthony smiled after setting down his water glass. "For my favorite girl? You know I will." Little did she know, Anthony had a surprise of his own waiting.

He opened the book and scribbled something on the inside cover. He closed it and slid it back to her. Debra turned the book around and opened it.

Anthony got out of his seat as she read his words. The orchestra was just starting to play Ravel's *Bolero*, which Anthony thought was perfect for the occasion. He shoved his hand in his pocket as he awaited Debra's reaction. When he registered her shock, he stooped to one knee, removed the box from his pocket, opened it, and looked for her response.

Debra's hand went to her mouth and covered it in shocked surprise. She fanned her face. Her bottom lip trembled and she noticed that the nearby patrons were watching in anticipation. Tears welled in her eyes when she saw the ring presented to her, and then looked at Anthony's vulnerable, questioning face. She was choked up and couldn't speak, so she nodded vigorously.

Anthony removed the ring from the box, placed it on her quivering finger, and leaned in to kiss her. The surrounding diners who had witnessed the proposal clapped and smiled. Some bobbled their heads approvingly and whispered to their spouses.

Roger got out of his aging car and went to the mailbox. He was anxiously awaiting a response from the sixth agent he had queried about his latest novel, *The Black Talon*. The previous agents he'd queried had all sent rejections. Roger was beginning to get used to them. It was par for the course.

He sought the articles in writing magazines by other writers commiserating about coping with rejection. In a way, it pleased Roger to know he wasn't alone. It was his way of dealing with the suffering. The advice was always the same: never take it personally; develop a thick skin; keep persevering. Roger tried to follow the advice, but it became hard not to take it personally when he read that no one wanted to publish his work. He felt ostracized from the publishing circle. "It's just not the right fit for us", in his mind translated to "take this shit somewhere else" and "best of luck in your publishing future" just meant "see ya, chump"!

Worst of all, however, were those agents that never responded to his queries. Although it was rare, this pushed Roger's buttons like nothing else. It was as if they wouldn't even waste their precious time with him.

He pulled the mail from the box and thumbed through it. Among the letters was the latest copy of *Writer's Digest*. An envelope caught his eye. He saw it was from The Carol Tinney Literary Agency, where he'd mailed his last query. His heart stuttered.

Roger hurried into the house and went straight to his den. Still holding the envelope from the agency, he tossed the rest of the mail on the desk. He opened his top drawer and removed the letter opener. He tore a slit and withdrew the folded paper.

Thank you for your query letter, it began. Roger scanned the rest of it quickly. *We regret to inform you...* He didn't have to read further. Instead, he crumpled the paper and tossed the ball in the waste basket. Another rejection.

Roger slunk into his chair, opened the desk drawer and dropped the letter opener back into it. The silver whisky flask was peeking out at him from the shadow. He grabbed it and set it on the desk in front of him.

He stared at it a moment before opening the top and taking a long gulp.

He sat alone in his study, in the empty house. Elizabeth had left him two months earlier, informing him that she was going to file for divorce. He had received the papers from her attorney last week. "Irreconcilable differences" it said. Liz had told him they simply grew apart. Maybe that had a little to do with it, but Roger knew that growing apart didn't drive you into another man's bed.

That coupled with the continuous rejection letters from agents and publishers alike made it easy to devalue his self worth.

Roger wasn't one to give up so easily though. He knew he'd eventually catch a break, with or without Elizabeth by his side. He reasoned that she just couldn't handle the sacrifices that came with the trials and tribulations of being a novelist's wife. She lacked the fortitude and integrity it took to stick with something, evidenced by her illicit affair with another man.

Roger had learned of the tryst the day Liz packed her things and left him. That was two months ago, when he arrived home from work and found her putting her suitcases in the trunk of her car.

"What's going on?"

Liz turned to him, her face solemn, matter-of-fact. "I'm leaving, Roger."

"What do you mean, you're leaving? Going where?"

"I'm going to go straighten things out in my head. You and I've grown apart. You're never there for me anymore. You're—"

"What do you—"

She held up a hand that cut off his question. "You've isolated yourself in the den, always working on those *damn* stories. We don't go out. We've stopped eating together, sleeping together. And, I know you sit in there and drink. I don't know what's happened to you and you won't talk to me. So…" She hesitated, looked down at her feet. "So, I've found someone who will listen to me, who cares about me." Another pause while she let him digest all of this, turn it over in his mind. "I'm leaving. I talked to an attorney and filed for divorce."

"Liz. Come on. I—" Again, she silenced him with an upheld hand.

"No. It's too late, Roger. I'm moving on. Don't make this harder than it already is."

Reliving the events in his memory still stabbed and hurt as much as the day it happened. Roger turned the flask up to his lips again, thinking about that last remark she made before getting into the car and backing out of the driveway, out of his life. *"Don't make this harder than it already is."* Harder for who, he wondered. It was hard all right, for him.

Bitch!

He looked at the story in the typewriter. A new novel called *The Show Must Go On*. The title seemed fitting, life imitating art. This was his third novel, about a man whose wife says she's leaving him for another man. The main character has other plans, however, seeking to save his marriage by killing his wife's lover.

Since Liz's disappearing act, Roger had found a new pleasure in the story, losing himself in his runaway imagination where he could get revenge. Originally, the story was conceived when one of Roger's friends informed him that he and his wife were divorcing because of another man. Now, Roger found himself in the same boat.

Must be something in the water.

The liquor was softening his mind, loosening him up. He stared at the paper resting in the carriage, at all the words he typed the previous day and suddenly he didn't feel much like writing.

He fanned out the mail and selected the magazine from the bottom. A young man was on the cover. *Robert Beechum*, it said. *Author of the breakout bestseller*, When the Clock Strikes Three. A circuit connected in Roger's fuzzy head. The title set off an alarm. That was the title of *his* story!

He reread the blurb beside the author's picture on the cover to make sure he'd read it correctly the first time. He had. The story was on page 42. Roger opened the magazine and flipped through to the interview. He skimmed some of the questions and answers. This was the asshole that had somehow beaten Roger to the publisher with another version of Roger's story. Roger didn't know how, but this little prick had stolen Roger's work! Currently, his addled mind was in no shape to consider how this guy could have pulled off such a stunt. As far as Roger knew, the two had never met.

Roger threw the magazine at the wall and watched it flutter to the floor. First Liz had left him and now this. He was disgusted. He wouldn't let it happen again. Fueled by his acute anger, Roger turned to his typewriter, channeled his emotions into his writing, and began typing.

CHAPTER 20

Debra quit her job at Red Lobster shortly after Anthony's proposal. They bought a house together in Acworth and Debra worked as Anthony's manager. Who better to look after his personal affairs than his wife?

They were married in the spring of 1976, which was tricky because Anthony didn't have a birth certificate to get their marriage license. Fortunately, he found someone who was able to fashion a fake for two hundred dollars. The ceremony was performed at Debra's mother's church. Of the eighty-three people in attendance, most were Debra's friends and relatives. Anthony invited his agent, editor, and a few author friends he'd met at book conventions.

Four months after their marriage, Anthony's third novel was published. *The Show Must Go On* hit number twelve on the *New York Times* bestseller list and rose to number four within the next few weeks. He had already begun transcribing the fourth book, a favorite of his titled, *The Shadows Have Eyes.*

Anthony was living the life he always wanted and occasionally found himself pondering who he really was and where he'd come from. Knowing the truth seemed surreal once he'd gotten caught up in his current lifestyle. He wondered about his parents, what they were doing in the future, how they'd handled the news of his disappearance.

He looked at the wall clock. It was 11 AM. He'd been entertaining his deep philosophical thoughts for fifteen minutes.

His past self was six years old this year, attending school at Hightower Elementary. When he dredged up memories of that time, he remembered that those had been fun years at a great school. He had plenty of friends. His curiosity was piqued when he considered the opportunity to see his past self. Hightower was only thirty miles away.

He grabbed his car keys and headed for the door. "Hon, I've got to run out for a bit," he said, hurrying down the hall.

Anthony climbed behind the wheel and set out for Doraville. Although his memory of that age was spotty at best, Anthony thought that catching a glimpse of himself at school might rekindle some of those embers. If he was lucky, he might see himself on the playground.

When he arrived at the school, it was a quarter past twelve. More than likely his young self would be in the lunch room. He couldn't recall what time he went out for recess, before lunch or after. Anthony pulled around to the side and parked in the area designated for faculty.

The rear lot of the school had one large paved area divided into three basketball courts. Next to that, the hill sloped down slightly then leveled out where there was a wooden jungle gym, some stand-alone monkey bars, and a mesh dome constructed of metal bars for children to climb on. A longer and steeper hill on the adjacent side of the basketball court gave way to a large dirt field covered with tiny pea-gravel. Three sections of chain-link fence formed backstops at three of the field's corners. This lower field was where kids played kickball, flag football, and softball. It was also where the school conducted its annual Field Day activities.

Anthony was not a very athletic person. He had never enjoyed the Field Day festivities, although he did enjoy being outside of the classroom and the camaraderie of his friends.

As Anthony stepped out of his car and approached the edge of the parking lot, he noticed several older boys—probably sixth or seventh graders—playing basketball on the nearby court. He could hear other younger children screaming and laughing as they ran around on the playground. A teacher sitting in an orange plastic chair at the top of the slope kept watch over both groups of children.

Anthony surveyed the boys dribbling and passing the basketball. At first, none of them seemed familiar, but after a moment, he realized that he recognized two of them. Both were boys from his old neighborhood. Seeing them pushing the other boys away jogged his memory. They were a pair of older bullies who had terrorized him and his friends. Now, through the eyes of an adult, they appeared so young and innocent. In the memory from his childhood, however, they seemed much older, mean, and intimidating.

As he watched them weave around their fellow students bouncing the ball, they appeared completely harmless. But, Anthony knew that the chubbier of the two, Billy Nuesome, would later develop a drug habit and have run-ins with the police. Anthony wasn't completely sure of the fact, but it was rumored that Billy took up burglary to support his habit and was eventually sent to a camp for wayward teens in an effort to straighten him out.

The other boy was Allen Pruitt. He was taller, skinnier, a shock of red hair you couldn't miss, and pale skin riddled with freckles. Allen was the friendlier of the two, kind of a Dr. Jekyll and Mr. Hyde thing going on there, but later on in life he would also turn to drugs and begin associating with more nefarious people. Anthony didn't know whatever became of Allen, but he knew that Allen had also had his fair share of encounters with the law.

When the teacher stood up from the chair and turned around, Anthony recognized her, too. She was his second-grade teacher, Mrs. Hargrave. He figured she was pulling double duty overseeing her students on the playground as well as the seventh graders on the ball court. She saw Anthony, shielded her eyes from the sun with one hand, and began walking in his direction.

Uh oh.

"Can I help you, sir?" she asked.

"I used to go to school here and decided to stop by to see it again."

She was still shading her eyes with her hand. "You're supposed to sign in at the front office if you're visiting."

"Oh. Okay. I didn't know that," Anthony said.

Mrs. Hargrave smiled. Anthony turned and walked away. After several steps, he stopped and looked back at her. She was already strolling across the grass to her chair. She looked a lot different with his adult perspective. In his memory, Mrs. Hargrave seemed so much older, but still strangely attractive. In his opinion, she had been a great teacher, favorable among the students, not mean and heartless like his later teachers were thought to be. Of course, that latter opinion was probably the product of an immature mind. When he looked at Mrs. Hargrave now, however, she didn't seem old at all. In fact, if he had to guess her age, he would put her

The Old Royal

in her late thirties. Probably a few years older than Debra. Mrs. Hargrave's complexion was smooth and clear. Her face exhibited only the faint hint of makeup. This ran counter to his memory, formed at an age when girls had cooties and any person over the age of twenty-five was considered an irrelevant dinosaur. He thought it funny how such perspectives could change so drastically with the passage of time.

Anthony decided to grab a quick lunch and return closer to 3:15 when school let out. Throughout his years in elementary school, Anthony had always been a walker. That is, he lived so close to school that he walked to and from home each day. In an effort to kill time, he decided he would drive through his old neighborhood after lunch to see how it looked. Since his last visit in 2002, it had changed plenty over the decades.

Anthony was flooded with memories as he drove down his old street. He looked at houses on each side of the road. Some had been home to his friends that had played kickball and touch-football in the street. The older kids, most of them bullies, had lived in some of the other houses near one end of the neighborhood. This neighborhood had plenty of those; bigger boys who enjoyed pushing around the smaller ones.

Anthony's brakes squeaked when he pulled to a stop in front of his old house. He expected it to appear as it had the last time he had seen it, sixteen years after his family had moved. The house and neighborhood had changed significantly since his last visit in 2002, but now it looked the same as he'd remembered it. Why wouldn't it? After all, his family was still living here. This was where Anthony had spent the first fifteen years of his life.

Not wanting to be seen by his parents, Anthony quickly scanned the street and yard. He doubted they would know him. He was an adult now, but that spark of familiarity might be strong and the last thing he wanted was to affect anything in the past which might alter his future. He needn't worry though, no one was home. He was still at school and his parents were at work at this time of day.

As he sat in his idling car, Anthony recalled the many Christmases spent there. Waking up in the small hours of the morning to emerge wide-eyed in the living room where toys awaited discovery in the dazzling glow of the twinkling tree. His most memorable Christmas rose to the forefront. That particular year, his parents' closest friends showed up late at night with their kids (who were really more like a second family) in tow. They parked in the driveway and began singing Christmas carols, much to the chagrin of the sleeping neighbors. Anthony heard the noise and stood up in bed to peer out his window at them. Something about that memory seemed magical.

The sentimental train of thoughts passing through his mind began to pick up speed. He thought of the week his cousins stayed with them during the summer. That was the same week his cousins stood up to three of the local bullies…and won! Trips to the city pool where Anthony developed a crush on a teenager named Shannon. She was obviously out of his league due to her age, but she would actually stop if she saw him and talk instead of snubbing him. Then there were all the evenings spent running through the neighbors' yards at dusk collecting lightning bugs in glass jars. Countless games of kickball played in the street between his friends, Tommy and Mark's houses.

Anthony glanced down the street at the two manhole covers in the asphalt that acted as home and second base. Good memories.

He took his foot off the brake and rolled slowly down the road still lost in reverie. He parked beside the curb, got out, and walked the length of the street from one end of the neighborhood to the other and back again. It was odd how this road seemed much longer when he walked it in his youth. As an adult, the walk took only a matter of a few minutes.

Anthony looked at his watch. When it was 3:15, he parked at the end of his neighborhood by the curb where several streets intersected. From this vantage point, he could watch the intersection where the school kids would pass. He didn't have to wait long until he witnessed the familiar exodus of children appearing at the crosswalk where Mrs. Young, the crossing guard, waited to escort them across the street. So many recognizable faces approached and turned onto his street in a sporadic procession.

Anthony finally saw what he was waiting for: himself. The young version of him came be-bopping down the road at 3:25 carrying a tattered book bag. Little Anthony held the straps of the bag over his shoulder while kicking a stick along the curb's gutter. Two other boys flanked him. Anthony identified them right away. The slightly taller, dark-haired boy on the right was Brian. The shorter, olive-skinned kid was Matt. They had been close friends throughout his childhood and only lost contact when Anthony's family moved away in the mid-80s.

Anthony's heart sped up at the sight. It was so surreal to observe himself and his friends walking home to spend a late afternoon playing. Anthony longed for the innocence of those days. He wiped at his eyes after a tear coursed down his cheek. He hadn't thought this would be such an emotional occasion. Once little Anthony had turned the corner and gone out of sight, older Anthony decided he should return home. Debra was probably wondering where he was. He cranked the car, drove slowly by the school, and headed for the highway. He never mentioned this little excursion to anyone.

Roger's plan was to eat lunch somewhere and then go to the bookstore to walk among the shelves. Roger had always loved the bookstore. It was a place where he felt he could relax and unwind. Turning through the pages of the newest novels was always a comfort. He didn't know why that was exactly; maybe just to daydream of the day he would see his own books on the shelf.

But, all of that came crashing down around him when he learned that *his* story was already in print, with *someone else*'s name. When he had read the title and Anthony's pseudonym on the cover in a storefront window display, Roger nearly lost his mind.

The cover's artwork is what caught his eye. He removed a copy from the cardboard stand. The author's name above the title enraged him. He opened it, thumbed through the pages, stopping periodically to read certain passages. The more he read, the more convinced he became that it was *his* story. When he reached the end, he studied the author's bio and stared at the picture of Robert Beechum. Roger's neck and cheeks flushed with the heat of his rage and he realized he was clenching his jaw.

That should be my *picture and* my *name!*

Although it put money in the other guy's pocket, Roger carried the book up to the cashier and purchased it. After the fact, he wasn't sure why he'd done it. Proof, he guessed, of the fact that his work had been plagiarized.

As Roger sat in his car staring at the cover and the other man's photo, his anger simmered, on the verge of boiling over. What was he going to do about it? What *could* he do about it?

I'm going to write a damn letter to the publisher, that's what!

Roger returned home from Barnes & Noble. He slammed the front door and stormed into his den where he threw the new book he'd purchased on the desk. The book was *The Black Talon*. Roger dropped into the chair behind his desk, jerked out the paper from his typewriter, threaded a fresh sheet, and began composing a letter to the publishing house. His fingers danced across the keys as he unloaded his emotions onto the paper.

By the time he'd finished, a scattered array of wadded paper balls circled his waste basket. He'd gone through twelve variations of his letter to the editor at Simon & Shuster when he realized that none of the first few versions would be taken more seriously than the rants of an irate lunatic. Roger had taken several slugs of whisky to help calm his nerves and get his mind right before putting his words down on paper. The last couple of revisions were his attempt to correct lapses that occurred due to the alcohol's effect.

When he pulled the latest copy out of the machine he read it over carefully. Satisfied, he folded it, tucked it into an envelope, and wrote out the addresses. He wasn't content with sitting idly by while some asshole reaped the rewards for his hard work and he fully intended to bring the matter to the publisher's attention. When finished with the letter,

The Old Royal

Roger went out in his back yard with a can of lighter fluid and promptly burned the book he had just purchased. The sight of it, as well as the author's photo, made him sick to his stomach.

CHAPTER 21

The telephone rang. Debra must've answered because it quit ringing. A moment later she called to Anthony from elsewhere in the house.

Anthony was concentrating deeply on listening to the words as he typed up the last few pages of the third book, *The Show Must Go On*, when Debra interrupted him.

"What?" He stopped the tape machine.

She appeared in the doorway. "I said Stuart's on the phone for you."

He thanked her and picked up the handset. "Hey, Stuart. What's shakin'?"

There was a rattle on the line as Debra hung up.

"Hey, Anthony. How's everything?"

"Good. Just finishing up a revision for the next book."

"This the one you talked about last time?" Stuart asked.

"Yeah," Anthony said. He and Stuart had last talked two months ago regarding Anthony's third book in the contract. Stuart had informed Anthony of Simon & Shuster's interest in renewing the contract for another three books, but Anthony said he wanted to negotiate for more money. "Have you heard anything about the offer? Are they willing to go higher?"

"We're still haggling. Look, I heard something and wanted to confirm it with you." The tone in Stuart's voice was secretive yet matter-of-fact. It made Anthony perk up in his chair.

"What is it, Stuart?"

"Well, the editor at Simon and Shuster received a letter from someone claiming that you plagiarized their work. They even went so far as to send in some sample pages from their so-called manuscript. I just have to ask if you know anything about this."

Anthony had already considered this angle when he first conceived his plan and was prepared with an answer. "Stuart, that's ridiculous! Someone out there's claiming I stole their story? You know I make it a habit not to read anyone's unpublished work. So, how would I have done it?"

"Hell if I know! Ever heard of a guy named Roger Kurrey?"

Anthony snorted. "Nope. You ever hear of a guy named Allen Pruitt?"

There was a pause as Stuart considered it. "No. Why?"

"He's a guy I knew growing up. He's nobody, just like this Roger guy. My book's already out there, Stuart. This guy probably wants to be a writer or something and fashioned the story hoping to cash in. I'm sure this isn't the first time something like this has happened."

Stuart admitted it was true. When an author hit the big-time and landed on the bestseller list, there were always some contenders to the throne claiming to have been ripped off.

Anthony added, "Where would I even have gotten his manuscript? It's not like I'm getting any advance copies to blurb."

"True," Stuart said. "Ever been to Connecticut?"

"Never been above the Mason-Dixon," Anthony said.

"You're right." Stuart laughed. "I'm sure he's just looking for a hand out. That's what I thought when I heard about it, but still, I had to ask. You know?"

"No worries. So, no word from Simon and Shuster, huh?"

"Nah. Not yet, but I imagine they'll concede. Especially since this last book is still on the bestseller list. I imagine if the next book does as well or better, they'll be in our corner."

"That's nice to hear, Stuart."

They chatted a little longer before Stuart hung up so Anthony could get back to work. When Anthony hung up, he had a deceptive smile. This was exactly what Anthony had been waiting for, that Roger would eventually say something. Anthony was pleasantly surprised at how easy it was to deal with this part of his plan.

Roger's heart raced as he ripped open the envelope from Robert Beechum's publisher. He expected to find a letter of humble apologies. As he walked through the front door, he unfolded the paper and read.

Dear Sir:

Thank you for contacting us regarding your recent suspicion of plagiarism on behalf of one of our authors. While we take this matter very seriously and made exhaustive efforts to investigate, we have concluded that there is no merit to your claim.

The work that you cited is, to our knowledge and that of the author's, the original material and concept from said author. Since the work in question has been available in print to the mass market for some time, the burden of proof is on the accuser to produce evidence of plagiarism.

We sincerely thank you for bringing this concern to our attention and hope that you will continue to enjoy other books offered by Simon & Shuster.

Roger wadded up the paper and threw it across the kitchen. He slammed his fists down on the island's countertop. "SONOFABITCH!"

The overall flippant tone of the letter was a punch delivered to Roger's gut. The author's photo materialized in his head and caused his hatred to boil over. It seemed that everyone was conspiring against him.

There had to be some other way to receive justice. But, how? He considered bringing about a lawsuit. Yeah. Initially, that idea sounded good. However, when Roger considered it further, he realized that attorneys were expensive and he didn't have the kind of money or attorneys that a large corporation like Simon & Shuster had.

Roger took the flask out of his drawer in the study and went into the living room. He turned up the container, emptying the last little bit down his throat. Before going to get the bottle from the kitchen, he pondered the lawsuit. His financial disadvantage was a deterrent, but Roger knew without a doubt that he was in the right. It was just a matter of convincing the court that he was the victim here. The burden of proof rested on his shoulders. If he could do that, he could seek monetary damages. The financial gain would probably be worth the pursuit.

He had his original manuscript. That would be his primary evidence. Then he recalled what the publisher's letter said—the book was available to the public nationally and had been for some time. Who's to say Roger didn't steal from the book after buying a copy? The book had been available for a few weeks now. There was no way he could prove that he had begun writing his story prior to the book's publication. As Roger sat turning over his options, he negated each one. His case grew flimsier by the moment until, eventually, he realized it was frivolous. Yet he knew he was the victim. Acknowledging that fact as well as the inability to do anything about it made Roger's hatred and rage flare to the point that he could barely keep control of it. He wanted to lash out at someone, preferably the writer—that Thief!—whose picture was in *his* book.

Instead, he retrieved the bottle of Glenlivet from the pantry, uncorked the top, and turned it up to his lips. The whisky burned his throat as it went down and began to warm his stomach. He gulped down a quarter of the bottle, letting the alcohol quell his temper.

CHAPTER 22

The year was 2010. Anthony's dreams were now a reality. As he sat at the patio table beneath the umbrella, Anthony looked over the top of the book he was reading just in time to see Debra dive into the shimmering clear water of their pool. The numerous films and TV-movies that had been made from his bestselling books over the years made him a household name, a revered author, and he had plenty of money. He took pleasure from the fact that he was living his dream.

Anthony and Debra had moved away from Georgia to a large house in a suburban neighborhood in Virginia following the publication of his third book. As the royalties accumulated throughout the years, they were able to afford pretty much anything they wanted. Bills were no longer a concern for them and Debra had expressed an interest in moving somewhere that actually experienced four seasons instead of only the ungodly Georgia heat and mild winters.

Anthony had recently turned in his latest manuscript. Unlike every story prior to it, this one was an Anthony Jessup original. It was the first one he had given to his agent. Now that his writing had reached a certain level of notoriety, Anthony figured he would attempt to get his original stories published. Besides, Anthony had exhausted all of Roger's books. *Banshee* had been published the previous year. Unless he was prepared to retire from writing, Anthony now had to rely on his own material since he had no intention of quitting. As a result, *The Wind Screams My Name* was slated to hit bookstores in the fall.

The cordless phone on the table rang. Anthony lifted it and hit the button to talk. "Hello?"

"Anthony? Stuart."

"Hey, Stuart. How's everything?"

"Fine. Just fine. You got a minute? I wanted to ask you about the book tour."

Anthony watched as his wife climbed out of the pool. Despite her age, he thought she still looked sexy in a bathing suit. "Sure, Stuart. I was just reading by the pool."

"Well, with the latest book due out in a few months, the publisher wants to know if you're willing to add ten more cities to the tour. They—"

"Did they say which cities they had in mind?"

"Not all of them. They have a preliminary list of about six or seven that I've seen. They're supposed to give me the complete list no later than tomorrow."

Debra walked over and stood beside Anthony. She touched his shoulder with her wet hand. Anthony covered the receiver and looked up at her. "It's Stuart. He says the publisher wants to add ten more cities to the tour."

Debra raised her eyebrows, nodding, and patted his shoulder. He uncovered the phone as Debra toweled off.

"Okay, Stuart. Sounds fine. Get me a copy of the list as soon as you can so I can make preparations, will ya?"

"Sure, Anthony. No problem. Have a wonderful rest of the day. I'll talk to you soon."

Anthony hung up.

"Ten more cities, huh?" Debra said as she eased into the adjacent seat. "That puts it at what? Sixty?"

"Yeah. I told him it was fine. He's going to send me the list tomorrow."

Despite the years spent accumulating rejections for his novels, Roger Kurrey had continued his routine of finishing a novel and submitting query letters to prospective agents. Although he hadn't sold any of his novels, he had sold a couple of obscure novellas and plenty of short stories to magazines.

The Old Royal

When most people would have given up and thrown in the towel, Roger persevered. He had the thickest skin of any writer out there and was probably the most stubborn.

He was looking through the latest edition of *Writer's Digest* when he came across an announcement for the book tour marking Robert Beechum's twenty-first novel, *The Wind Screams My Name*. It had been decades since Roger had written the letter addressing Robert Beechum's act of plagiarism, yet the author's name still sent Roger's blood pressure soaring whenever he saw it. This time was no different.

Roger was clenching his teeth as he scanned the list of cities and had to relax his jaw muscles or he'd develop a migraine. Roger's finger stopped on the list when it came to Newark, Delaware. This was the closest city where Beechum was scheduled to appear during his book tour. The date indicated that he would be there in two and a half months. Roger put the magazine on his desk and went into the spare bedroom. He came back with a paper bag that contained all of Beechum's novels throughout the years, all paperbacks. Roger wouldn't have given the smug prick the satisfaction of buying the more expensive hardcovers.

Roger planned to confront the author with the books, see what he had to say for himself.

CHAPTER 23

Anthony sat behind a folding table in the corner of Book Worms off Center Street in Newark. It was the final stop on his sixty-city book tour and Anthony was exhausted. He'd spent too many days on the road, on planes, in hotel rooms, and away from home. Mostly, he looked forward to wrapping it up so he could return to Debra and unwind.

He'd returned only fifteen minutes ago from Catherine Rooney's Irish Pub, where he grabbed a beer and a bite to eat for lunch. Before resuming the last few hours of his book signing marathon, Anthony opened his cell phone and called his wife.

"Hello?"

"Hey, hon. I'm almost done." He sighed. "Just wanted to call and tell you I'm going to drive straight home tonight."

"Well, don't kill yourself trying to make it all in one trip. The roads between here and there might be icy." A premature snowstorm had swept across the eastern seaboard leaving several inches of fresh powder between Virginia and Delaware.

"Don't worry. I'll drive carefully. I just want to get home and be with you. I've signed so many books; I think my hand may stay this way." Debra couldn't see him miming a claw with his right hand.

Debra laughed, imagining his poor tired hand. "Okay. If I'm not here when you get home—I suspect you'll get in later this evening—it's because Mary's in town and we've gone to dinner. I told her I'd take her out."

Mary was Anthony's sister-in-law. She stopped in to visit once in a while when her job brought her near Richmond. Since Mary lived in Spokane, Debra made it a point to take her sister out to eat because it was one of the few chances they had to catch up with one another.

"Okay. I've got to get back to work. Love you."

"I love you, too."

Anthony waited to hear his wife hang up the phone before closing his. He tucked the cell phone into his pocket, stretched his hand a couple of times, nodded to the manager to let the attendees come forward, and picked up his black Sharpie.

A heavy woman wearing a cold wet parka approached and placed a copy of his latest hardcover on the table in front of him. Her face was beaming with joy and she clasped her hands together over her breasts. "Oh, Mr. Beechum, I'm such a huge fan…" yada, yada, yada.

Although he'd heard the sentiment a million times, if not more, Anthony still smiled. He understood their excitement first-hand and vowed he'd never take it for granted. He asked her name, opened the cover, and began to write. Although his hand hurt and he battled the urge to close his weary eyes, Anthony kept up his smile and good-natured banter with the fans. When he finished with the woman's book, he leaned forward to peer at the line trying to determine how long it was. It stretched across the store to the entrance and out the door where he lost sight of it. Everyone waiting wore coats, knitted caps, scarves, gloves, and held copies of his latest book.

He thanked his lucky stars for being in the position he was. His days working in technical support for meager wages still lurked in the back of his mind, reminding him just how lucky he really was.

A portly older man stepped forward and passed his copy of *The Wind Screams My Name* to Anthony. The man pointed at the book as Anthony pulled it closer and said, "That's a fantastic book, Mr. Beechum. Different from your others, but still good."

Anthony thanked him, wondering if the man's accolade was genuine or just something to say since they were face to face. Anthony had read plenty of reviews since the book's release. It was a product of his own imagination and no one else's, unlike the previous books which were really Roger Kurrey's creations. The recent reviews had been unflattering. Anthony was lucky the previous novels had done so well or the reviews might have been more severe. As one critic put it, "A writer can't knock them all out of the park. At some point they strike out, too."

Thinking of that review made Anthony's stomach sink. Maybe he should quit while he was ahead. Who was he fooling? All of the agents and editors he'd originally queried with his own work had shot him down in flames. Certainly that was a good indicator of Anthony's lack of writing skill. He didn't want to admit defeat though, even if this book only reinforced that idea.

While the story's plot was engaging, Anthony's poor character development left the characters feeling as flimsy as cardboard cutouts instead of someone the reader might root for or empathize with. Anthony didn't want to dwell on that right now, though. There was a light at the end of his tunnel. Only four hours remained until he could stick a fork in this tour and call it done. He just wanted to get home and relax.

Roger held three of Robert Beechum's older paperbacks. He had decided against bringing in all twenty novels. That was a little excessive and also unwieldy. He could make his point just as well with three books. He had finally entered the store and gotten out of the flurry of snowflakes. The heat inside stung Roger's cold cheeks.

He unwrapped his scarf and let the ends dangle, then picked up a copy of the newest hardcover. *The Wind Screams My Name*. Unlike all of the previous books, Roger didn't recognize the title. It wasn't one of his.

Probably why it's not on the bestseller list.

He smirked. What had happened to the guy? Why hadn't he stole Roger's latest story? He had no answer for this. Hell, he didn't even know how the guy had stolen his previous ideas. Did he have a crystal ball or something?

Beats the hell out of me.

He edged closer to the table as the line shuffled forward. He still couldn't see the thief sitting behind the table but, by craning his neck, he caught glimpses of the man's hands as he reached out to accept the books proffered him.

Roger's hatred bubbled to the surface. If he could see his own face in a mirror, he wouldn't be surprised by the scowl plastered on it. The people in line around him must've noticed it because they turned away, pretending he wasn't there. Roger stuck his hand in his coat pocket and felt the cold metal of the little sub-nose .38 revolver.

It was the gun his dad had given him long before dying of a heart attack. Before the old man kicked the bucket, he'd told Roger that he wanted him to have it "in case he ever needed to protect himself". Well, Roger had convinced himself, this isn't exactly what Pop had in mind, but, in a way, he *was* protecting himself.

In his mind, Roger imagined himself stepping forward with the books, which he planned to lay out like a hand of cards. When the thief registered the contempt on Roger's face and looked back at the books, Roger would pull out the nickel-plated pistol and jerk the trigger repeatedly, emptying the cylinder into the man who'd stolen his fame, his fortune, his life. Pandemonium and chaos would follow the percussive bangs. That's when Roger would make a break for the doors, exiting into the streets just as John Wilkes Booth had after assassinating Lincoln.

As the line edged closer to the table, however, Roger found his nerve slipping. He wasn't really a cold-blooded killer. The rational part of his mind knew this and reminded him. However, when the irrational side piped up, it reminded Roger that this was the guy responsible for wrecking his writing career. He envisioned Anthony enjoying his millions of dollars in a nice big house without ever having to worry over the problems of the middle class. Roger found himself gritting his teeth and clenching his fists.

The rational side emerged again, flashing images of metal bars and a life spent in prison. A mental tug of war was taking place and the rational side of Roger's mind was slowly winning as he neared the man sitting behind the table. The room seemed to be getting warmer. Roger unbuttoned his coat; his cold cheeks were red against the heat.

When Roger reached the head of the line he had lost his nerve but his anger was still there. His face remained deadpan instead of cheerful. He laid the books in front of Anthony, who looked up from the old paperbacks at the man he had wronged. There was a moment of hesitation as the two men's eyes locked.

"Oh, I see you're a long time fan," Anthony said, feigning a smile.

Roger didn't return the smile. He simply stood there looking down at Anthony like an automaton, cool and uncaring. Roger's eyes drilled into Anthony as he opened the book and quickly signed each copy.

Watching Anthony carry on so smugly, scribbling into Roger's books set off a wildfire inside him. The thought of jerking the trigger until there was nothing but empty clicks ran through Kurrey's mind once again.

Anthony closed the last book, stacked them neatly on one another, and slid them across to Roger. Anthony's face still bore that empty smile. "There you go. Thanks for reading."

Roger picked up the books, still staring with that emotionally void expression. He turned and walked past the line of fans and into the cold blustery air.

Anthony sighed as he watched the back of Roger exit through the store's front doors.
Well, that could've gone worse.
His smile returned, now filled with genuine happiness as the next person in line approached. Anthony likened himself to Santa Claus at a retail store, seeing each child in line who wanted nothing more than to see the man who could give them the happiness they wanted. Roger, he thought, was just one of the unruly, pouty kids. It was over now, and Anthony was happy that Roger hadn't caused a scene.

When the last person had received their signed copy and gone, Anthony got his coat and walked with the manager to the front of the store. It was 5 PM and the sky was gunmetal gray. Snow flurries danced in the wind outside.

"I want to thank you again for coming, Mr. Beechum," the manager said, shaking Anthony's hand.

Although it was just a pseudonym he'd begun using thirty years ago, Anthony decided way back to not correct anyone who called him by it. Rather than getting into an awkward explanation that Robert Beechum was only a pen name, he found it easier to just go along. "Well, Mr. Darcy, it was my pleasure. Thanks, again, for having me."

"Oh, are you kidding? Hosting a book signing for a multiple bestseller is our pleasure. Really."

Anthony threw the ends of his scarf around his neck and turned toward the parking lot.

The store manager waved. "Be careful driving out there."

Anthony got behind the wheel of his BMW and waited with the engine running to warm the interior. He flipped open his cell phone and called home.

"Hey, honey."

"Anthony?"

"Yeah. Just finished up here." He glanced at his watch, 5:10 PM. "I'll probably be home around eight."

"Okay. Be careful. Some of the roads are pretty icy."

"Yeah, that's what I figured."

"Remember, I may be out with Mary," Debra reminded him. "Want me to bring you something home?"

"Nah. I'll fix something. I just want to get there, then I'll worry about eating."

He told her he loved her. She did the same and they both hung up.

Anthony tucked the cell phone in his pocket, put the car in gear, and slowly pulled out of the parking lot.

Debra had been right; the roads between Newark and Richmond were in sad shape with spots of ice.

Anthony drove carefully, occasionally passing cars that had slid onto the shoulder or had small fender benders. In some places, police cars sat with their lights flashing and road flares burning near potentially hazardous conditions.

Despite wanting to get home quickly, Anthony took his time. He wanted to get there in one piece. Once there, he could warm up in a hot shower and relax.

The book tour was over. The idea for his next book had already begun to take shape in his head. He was anxious to begin writing it. This current novel may not break onto the bestseller list, but Anthony was confident that the next book, another one of his originals, would. He had faith in it. You had to in this business. The story was begging to be written.

As Anthony drove, he paid close attention to the road and the surrounding cars, but his mind also turned over the plot of the next book, looking for potential holes.

Roger squinted through the swishing wipers and oncoming snowflakes in an effort not to lose track of the black BMW two cars ahead of him. He had been following it since it pulled out of the Book Worm's parking lot an hour and a half ago.

Most of the daylight had already drained from the sky, but the clouds remained, dropping their wintry flakes down on the procession of cars. Roger had the heater wide open in his old Nissan. He did a double-take when he passed the sign welcoming him to Virginia. He looked at his watch. 6:40 PM.

Virginia? How much farther is he going to go?

It was 8:20 when Roger saw Anthony's car turn into the driveway of a large house. The other houses nearby were also large, sitting in the middle of expansive lots. The car Roger was watching stopped just short of the garage doors as they slowly started to ascend. Roger switched off his idling motor, got out, and began running toward the house. It was dark out and the lack of street lights made it hard for anyone to see him.

The fresh snow crunched under Roger's feet as he ran. He watched the car's brake lights blink out as it eased into the garage. The door began to descend just before Roger reached it, stepped over the invisible beam at the bottom, and crept around the passenger's side. The hot engine ticked as it rapidly began to cool. Roger had his hand stuffed inside his coat pocket.

The driver was oblivious of the intruder skulking around his car when he threw open his door. The dome light illuminated the interior, casting a glare on the windshield and side windows. A faint dinging alerted the driver that his headlights were still on. He reached and flipped them off, then continued sliding out from behind the wheel. Once out, he turned to his left and grasped the doorknob leading into the house.

CHAPTER 24

A shuffling sound caused Anthony to stop and turn. When he did, his heart froze between beats. His brain had enough time to register a large man in his garage, making his way hurriedly around the front of the car. The stranger advanced quickly, but attempted to remain stealthy. Maybe he didn't want to alert anyone in the house. Of course, he didn't know the house was empty, that Debra was out having dinner with her sister.

As the looming silhouette drew nearer, Anthony recognized the man's face.

Roger!

He opened his mouth to say something, but before he could…

Bang!

Out of the ensuing chaos, a white hot pain gored Anthony in the stomach. It felt like being punched with a red hot poker. His bowels loosened and then clenched. He fell to his knees, and watched his former idol, now a desperate man, push the garage door button, stoop to duck through the widening gap, and flee into the wintry night.

Anthony pulled his hand away from his stomach, cringing at what he might see—intestines protruding, perhaps. His hand was dark red, almost black with sticky warm blood. The sight of his own blood made his heart beat faster. He pulled back on the reins of his runaway thoughts and told himself to get a grip, that panicking would only cause him to bleed out much faster. His mind felt fuzzy as he grew light-headed. Anthony pulled himself up onto legs that were wobbly and didn't want to cooperate, but he forced them. He turned, everything wavering, and went into the house. Crimson droplets marked his progress across the cream-colored floor tiles in the kitchen to the hallway.

Gotta get to the Royal.

He staggered along. Breathing became a struggle.

Just pull out the page!

Anthony twisted the closet knob and threw back the door. Inside, on a shelf beside the coats and umbrellas, sat the musty old machine. The thirty-year-old paper still rested securely in the carriage.

The edges had begun to yellow and deteriorate in some places from years of sitting in dark storage.

Anthony grasped the paper with trembling red fingers. He jerked. The typewriter refused to give up its possession, teetering on the edge of the shelf before the paper tore in half. He let go of the scrap in his hand, but his sticky fingers acted like glue that still held it. He shook it loose and let it flutter to the floor. As it twisted and spun, Anthony noticed the bright red smudges on it. The typewriter cantered and fell onto the floor with a clatter, still holding the remains of the page.

Anthony's knees gave out. With his back against the door, he slid down to the floor, leaving a red smear. He clutched at his fiery guts and tried to catch his breath. He winced as he reached for the paper protruding from the machine. When his fingers clasped hold of it, he closed his eyes and gave a final yank.

CHAPTER 25

Roger ran from the garage into the frosty night with the pistol jammed into his coat pocket. His breath streamed out before him like an antique locomotive. He hurdled over the shrubs at the edge of the yard, lost his footing in the slick snow when he came down, and tumbled into the street. He righted himself, got his bearings, and dashed for his car. When he reached it, he threw open the door, hopped in, fumbled his keys until he found the right one, and started the engine. He slammed the gear shift into DRIVE, nailed the accelerator, and spun away from the curb.

The Old Royal

When Debra arrived home, she saw that the garage door was open, but the light was off. Her headlights shone on Anthony's BMW.

He forgot to shut the door again.

She unlocked the front door and stepped inside. She placed her things on the little table in the foyer. "Honey? You left the garage door open again."

She shrugged off her coat and turned into the hallway to hang it in the closet. But, the door was already open. From her vantage point, she could see Anthony's leg extending from behind the door. The tip of his loafer pointed toward the ceiling. Her hand went to her mouth and she gasped. With a whisper she called his name, "Anthony?" She took some hesitant steps forward. "Honey?"

Her trembling hand was at her neck as she craned to look around the closet door.

Anthony sat with his back against it. One hand still clutched his stomach, the other rested by his side with the torn page at his fingertips. A scarlet ring of dried blood encircled her late husband. His filmy dead eyes looked straight ahead into eternity.

Debra screamed and fell to her knees.

EPILOGUE

The store manager at the Oakwood Barnes & Noble carried the cardboard promotional display to the front of the store. When he got to the window beside the entrance, he set the base down and unfolded the cross member in back that would allow it to stand up on its own. He repositioned it until he thought it was at the proper angle, stood back, and evaluated its placement.

On the front, there was a long road segmented by the perspective of rolling hills. The asphalt laid itself out toward a fiery orange sunset. Flanking the road was a sea of skeletal winter trees. At the top, it said, *The Long Journey*. At the bottom, where the road began, were the words *by Roger Kurrey*. Smaller text below that said, "If you like Robert Beechum, you're going to love Roger Kurrey".

Roger had finally made it. His debut novel garnered him a substantial advance and a three book contract with HarperCollins. The deal was featured in *Publisher's Weekly* as well as *Writer's Digest*.

Susan Roberts arrived home from work for lunch and reached into her mailbox as usual. Her hand came out holding a typical-looking stack of mail: a flyer for a local tree trimmer; two bills—one from the cable company, the other for the electricity; a new issue of *Rolling Stone* and *Entertainment Weekly*; and...an envelope sent from Pritchett, Mathers & Goldblatt, attorneys at law.

Susan's eyebrows pinched together quizzically as she read the sender's address.

Who the hell are Pritchett, Mathers & Goldblatt?

She went inside and dumped the mail on the coffee table, not bothering to flip through the pages of EW as she was accustomed to doing. Her curiosity piqued, she worked her thumb beneath the flap and tore it open. She unfolded the letter that was inside.

As she read, her eyebrows relaxed, but her eyes grew wider and wider. The words she was puzzling over were *inheritance*, *substantial amount*, and *contact us at once*. Normally, she would have tossed the letter into the trash along with the other junk mail, but something about this correspondence screamed that it was official.

She picked up the phone and dialed the office number in the upper corner of the letterhead.

"Pritchett, Mather, and Goldblatt. This is Donna. How may I help you?"

"Hi. My name's Susan. I just received a letter from your firm informing me of..." she glanced at the letter again, unable to comprehend exactly what she was trying to convey, but also with a bit skepticism, "an inheritance, I guess."

"What is your last name, ma'am?"

"Roberts. Susan Roberts."

"Can you hold, please?"

Susan said she could and listened to Vivaldi's *Four Seasons* as she waited. A moment later, the line clicked and a man's voice spoke.

"Ms. Roberts?"

"Yes."

"Hi. My name's Daniel Mathers. I'm a partner here at Pritchett, Mathers, and Goldblatt."

"Okay." Susan's voice was still apprehensive.

"We're executing a will and it seems you're listed as one of the beneficiaries. According to this, you've been left a substantial windfall."

"A will? Whose will?"

"Uh—" The sound of some paper rustling came across the line. "A Mr. Jessup. Anthony Jessup."

It had been nearly eighteen months since Anthony had gone missing under suspicious circumstances, and the name still caused Susan's heart to flutter. Her stomach sank and her knees felt weak.

"It seems he's left you two hundred and fifty thousand dollars."

Susan couldn't find her voice. Memories of Anthony danced through her mind. She had to sit down. "I…uh, I…"

"Ms. Roberts? You still there?"

Debra's house had been a circus during the fallout. The police had shown up first, the forensic team shortly after. Lights, men in suits, yellow police crime-scene tape, questions. Debra had answered the questions. Pictures were taken. They even dusted for fingerprints. What had been discovered? So far, nothing.

Debra buried her husband three days later and tried to sort out her life. She hired a moving company to pack most of their possessions from the house. Debra had designated some things to be set aside and donated to charity; the rest was to be auctioned off. She couldn't live in the house any longer. Not after what had happened there. She wanted to relocate back to Georgia, or maybe even Florida. She was done with the cold and lonely winters. She would make up her mind later. In the meantime, she was going to move in with her mother until she had finished grieving and straightened out her mind.

Among the items in the pile of things to be auctioned was the Royal typewriter. Debra had only seen it a couple of times during her marriage to Anthony. When they'd moved into the house in Virginia, Anthony had placed it on a shelf in the hall closet, where it had stayed all of these years. She had been surprised to see it on the floor when she discovered her husband's body and still didn't know why it was there or how it had gotten there. She didn't care and didn't want to think about it either. She doubted the typewriter had meant very much to her late husband since he had kept it stored away for so long. She hefted the antique machine and placed it in a cardboard box, along with other items that were to be donated to charity. As she folded the flaps on the box and secured them with tape, she found herself thinking about the many experiences she and Anthony had shared. Looking back on those cherished memories of her marriage only reignited Debra's grief. She would have gladly given up everything to return to the past, to be with her husband in happier times. As far as she was concerned, there was nothing on Earth that could bring back her Anthony.

Key West, FL
December, 2011

CPSIA information can be obtained
at www.ICGtesting.com
Printed in the USA
BVOW03s0225211217
503370BV00001B/11/P